GET YOUR FREE STORY!

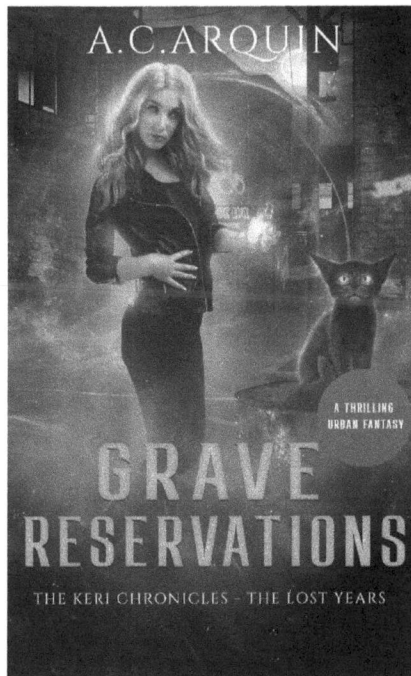

A.C. ARQUIN

A THRILLING URBAN FANTASY

GRAVE RESERVATIONS

THE KERI CHRONICLES - THE LOST YEARS

1

Valora Keri stood in line, breathing in the scent of Zombie Coffee. Thankfully, this was not the reek of putrefaction suggested by the name, but rather the more pleasant earthy smell of rich coffee beans. Her eyelids sagged. It had been a long day. A long week. A long month.

"A long life?" Mister E put in. He floated in the air beside her, wearing his Cheshire Cat grin, blowing smoke rings with his candy cigarette. Even with her eyes closed, Val could feel the intensity of his golden gaze.

"Speak for yourself," she murmured. "You're the one who's been around for centuries. I've still got my whole life ahead of me."

Mister E snorted. *"At the rate you're making enemies, you'll be lucky to see thirty."*

Val wanted to snap a sharp comeback, but she didn't have the energy. She'd been working out every day that week and she was exhausted. Mister E had proven to be a demanding mentor. It was amazing how standing still and channeling magic for fifteen minutes could leave her more exhausted than an hour of sparring at the gym.

Besides, the demon-cat had a point. In the past month, Val had pissed off a vampire cabal, a ghost, a witches' coven, a cult of seraphim, and the San Francisco Police Department. Any one of them would be cause for concern. Together, they made her want to bury her head beneath her blankets and never get out of bed again.

She rubbed her temples. "One nice thing about living in a hipster town. Everyone wears black, so no one can tell when you're depressed."

"I blame Steve Jobs."

"Nice try, but San Francisco was into black turtlenecks long before Steve started wearing them. They were all the rage with the beat poets. Maybe even before that."

"Nothing says 'gold prospector' like a black turtleneck."

Val chuckled, her eyes drifting closed again. "Now I'm picturing Forty Niners with scraggly beards, pipes, turtlenecks and overalls."

"How the West was truly won," Mister E smirked. *"With haiku."*

Val's laughter died on her lips as she saw a young woman bent over a sketch pad across the room, the light sparking blond highlights in her close-cropped hair. Her lips pressed together in concentration, creating faint dimples in her cheeks.

"There's Sandra." The girl had been her roommate for a short time —until Val abruptly evicted her one morning in a fit of temper. "I should probably apologize."

"What for? You had a moment of anger. All the great warriors have tempers."

Val gave him the side-eye. "Great warriors? Is that what you think I am?"

Her hand strayed to her heart, unconsciously tracing the lines of the memento mori tattoo beneath her jacket. It stretched from her heart up over her left shoulder: a memorial to all the people she'd hurt or killed over the years.

Starting with her mother when she was only six years old.

She squeezed her fists so tight her nails bit into flesh.

"You are far from a finished product," the floating cat said. *"But you're well on your way. Our training sessions will level you up in no time."*

Embracing her power meant facing the things she'd done. And the things she'd failed to do. Accepting responsibility for them.

She was tired of running, truth be told. She'd been running her whole life. Running from her mistakes. Her guilt. It was time to do something different.

After years of nagging, she'd finally agreed to let Mister E train her. She still wasn't sure it was a good idea. But neither was fighting her enemies with only her instincts and raw power. She needed as many tricks up her sleeve as she could find.

Lightning flashed. Thunder shook the big front windows as the skies opened up outside. Someone scurried in the door, bringing a blast of cold, wet air with them. Val snugged her leather jacket up around her neck as she breathed in the electric tang of magic in the air.

A Wild Storm.

The Wild Storms had been coming more frequently lately, bringing unpredictable magic with them, filling the city with more weirdness every day.

All the more reason for her to learn to control her own power.

She wasn't sure why she'd resisted letting Mister E teach her for so many years. If she had to guess, she'd say it probably came down to guilt. Using her power always reminded her of the awful things she'd done with it.

The barista finally called her name, and Val gratefully collected her butterscotch latte. As she turned toward the door, her eye caught on Sandra again, still bent over her sketch pad. Another mess she needed to clean up.

She sighed and looked away. Apologizing to Sandra could wait until tomorrow.

Clutching the warm cup like a lifeline, Val pushed out into the pounding storm.

———

Sandra felt sick as she watched Val leave Zombie Coffee. Her former roommate obviously hated her. She knew Val had seen her sitting there sketching, but Val had avoided Sandra's eyes and slunk out the door without a word.

Sandra didn't understand what she'd done to provoke Val's hatred, but then again, people often mystified her. Social interactions felt like some big game where she was constantly trying to understand the rules. Every time she thought she'd finally grasped them, the rules changed, and people ended up hating her.

Like Val did.

She frowned and turned her attention back to her sketch pad. Her pencil traced an improbable, towering spire arcing out over a bumpy landscape of hills and gullies. Her art was the only place Sandra really felt comfortable. Creating secret fantasy worlds she could get lost in.

Her stomach growled, pulling her back to the real world. She surveyed her drawing with a critical eye. Yes, she decided, there might be something there. The composition was a little off, but if she added a small detail in the lower left quadrant, that should balance things out. Another few hours and she might be happy with this one.

Lightning flashed outside, and she started, surprised to realize it was raining. Pouring, really, the gutters transforming into raging rivers. It looked like one of those crazy storms that boiled up out of nowhere and dumped a week's worth of water in ten minutes.

What had Val called them? Wild Storms?

Sandra smiled to herself. It was an apt name. Every time she got caught in one she half expected to get swept away to the land of Oz. It hadn't happened yet, but she kept hoping.

She cursed and fumbled in her satchel for a plastic bag as she realized her bike seat was getting soaked, then dashed outside and secured the bag over the seat. She regarded it doubtfully. The seat was already soaked. The plastic probably wouldn't do anything to help at this point.

Cold water ran down the back of her neck. The rain tingled on her scalp. She shuddered. Why was she standing there getting drenched? She turned to dash back into the coffee shop and ran into a small man in a dark overcoat. He staggered back and sat in the gutter, his pants getting soaked.

"Oh, excuse me!" Mortified, she reached down to help him up.

The man peered up at her. He had lively dark eyes, and dark hair that curled around his large ears. His long face drooped like a dog's.

He reached up and took her hand.

An electric shock passed through her as she pulled him to his feet. She snatched back her hand with a gasp. The man gave her a sly smile.

"It pays to look before you leap." His voice had a slight burr to it, and his smile exposed long canines. "You never know where you might land."

She hesitated at that smile, full of sparkling mischief.

"Right. Well. Sorry again."

She ducked past him and tried to dry herself with a handful of napkins.

"That'll never do."

Sandra jumped. The man was standing at her elbow.

"Let me help."

Before she could react, he reached out and touched her hand again. A wave of warmth passed through her. He cheeks grew flushed. She didn't feel any drier, but now it was a warm dampness. As if she'd just stepped out of a hot bath.

"What did you...?" She looked up, but the long-faced man had disappeared. She spun around but there was no sign of him anywhere. He was just... gone.

Sandra's stomach growled again, loud and urgent. She flushed, glancing around self-consciously, but no one seemed to be paying her any attention. Hopefully, the sound of her stomach's complaints had gotten swallowed up by the general hubbub of the busy shop. Still, she'd better feed the beast before it got any louder.

She took a step, and a wave of dizziness swept over her. Sandra leaned against a table, ears ringing, the world dimming. Pins and needles pricked her hands and feet. She hung on grimly as the world went entirely black. She hoped she wasn't about to pass out. That happened sometimes—a product of her low blood pressure. The world would go black without warning, and she'd find herself lying on the floor with a crowd of concerned faces staring down at her.

Fortunately, this wasn't one of those times. The blackness slowly receded while the ringing left her ears. She flexed her hands to chase away the pins and needles.

Her stomach growled again, churning like there was an alien baby growing in her gut. She needed food. Now.

Sandra went to the end of the line, but her friend Matt saw her and waved her up to the pastry counter.

As she skirted the line, a thick-shouldered guy in a blue shirt said, "I guess the rules aren't for everyone." Sandra's face grew hot.

"Ignore that dude. You don't have to stand in line. What do you need?" Matt grinned at her beneath his shock of green dreadlocks.

"I didn't want to presume," Sandra explained. She could feel everyone's eyes on her back. "I can wait like everyone else."

"Forget that," Matt said cheerfully. "You're my friend. Friends don't wait in line. What can I get you?"

Before she could answer, Sandra's stomach spasmed again, so strong it doubled her over, arms wrapping around her midsection. The room swam.

"Hey, are you OK?" Matt peered at her over the counter.

She waved him off. "I just need some food."

"How about a bagel?"

"That's fine. Thank you."

As Matt opened the pastry case, the guy in the blue shirt called out, "Don't mind us, we're just the nobodies waiting in line."

Sandra felt a flash of intense irritation. It wasn't her fault her friend had called her to the front. Why couldn't the guy just drop it?

The churning in her stomach intensified. Sandra groaned as sharp pains lanced through her midsection. She panted, sweat beading her forehead. What was going on? These weren't like any hunger pangs she'd ever experienced. It felt like there was a creature inside her, trying to claw its way out.

Her ears were ringing, and she leaned against the pastry case, the world around her going all soft-focus. She whimpered as the pins and needles came back tenfold. It felt like a colony of ants was eating her extremities.

She heard someone say, "Instant karma." The asshole in blue, no doubt.

Rage turned her vision red. Suddenly, she wanted to rip the guy's head off.

The pain in her stomach doubled. The ringing in her ears rose to an all-encompassing drone, roaring like a jet engine. Her guts burned beneath a red-hot brand.

She groaned and writhed.

Something was happening in the line behind her. Bodies jostling and pushing. Voices rising in alarm. Hot liquid splashed her skin.

But Sandra was unaware of all that. Her mind had retreated from the pain, fleeing to some far-off inner kingdom. Somewhere she would be safe.

Then the screaming started.

2

The wind always howled around Twin Peaks, but today was exceptional even for these heights. The air tried to shove Val off her feet, forcing her to lean into it to keep from staggering. The rain slashed down sideways, while low black clouds boiled and churned, swallowing the peaks whole.

"It's like the apocalypse up here," Val complained.

"What better place for a wind witch to train than the windiest place in the city?" Mister E replied. *"The storm ensures we won't be disturbed. No one else is going to come to the peaks on a day like this."*

"Maybe because everyone else has more sense than your average houseplant." Cold water trickled down her neck. Val shivered and snugged the collar of her leather jacket. She wished she'd worn a scarf.

"Complain all you want. But no one ever improved at anything by complaining. Or by reading about it, for that matter. The only way to learn something is to do it."

Val sighed and blew on her frozen fingers. She supposed she shouldn't be surprised that an ancient being who took the shape of a Cheshire Cat was an action-not-words kind of teacher. And to be fair, Val was an action-oriented kind of girl. So his practical magic instruction made sense for her. Most of the time.

"Until the day you find yourself standing on the top of Twin Peaks in the middle of a storm," she grumbled under her breath.

"Don't like the weather?" Mister E asked cheerfully. He floated at eye level, wearing a lazy smile while he let the rain and wind pass right through his incorporeal body. *"So why don't you do something about it?"*

"Like what? I can't dispel a storm. It's too big."

"No, but you can direct the local air currents easily enough." Her mentor spoke slowly, as if he were talking to a small child. Val ground her teeth. *"Unless you enjoy freezing rain pelting you in the face."*

The demon-cat looked up at the storm and grinned. *"Personally, I find it invigorating. So much drama! So much action!"*

"So much hot air," Val grumbled.

Still, the cat had a point. Setting her jaw, she turned to face the wind and focused.

As she reached out with her power, she discovered the air was moving really, really fast. The wind had been traveling unobstructed across the Pacific Ocean for thousands of miles, and it had built up a lot of momentum. Twin Peaks was the first bit of land to get in its way in a long time, and the wind did not seem happy about that. At all.

Trying to get a hold on that wind, Val felt like a single grain of sand trying to stop a breaking wave. The power facing her was immense. World-spanning. And Mister E thought she could just bend it to her will? The idea was laughable.

"It'd be a lot easier if I let it carry me away," she snarled. "Can't we do flying lessons instead?"

Mister E's grin vanished.

"Do you know where taking the easy way gets you? North America. When you were trying to find a passage to India by ship. And what do you get then? Entire native civilizations wiped out. Death and destruction. Then Queen Isabella throws you in jail for gross incompetence and crimes against humanity." He fixed her with his golden stare, eyes glowing with irritation. *"Is that what you really desire?"*

Val rolled her eyes. She had no idea what he was going on about, but unless she wanted to spend the next twenty minutes listening to a convoluted lecture on history, she knew better than to question the deranged cat. Better to just bear down and try to do what he wished.

But how could she get control of the wind?

Creating wind out of nothing was a snap. Air always desired to move, so convincing still air to start flowing in the direction she wanted was easy. But this air was already moving fast. This was the type of wind that sculpted cliff faces the length of the coast. If solid stone couldn't stop it, what chance did she have?

Val tried to block it with a spinning barrier of air, but the wind ripped her feeble cyclone away before it even got started. She tried creating a wall next, bracing herself and throwing a pocket of stillness before her like a shield.

The roaring wind trampled her effort like a herd of elephants charging across the savannah. It knocked her off her feet and sent her skidding across the asphalt. The skin peeled painfully from her palms.

"Flying toads." She cursed as she picked a small rock out of her finger. "This is impossible."

Mister E laughed.

"You are approaching the problem from the wrong angle. Do you really think you can stop a wind like that in its tracks? You're not a continental shelf. You'd need several tons of stone behind you to even think about doing that."

"Isn't that what you told me to do?" Val barked in exasperation.

The demon-cat rolled his eyes. His body followed until he was floating on his back.

"I said no such thing. I suggested you could do something about the weather. I never said you should throw yourself against it like a gnat in a lantern."

"What should I do then?"

He sighed dramatically and pulled a gold monocle out of the air, placing it over his left eye. His tone became didactic.

"Do you recall that famous thought experiment where a speeding train is bearing down on a bunch of people who are tied to the tracks? If it continues the way it is going, it will kill many people, but if you pull the switch, the train moves onto another track, and kills only one person?"

Val's scrunched up her forehead. "What does that have to do with anything?"

"The experiment is always presented as a binary choice, yes? One track or

the other? But both choices are inherently flawed. Someone dies no matter which way the train goes."

"Yes..."

"Why do you suppose no one ever suggests simply stopping the train? Wouldn't that save everyone?"

"Because that's impossible. The train has too much weight and momentum. You can't stop the train."

"Ah! And how can we apply this lesson to our current situation?" Mister E cocked an expectant eyebrow at her.

Val scowled. "This wind is like the train. I can't stop the wind in its tracks. Got it."

"But?"

"But..." She thought for a moment. "I can move it onto another track?"

The cat sighed. *"You are distressingly literal, but yes, that's the general idea. You only have to divert the wind by a tiny degree to make it miss you. Doesn't that sound simpler than trying to stop it?"*

Val ground her knuckles into her eyes. It sounded so reasonable when he said it. Sometimes Mister E made her feel like she was six years old.

She gathered her power again and closed her eyes. She could feel the wind currents pushing at her, the rain soaking her hair. She took a deep breath. This time, instead of stopping the wind, she visualized herself cradling it in her arms and letting it flow around her. Softly diverting its force just enough so that it missed her.

To her surprise, the results were instantaneous. The air around her went from a violent howl to a gentle swirl. The rain became a spattering of droplets. Then it died completely.

Val opened her eyes and found herself in a pocket of calm. All around her, the storm still raged. If she stretched her arm to the side, she could feel the transition zone. She pushed through it and her fingertips became soaked, while the rest of her arm remained dry.

"Well done. You've created your very own eye in the storm."

Val grinned... then the sky went white while the world exploded.

3

One moment, Val was standing in the calm center of the storm, enjoying the peaceful pocket she had created. The next, she was flying through the air.

Val yelped, twisting and clawing at the air as her little bubble of calm collapsed. The redoubled force of the storm rushed back in like a vengeful god bent on retribution. It swept her up as if she were weightless, and in the blink of an eye Val was ten feet above the ground and rising fast. Freezing rain pelted her face and hair as she entered the churning clouds, tumbling into a twilight maelstrom.

"What the flock just happened?" she yelled.

"It's a Wild Storm," Mister E said grimly. "Didn't you see the lightning? Don't you feel the magic in the air?"

Val cursed. As if she didn't have enough trouble controlling her power. Wild Storms created unpredictable fluctuations that caused magic to spike. They could twist reality and cause just about anything to happen.

She fought to contain her panic as the wild energy tingled over her skin. One thing at a time. First she needed to arrest her flight before the storm carried her across the bay.

Fortunately, she'd been practicing flying a lot. Not only was it fun, but it was the fastest way to get across town in a hurry. And she'd been beating herself up over the way she'd eaten asphalt while chasing the gunmen who had killed Andrei Vasilevski, letting them get away. She didn't need more of that kind of guilt on her conscience. She had quite enough guilt already, thank you very much.

The first challenge was figuring out which direction was down. Not the easiest task when you're being tumbled about like a leaf in a cloud and can't work off any visual clues.

Val concentrated on bending the storm around herself as she had before, slowly forming a pocket of stillness inside the cloud. As her flight slowed, gravity reasserted itself and down became obvious.

Almost too obvious. She fell out of the bottom of the cloud, dropping fifteen feet in the blink of an eye.

Clutching at the air like a drowning swimmer, Val managed to stop herself inches above the ground. She hovered there, hyperventilating and trembling, soaked from head to toe and bleeding from both palms.

"Perhaps that's enough for today," Mister E said. *"This Wild Storm makes things too unpredictable for edifying instruction."*

Val couldn't agree more.

The rain came down even harder as Val steered the Ural back down the mountain. She flipped her collar up and hunched over the handlebars. Beside her, Mister E lounged in the sidecar smoking his candy cigarette, ignoring the rain completely. Which is easy to do when you're non-corporeal.

Riding a motorcycle in the rain sucks. First, the visor of your helmet gets spattered with raindrops, making it almost impossible to see. Second, no matter what kind of rain gear you wear, water invariably finds its way through the seams—dripping down your collar and wrists, trickling under your waistband—and you end up wet and cold. And that's if you bother to wear rain gear at all, which, for reasons she couldn't entirely explain, Val did not, trusting to her leather jacket instead. Call it stubbornness, masochism, or stupidity. Whatever you called it, the result was the same—a miserable ride.

She was tired, wet, and hungry, so when Val saw a little corner market ahead, she found a spot and parked the old motorcycle.

"Going to buy an umbrella?" Mister E grinned.

"Funny. I need to get something hot in my stomach to chase away this chill." Val eyed her scraped palms critically as she swung her leg off the bike and tucked her helmet under her arm. "Some bandages wouldn't hurt either."

Rounding the corner, she almost walked into a gang of grafters huddled beneath the market's awning. Grafters were like the science-fiction version of shifters. Punk kids who used skin grafts, cosmetic surgery, and gene mods to make themselves look like anthropomorphic animals.

This group's mods made them look like a herd of exotic beasts. There was a girl with tiger stripes across her cheeks and a thick man with a shaved head whose skin was gray and wrinkled—he even had a surgically implanted horn jutting from the center of his forehead. A lanky guy with a droopy face covered in short black fur leaned against the wall of the market. Another woman had a brilliant crest of feathers running down the center of her scalp and a small beak where her lips should be.

"Toad's milk," Val cursed quietly. She thought about turning around and walking back the way she'd come. But that might attract the gang's attention. Like most predators, grafter gangs loved a good hunt. If you ran, the pack would chase you. Instead, she hunched her shoulders and avoided eye contact, hoping the grafters would ignore her.

No such luck. The black furred grafter called out to her.

"Where are you hurrying off to?"

She pretended not to hear the question as she pushed open the door to the market. The bell over the door tinkled.

Inside it was a pretty standard corner market: shelves stocked with snacks, drinks, and an odd assortment of necessities like toilet paper and coffee filters. There was also a deli counter with a few stools. Val slid onto one. Maybe if she waited here a while, the rain would stop and the grafters would move on.

A Latina woman with a dozen silver hoops in her ears raised a questioning eyebrow behind the counter.

"Coffee please," Val said.

"I'll have to make a new pot. This one's been here since this morning."

"That's fine. I can wait. I just need something warm, you know?"

"Tequila is warm." The woman gave her a sly smile.

Val laughed. "Not that kind of warm. Do you have any food?"

"Sure." The woman slid a single-page menu across the bar.

A quick glance told Val it contained standard Mexican fare. Tamales, enchiladas, tacos, burritos, etc. Which was fine with her, as long as it was served hot. She needed all the ammunition she could muster to fight the chill of her wet clothes.

"I'll have two tamales. Some jalapenos too."

The bartender's eyes turned appraising as she gathered the menu and headed for the kitchen.

"I think you earned her respect with that jalapeno request." Mister E lounged on the counter in front of her, blowing candy smoke rings up into the air.

"Latinas like spice," Val confirmed. "We have that in common."

The woman came back and set a fresh cup of coffee in front of her. "Cream and sugar?"

"Please."

"Spicy and sweet. I like that." The woman grinned. "My name's Rosa."

Val returned the grin, carefully weighing Rosa's smile. Was she being professionally friendly? Or was the woman flirting with her?

As a bartender, Val knew that most of the time putting on a smile was simply part of the job. You had to pretend to be everyone's friend. Very rarely did you mean it.

Still, there were exceptions. And the woman was cute.

Val turned up her own smile a notch.

"I'm Val. Is it always this quiet in here?"

Rosa rolled her eyes. "Nah, it's the stupid weather. People think they're gonna melt if they get wet."

"San Francisco: Home of the Wicked Witch of the West."

The woman laughed at that. "I mean, I do know a lot of witches, so you're probably onto something there."

Val's antennae went up at that. "Witches?"

She hadn't found any other witches living in San Francisco. As far as she knew, she was the only one.

"Of course. My family is full of them. My abuela reads coffee grounds. She predicted my cousin would have twin girls. Nobody believed her, but when the twins arrived, they all changed their tune real fast. I've got a tía who reads tarot cards. She said my cousin was going to end up in jail if he didn't change his ways. He didn't listen. Guess where he is today?"

Val sagged back onto her chair and tried to hide her disappointment. These weren't real witches. Just normal people who believed in tarot decks and tea leaves. She was as alone as she'd always been.

The bell over the door tinkled and Rosa's eyes widened as she glanced at something over Val's shoulder. Val sighed. She knew that look. It meant trouble.

4

Val turned to find the lanky grafter with the black fur leering at her. He had dark curling hair on top of his fur, and up close his facial structure was long and doglike: nose flattened, cheekbones widened and sharpened. The overall effect was unsettling, like a shifter caught halfway through a transformation.

"What brings a pretty little thing like you to a place like this?" He sauntered up and leaned on the counter. There was a slight lilt to his voice that reminded Val of her friend Padraig O'Ceallaigh.

"The weather. It's not a nice day for a ride." Val pushed her wet hair back to emphasize the point.

The man's laugh grated like steel on asphalt. It wasn't a pleasant sound. "I hear that. I hate the rain myself. I grew up on a green island. Everything covered in moss. Rotting away. It's disgusting. Give me sunny skies and heat."

"What brought you here then?" Val skillfully turned the conversation away from herself. It was an old bartender's trick. People loved to talk about themselves. If you asked the right questions, you could get people to carry a conversation single-handedly most of the time.

The grafter took the bait. "That island was too small for me. I need action..."

She let him ramble on, asking questions when necessary and listening with one ear while she kept a wary eye on his friends. The gang had propped the door open and some of them were smoking under the awning.

An explosion shook the market, a blinding flash lighting up the sidewalk.

Val yelped, pressing her palms to her eyes. She heard screams and cries of pain from outside, but she couldn't see a thing. The entire world was a bright red smear. She felt like her retinas had been barbecued.

"What's happening?" she murmured under her breath to Mister E. Or at least she thought she did. Her ears were ringing too—it was impossible to tell if she was whispering or shouting.

"Lightning struck the people standing outside." Mister E's voice sounded like it was coming from a long way away.

"Lightning? Seriously?"

"Yes. I don't think it was a mundane strike either."

"What do you mean?"

"This is a Wild Storm. The lightning did something to them."

Val squinted in the direction of the sidewalk, but all she could see was red and black spots. She growled in frustration.

"Did something? Can you be more specific?"

"It is changing them into beasts."

"What?" Now that he'd said it, Val noticed growls and snarls coming through the open door. "What does that mean?"

"Well, they were already pretending to be animals with their skin grafts and surgeries. It seems the Wild Storm has granted their wish. They are becoming what they longed to be."

Val struggled to wrap her brain around that. "They're becoming shifters?"

"Perhaps. But shifters can shift between forms. I don't think these will ever be human again. They are simply becoming beasts."

As the ringing in her ears slowly receded, Val heard a steady stream of profanity behind her. It took her a moment to realize it was Rosa.

Someone grabbed her elbow, and Val lashed out instinctively, her fist connecting with soft flesh. She heard a grunt and a curse. Squinting in that direction, she could just make out the dark shape of the furred grafter picking himself up from the floor.

"Stay back," Val snarled. She drew her knife and waved it menacingly. She might be mostly blind, but he didn't need to know that. "I don't want to hurt you."

The sounds from outside had changed. Now she heard cries and screams of pain.

"What's happening out there?" she hissed.

"The transformations appear to be complete," Mister E told her. *"Those who have transformed are attacking the ones who haven't changed. They're tearing them apart."*

"We have to get out of here. I can't fight them off when I can't see. Can you guide me to the door?"

"Certainly. Though I'd like to lodge a formal protest. Even without eyes, you should be able to handle these animals."

"Your protest is noted. Now get me out of here."

As she turned toward the door, she saw the black-haired grafter slipping out. Rosa stood frozen behind the bar. Val realized her vision must be clearing because she discerned the woman's face. The shopkeeper was staring toward the door, her eyes wide with terror.

Val cursed. She couldn't abandon the woman.

"Run," Val barked at her.

Rosa started, glancing back and forth from Val to the monsters outside. She didn't move, her limbs locked with terror.

Val reached over the counter and shook her. "Wake up. We've got to get out of here. Now."

The woman looked past Val, her face going ashen.

"Too late," she squeaked.

The pit of Val's stomach dropped. She turned to face an abomination.

Squinting, she could barely recognize the hazy shape of the girl with the tiger stripes on her cheeks. Now she had tiger stripes and fur over her entire body, along with slitted feline eyes, long canines, and a tail that lashed behind her. There was blood on her lips. She looked more tiger than human, slinking toward Val on all fours, her ears pinned back, shoulders low. Stalking her.

Val held out her hands. "Easy there. We don't have to do this. I know you're probably a little confused right now, but I'm sure we can handle this peacefully." Even as she spoke, Val gathered her power, preparing to defend herself.

The tiger girl pounced.

5

Val threw up a shield of wind, sending the tiger girl spinning into a rack of sunglasses. The creature snarled, landing on her feet and springing back at Val in one smooth motion.

She turtled, surrounding herself with a fierce cyclone. It wasn't the most active plan, but the transformed grafter wouldn't be able to get through the spinning barrier of wind. It should keep her safe until her vision cleared.

Unfortunately, she wasn't the only person in danger. Rosa's scream rose above the roar of the wind, freezing the blood in her veins.

She whirled in the direction of the screams, but her retinas were still fried. She could only make out shadows and smears of red.

"Mister E, I need your eyes."

"*I thought you'd never ask.*" The demon-cat's tone was amused.

Val's point of view shifted. She was now floating just outside her cyclone, above and to the left.

As she took in the scene, her breath caught in her throat.

The tiger girl had Rosa backed against the door to the kitchen and holding a broom handle in front of her like a sword. Val could tell at a glance Rosa didn't know how to use it. She was just mimicking what she'd seen in movies. That wouldn't help her against the predator stalking her.

Val punched a gust of wind toward the grafter, but all it did was scoop a stack of cocktail napkins off the bar and scatter them everywhere.

"I need some new tricks," she growled. She cut Mister E off before he could reply. "Yes, I know. I've already agreed to let you train me. Unless you have a useful suggestion, shut up."

"Sometimes the old tricks are the best."

"You're right." In one smooth motion, Val dropped her protective cyclone and tossed her knife.

The tiger girl let loose a satisfying scream as the spinning blade sank into her shoulder.

Val grinned. "Just like the dartboard at the Alley Cat."

"Except the dartboard doesn't fight back."

The tiger girl whirled and sprang at her.

Val barely got her arm up in time to keep the monster from tearing out her throat. The tiger girl chomped down on her forearm instead, sharp fangs going through Val's leather jacket like it was taffeta.

Val snarled. Her poor arm had been chewed up by pavement and bitten on the same day. She really needed to open a gauze factory.

She punched the grafter with her other hand, but her blows had little effect. The tiger wrenched her head to the side, tearing a chunk out of Val's arm. Her claws raked across Val's ribs. Val screamed and cursed, blood spraying across the ancient hardwood floor.

The tiger girl was faster and stronger than she was. She needed to even the odds. Val tried using a directed gust of wind to fling dirt into the creature's eyes, but the tiger girl squeezed her eyes shut and kept slashing.

Val cast about, frantically looking for a weapon.

Then she saw it.

She reached up and grabbed the handle of her knife, which was still sticking out of the monster's shoulder. The tiger girl snarled as Val ripped the knife out and plunged it back in again.

But as she drew the blade back for a third strike, the transformed grafter seized her wrist. The tiger girl used her weight and leverage to slam Val's arm against the floor. Val didn't lose her grip on the knife, but she couldn't lift her arm off the hardwood either.

The tiger girl opened her jaws wide. Val tried to hold the creature back with her other arm, but it was practically useless after the tiger girl had ripped a chunk out of it. The pain twisting through her as she tried to push with the mangled limb was so intense that she almost passed out. Saliva dripped from the monster's canines as she closed in for the kill.

A broom handle cracked against the side of the tiger girl's head.

The creature turned and hissed up at Rosa, who was pulling the shaft back for another swing.

The momentary distraction was all Val needed. She slammed her knife home, sinking the blade deep between the creature's ribs. The tiger girl screamed in agony.

Rosa smashed the broom on the creature's skull once more for good measure.

The tiger girl collapsed to the floor and lay still.

"Thanks," Val croaked. She cradled her shredded arm. Her sleeve was soaked with blood. "Got a first aid kit?"

Rosa licked her lips.

"Yeah, but I think we've got bigger problems."

Val followed her gaze. The slaughter out front was finished, and the victors had now come inside the market. There were two of them: the rhino guy she'd seen earlier and another one so transformed Val had no idea what kind of grafter it had once been.

Naturally, the monsters were staring back at her.

The grafters were all the way across the room, though. That gave Val all the space she needed.

"I've got this."

She summoned up a gale, slamming the creatures right in the face. Caught off guard, the former grafters were blown off their feet. They tumbled back into a shelving unit, which collapsed on top of them, burying them in an avalanche of snacks.

Rosa flinched away from her. "What the hell are you?"

"Questions later. Outside. Shut the door," Val snapped. "Lock it."

To her credit, the woman didn't argue. She and Val dashed out of the market and Rosa swung the heavy door closed, then slammed the security grating into place. The doors boomed as the transformed grafters threw themselves against them, but the barrier held. It looked like they were safe. For now.

Only then did the pain really hit Val. She sagged against a bin of oranges, breath hissing between her teeth as she clutched her mangled arm.

"I don't suppose you brought the first aid kit."

Rosa shook her head, still watching Val with wide eyes. "No, but there's a roll of paper towels under the apple bin."

"Better than nothing."

Rosa didn't speak again until she'd gotten Val's jacket off and the wound wrapped. Then she cleared her throat. *"Gracias* for saving my ass."

"De nada." Val held up her paper towel wrapped forearm. "I'd say we're even. Nice work with the broom stick in there too."

That brought out a hesitant smile. "Yeah, well, this is my business. You've got to keep order, you know?"

Val chuckled. "Yeah, I do know."

A grafter slammed against the inside of the door, making the security grate boom. They both jumped. It slammed again, and a dent appeared in the metal.

"Is that going to hold?" Rosa asked.

"Maybe? Either way, I don't think we should stick around to find out."

Rosa's brow furrowed. "I can't just let them tear my market apart. Also, there's a dead body in there. What the hell am I supposed to do about that?"

Val's gut twisted. Minutes ago, the tiger grafter had been a young woman. Now she was a corpse. Another corpse Val had created.

She grimaced. "Best to let the police deal with that. Hiding dead bodies never ends well. Besides"—she gestured at the slaughtered grafters outside the market—"you've got dead bodies out here too."

"But what do I tell them?"

"Tell them the truth. They turned into monsters and attacked us. We defended ourselves. End of story."

Rosa looked sick. "Will they lock me up?"

"For what? Defending yourself from a monster? Don't worry, you didn't kill it. I did. If they lock anyone up, it'll be me."

"Oh good, another trip to the SFPD cells. I so enjoyed our last one." Mister E added.

Val was putting on a brave face for Rosa, but she was worried about that too. Technically, she was still awaiting trial for breaking into the SFPD morgue to talk to Stephen Hues. How would Detective Chen react to finding Val at the scene of yet another murder? And to her being the murderer this time, even if it was in self-defense?

She wasn't sure, but she doubted it would be good. At the very least, Chen would probably rescind her bail.

They both flinched as the monster slammed against the security door again.

Val realized Rosa was watching her. She tried to put on a reassuring smile. She wasn't sure how successful it was.

"Your security camera footage will back up your testimony. You do have a security camera?" At Rosa's nod, Val continued. "Anyway, we can worry about that later. Right now, we need to get you out of here. Do you have a car?"

"No, I live close. I walk."

"Even better. Let's go."

Stepping out from under the awning, Val was happy to discover that the rain had settled into a fine mist. She walked Rosa home and gave the woman her phone number in case she needed someone to corroborate her story.

Rosa peered out at her from the entrance to her ground-floor apartment. Her expression was equal parts fear and curiosity. "How did you do what you did back there? Are you a witch?"

Val gave her a tight smile. "Something like that. You take care of yourself." Then she turned and headed back towards the market.

"Looking for more play time?" Mister E floated along beside her, lounging on his back and blowing smoke rings with his candy cigarette.

"I can't let those things loose in the city. Anyone they hurt will be my fault."

"Are you sure you're not Catholic? You have such a well-developed sense of guilt."

"Laugh all you want, but it's true. If I don't stop them now, I'll have to hunt them down later. I might as well save myself a lot of work tracking them down."

"I can't understand your lack of enthusiasm for the hunt. Hunting is the fun part."

"You have a strange definition of fun."

They found the door to the market hanging open. Val sidled up to it and peered cautiously inside.

The market was empty.

"It looks like you'll get your hunt, after all." She sighed, then winced and clutched at her injured arm. "It's going to have to wait, though. I need to get this arm sewn up."

Mister E's grin was wider than his face. *"Goody goody gumdrops."*

6

V al was soaked and exhausted. It had taken her almost an hour to ride the Ural home one-handed in the rain. Thank the gods the motorcycle's sidecar made balancing easy, or she'd never have been able to pull it off.

Now all she wanted was dry clothes and a hot cup of coffee. Tripping over her vampire roommate's dirty underwear in the hallway did nothing to improve her mood.

"What the flock, Hillary!" she shouted.

Silence answered her. The flat was deserted.

"You have got to be kidding me." Val kicked the offending panties down the hall and ducked into her room to change.

Getting out of her wet clothes was difficult and painful, but ten minutes later, she was curled up under a blanket in the living room, wearing a fuzzy green bathrobe and cradling a warm mug of butterscotch coffee in her hands. She had replaced Rosa's makeshift paper towel bandage with medical gauze, but she was too tired to do more than that. Hopefully, Hillary would be home soon and stitch it up properly.

Val leaned against the wall in the window seat, looking out at the gray drizzle. Somewhere out there, monsters were stalking the city. She hoped she could find them before they killed anyone else. She sighed and leaned into her coffee, letting the steam envelop her face.

"On the bright side, you don't have anything better to do now that the Alley Cat has been closed. So you can devote all your energy to hunting." Mister E floated near the ceiling, grinning down at her.

Val made a sour face. "Thanks for the reminder."

The Alley Cat had been shot up during Andrei Vasilevski's assassination and closed by order of the SFPD while they conducted their investigation. Val had no idea how long it would be closed, but in the meantime she had bills to pay and a rapidly dwindling bank account balance.

The front door clicked open and Malcolm and Hillary came giggling into the apartment. They held bags from several shops.

"Oooo, is there coffee?" Malcom veered toward the kitchen.

Hillary turned to follow him.

"Your panties are in the hallway," Val snapped. "Why are your panties in the hallway?"

Hillary turned back sheepishly. "I don't know. Maybe they got caught on my shoe on my way out?"

"How many times do we have to talk about this, Hillary? If you want to be a slob in your room, that's your business. But keep your mess to yourself. I'm sick of it overflowing into the rest of the house."

"Actually, you should at least get the dirty dishes out of your room," Malcolm said. "That's how we get roaches."

Hillary glared in that direction. *"Et tu, Malcolm?"*

"Hey, I was up front about my OCD when you moved in. I like everything in its right place." Malcolm emerged holding a steaming mug of his own. A grumpy unicorn on the mug was saying, "I will stab you."

"This is your last warning," Val continued. "Next time I trip over your panties, you are out on the street."

Hillary turned to Malcolm. He sank onto the couch and shook his head.

"Don't look at me. You've already been here longer than our previous roommate. The queen has spoken."

"Thanks for nothing." The vampire stomped to her bedroom and slammed the door behind her.

Val sighed.

"What is it with roommates in this town, Malcolm? Either I'm an unreasonable bitch, or you are the only decent roommate in this entire city."

"Why not both?" Malcolm quipped.

"Thanks a lot."

"I'm not saying there's anything wrong with that. You can be an unreasonable bitch all you want. Trust me, it takes one to know one."

"That has to be the most backhanded affirmation I've ever heard."

"We aim to please." Malcolm smirked and started rooting through his bags.

Val frowned. "The two of you went shopping? In broad daylight?"

"Do you see any sun out there? It's perfect vampire weather."

"I guess it is. I never really thought about it before. Maybe all the rain is the reason the city has become infested with vampires."

"You might be onto something there. Does that mean they all used to live in Seattle?"

She laughed and took a sip of coffee, wincing as her wounded arm protested against the movement. Malcolm noticed.

"What happened to you?"

"I got mauled by a monster, what else? It's fine."

"It is not fine. There's blood soaking through your bathrobe. It's disgusting and frankly unsanitary. I'll get Hillary out here to stitch you up."

"After I scolded her?"

"She's a nurse, she has to help you. I think it's part of the Hippo-cratic Oath."

"I don't think that's how that works."

"No arguing. Sit still."

She rolled her eyes but sank back onto the window seat. Malcolm was right. She wouldn't be any good to anyone if she passed out from blood loss.

Apparently, physical wounds trumped emotional ones because Hillary took one look at Val's arm and switched into nurse mode.

Fifteen minutes later, the vampire had her wounds neatly stitched up, and the three of them were sitting in the living room, drinking coffee as if the whole dirty-panties incident had never happened.

"Now we know what to do to smooth things over the next time you have an argument with your roommates," Mister E murmured. He was floating on his back near the ceiling, his tail hanging straight down, exposing his little kitty butthole. Val did her best not to look at it.

"You mean all I have to do is get shredded by something with sharp teeth?" she muttered under her breath. "No, thanks."

The demon-cat laughed. *"I'm just saying. If it ain't broke, don't fix it."*

Malcolm made a little noise. "Oh, I almost forgot to tell you! The same thing happened at Zombie Coffee!"

"Something happened at Zombie Coffee?"

"Apparently there was some kind of monster. From what I heard, a couple of people were killed."

Val sat straight up. "When?"

"About two hours ago. We walked past on our way home and the cops had it all taped off already."

She threw the blanket from her legs and shot to her feet. "I've got to get down there."

Malcolm called out as she was reaching for the doorknob. "You might want to change first."

Val glanced down at her fuzzy bathrobe and flushed.

"Right. Good idea."

7

As Val wound her way through the press of emergency vehicles, it was clear Zombie Coffee had seen better days. Yellow police tape cordoned off the entrance, and one of the big front windows lay in jagged pieces. A table on the sidewalk had clearly been thrown through the glass. Paramedics clustered around injured people on gurneys, bandaging, disinfecting, and comforting as best they could.

Inside the shop, things were even worse. The big pastry display had been smashed, and tables and chairs lay scattered and broken. The chalkboard menu hung crookedly by one corner.

Then there were the bodies.

Two bodies had been covered with sheets, and another lay inside an already zipped body bag. The police on the scene stepped carefully over sticky pools of blood, snapping pictures and taking notes. Val was unsurprised to see a familiar face among them.

Detective Chen wore his customary scowl beneath his close-cropped salt and pepper hair. He looked tired, and Val wondered if the bags under his eyes were the result of long hours at work or insomnia. Given the crimes he investigated, she thought it was probably both.

She hesitated just beyond the yellow tape, unsure if she should call out to him. He wouldn't welcome her presence, but he was the only one who might tell her what had happened here.

The decision was taken out of her hands when he glanced up and noticed her standing there.

"Keri. Why am I not surprised?" He crossed to the doorway and stood opposite her, just inside the yellow tape.

"Good news travels fast."

"You heard what happened?"

"I heard a monster rampaged through the place."

Chen scowled. "That's just what we need. Rumors of a monster loose in the city."

Val's eyes widened as something in the cafe caught her attention. She ducked under the yellow tape and crossed the room with quick strides.

"Hey! Don't touch anything!" Chen bellowed.

But Val was too quick. She had already snatched up an abandoned sketchbook lying on a table by the broken window. She didn't need to see the drawings to know the book belonged to Sandra.

She whirled to face Chen. "Was one of the victims a young woman? Sandra Churchill? Round face? Shaved hair?"

"You know I can't share that information, Keri."

Val shook the sketch pad at him. "This is her sketchbook. It's her most valued possession. Sandra would never abandon it." She moved toward the closed body bags.

Chen stepped in front of her. "I know you like poking around in body bags, but don't even think about it, Keri."

She tried to go around the detective, but he seized her wrist. "I will charge you with obstruction. Don't forget you're still out on bail, Keri. Don't give me an excuse to haul you in."

Val ground her teeth. Chen had caught her poking around in SFPD's morgue when she was trying to find out where the soul of Malcolm's friend, Stephen, had been imprisoned. If Andrei Vasilevski hadn't bailed her out, she might still be rotting in a cell.

She knew she was on thin ice here. She stopped struggling and took a deep breath.

"Please, Chen. She's a friend. Just tell me if any of the victims match that description."

The detective held her gaze for a long moment, then he released her wrist.

He leaned in and spoke softly, "No. None of the victims match that description."

"Thank you." Relief flooded through her as she hugged the note-book to her chest. At least Sandra wasn't dead.

Val frowned and peered around at the chaos of the coffee shop. She looked down at the abandoned sketchbook in her hands.

If Sandra wasn't dead, and she wasn't here, then where was she?

Sandra's new housemates were not happy to see Val. A wiry boy with acne and a green mohawk glared at her through the open door. He looked like he was maybe sixteen.

"Did you come to gloat now that Sandra's dead?"

Val was shocked. "Seriously? What kind of monster do you think I am?"

"The kind who kicks their roommate out on the street without warning."

"I suppose I deserve that. But that doesn't mean I'd be happy if Sandra was dead."

The boy crossed skinny arms over an old Misfits t-shirt with the arms cut off.

"So why are you here?"

"I'm trying to find out what happened to her. I don't think she's dead."

The boy sneered at her. "The cops said she's missing. Missing usually means dead. Do you know more than the cops?"

Val took a deep breath, trying to be patient. "No, but there are things about this case they don't know."

"Like what?"

"Like what I just told you. Sandra might still be alive." She glared at the boy. "May I come in? I'm trying to figure out where she is. Is there anything you can tell me that might help?"

He still looked skeptical, but the boy slouched aside. "Sure, come on in."

A pair of scruffy teenagers lounged in the living room, playing cards. The room smelled of stale smoke and mildew, and curls of foam poked through the fabric of the battered couch cushions.

"Have either of you seen Sandra?"

One of them gave her the finger, his eyes still glued to his cards.

"A friendly bunch," Mister E observed. "I think I like it here."

"You would."

The threadbare carpet running the length of the hallway was worn through in places, and the entire flat had the well-trafficked look of a crash pad. The vibe was run down but colorful, with dozens of sketches and paintings haphazardly tacked to the walls. Val recognized some of them as Sandra's work, but there were other styles as well.

"Are any of these yours?" she asked the kid with the mohawk, who was trailing her suspiciously.

"Maybe."

She rolled her eyes. He was determined not to cooperate with her.

"Which room is Sandra's?"

He showed her to a small room at the back of the flat. She noticed spots of mold along the baseboards. She wouldn't be surprised if the apartment was a squat. Plenty of condemned buildings in the city still had people living in them.

Malcolm would have been appalled. Hillary would probably be right at home.

Sandra's room contained a worn mattress on the floor, an ancient dresser with peeling paint, some cinderblock shelves full of art supplies, and little else. Val frowned. The room was depressing.

Guilt twisted inside her. Val had driven Sandra to this. She'd lost her temper and kicked out the poor girl for the cardinal sin of vacuuming in the morning. If she were a better person, Sandra wouldn't be living like this. She wouldn't be missing. Sandra would still be safe.

If she had a few drops of Sandra's blood, Val could track her former housemate pretty easily. Without blood, it would be more difficult.

Hair would be the next best thing, but Sandra had short hair, and no hairbrush that Val could see, which complicated matters. She ran her fingers over Sandra's pillow and came away with half a dozen fine blond hairs. Better than nothing, anyway.

She looked around for clues to places where Sandra liked to hang out. Anything that might tell her where the girl might have gone to hide.

More of Sandra's sketches covered the walls. There were a few portraits, but they were mostly landscapes. Familiar locations in the city turned into fantastic places: buildings with trees growing out of their windows, streets that had become verdant fields of wildflowers. Val even recognized Zombie Coffee in one, transformed into a sheltered glade surrounded by high, rocky cliffs. A safe haven.

If only that had been true.

Val recognized a couple of locations from the sketchbook she'd found at Zombie Coffee. Places Sandra returned to again and again in her work: a grotto underneath the Golden Gate Bridge and a ruined park at the Castro end of the Market Street Chasm. Val guessed they must be some of Sandra's favorite places in the city.

She turned to find the boy still standing in the doorway, watching her with his arms crossed. She pushed past him. The card players didn't look up as she exited through the living room.

"Thanks for all your help," she said sarcastically, stepping out the front door and back into the gray.

Mohawk boy slammed the door behind her.

Finding Sandra felt important. Val's intuition said Sandra might lead to the monster that had torn up Zombie Coffee. And if she could find one monster, maybe that would help her find the transformed grafters from Rosa's market after that.

Her gut told her the monsters were all connected somehow. If she could slot one piece into the puzzle, the rest might begin to make sense. She just had to keep moving forward. Follow the clues until things started falling into place.

8

A fter the massacre at Zombie Coffee, Val knew Sandra would be confused and terrified. That meant she would run to a place that made her feel safe. Val performed a small tracking ritual beneath the ruins of the I-80 overpass, murmuring a few focus words and burning one of the blond hairs she'd collected from Sandra's pillow. The smoke drifted north, toward the Marina.

"Inefficient." Mister E sniffed. *"If we had some blood, we wouldn't need to burn hair."*

"I'm sorry, I don't take blood samples from everyone I come in contact with."

"Maybe you should start."

"Detective Chen would love that. If he searched my apartment and found a vial of blood with his name on it, I might have a hard time convincing him I'm not a serial killer."

"That sounds like his problem, not yours."

Val rolled her eyes and steered the Ural toward the Marina. The big motorcycle chugged past a gleaming high rise that was all glass and steel, with armed guards and high security doors protecting the inhabitants from the outside world. The guards looked bored and unhappy with their lot in life. Val didn't blame them. They probably resented their rich employers as much as the rest of the city did.

As she neared Marina Green, she stopped in a narrow alley and burned another hair. This time the smoke drifted west, toward the Golden Gate bridge. Val pulled out Sandra's sketchbook. Several of the drawings featured a grotto at the base of the bridge. Bingo.

As she neared the bay, the low rumble of breaking waves filled the air. Gulls wheeled and screamed overhead. Val breathed in the salty breeze, the moist air soft against her skin. She understood why people were drawn to the coast. The briny air called to some ancient part of her brain. The crash of the waves made her feel alive.

She parked near the base of the bridge. The support structure of the enormous span disappeared into an equally enormous pile of rubble. It looked like a tumbled-down foundation from a demolished factory, all red brick and broken concrete, grown over with scrub grass and stubborn vines. The debris was punctuated by rusted steel girders, old tires, shopping carts and discarded clothing.

In the shadow of the bridge, a shantytown squatted around and upon the rubble, with ramshackle structures built from cardboard, plywood, sheets of tin, old doors, panes of plexiglass—whatever the inhabitants could get their hands on.

Val pulled out Sandra's sketchbook and wandered around the perimeter of the camp, trying to see if any particular angle matched the sketches. A few of the inhabitants of the camp eyed her warily, but most ignored her.

One old woman, however, walked right up to her. "Can I help you with something?"

The skin on the woman's face reminded Val of sun-bleached driftwood, sweeping in graceful curves over high cheekbones to gather in deep crevices at the corners of her eyes and mouth. Her silver curls strove for freedom, barely restrained by a worn sun hat with a dandelion puff tucked into the band. Or at least it had been a dandelion puff at one time. All the seeds had been snatched by the wind, leaving only a sad, abandoned stalk. The woman's eyes were clear, bright, and mismatched: one was sapphire blue, the other clay brown. Her expression was mild, but the woman's gaze was sharp enough to strip flesh from bones.

"I'm looking for a friend," Val said cautiously. She wasn't sure what the old woman wanted, but she looked fairly lucid, and you couldn't beat locals for up-to-date information.

"Are you looking for any friend in particular? Or will I do? My name's Lucy." The woman grinned and spread her arms wide as if she were going to come in for a hug. Mister E hissed.

The woman's eyes darted his direction for a moment, then she laughed. "You should see your face right now! Don't worry, I'm not a hugger. I'm just messing with you. Who's your friend?"

"My... what?"

"Your friend. The one you're looking for."

"Oh."

For a moment, she'd thought the woman was referring to Mister E. Which would have been alarming, since Mister E was invisible to everyone but Val.

"Her name's Sandra. You might have seen her around here with this sketchbook. She's a big girl. Thick shoulders, square jaw, biceps that could crack walnuts. Close cropped, sandy hair."

Lucy's eyes lit up. "Yes, I know her. Quiet thing. Hard to get a word out of her. She likes to sit over there and draw." She gestured to a flat-topped boulder that afforded a good view of the shantytown.

"Have you seen her recently?"

The old woman put on a thinking face and toyed with her dandelion stem. "Can't say that I have. It's been a few days, at least."

Val frowned. "Thank you anyway."

Lucy watched as Val walked over and climbed atop the boulder the old woman had pointed out. She compared the view to Sandra's sketches. Yes, the angle and perspective were the same. This was definitely Sandra's spot.

The shantytown was surprisingly orderly, considering the whole thing was built around a pile of rubble. Most of the dwellings were neat and tidy—no big trash heaps or pack-rat clutter heaped outside. Very unusual for a shantytown.

"It's so neat and clean here. I wonder why that is?"

"Lucy runs a tight ship." Mister E yawned and stretched out on the rock beside her.

"You think she's in charge of this place? I didn't know shantytowns had governments."

"Most don't. But that woman has power. She's bending it to her will. Can't you feel it?"

Val eyed the old woman, who was still watching them from across the way. All she saw was a strong, wild, slightly addled old woman. Nothing out of the ordinary.

"Lend me your eyes for a moment."

Mister E obliged, and the world shifted. Colors became brighter, the edges of things sharper. Most importantly, everything Val looked at had an added dimension to it now, a range of color and texture layered on top. The cat could see magic the way infra-red scanners could see heat. This was one of the skills she'd been practicing, and her view no longer shifted to look out through Mister E's eyes by default. Now it was more like his sight was layered on top of her own.

Lucy shone bright to Val's altered senses. The old woman was definitely a witch, probably a strong one.

Which made Val grin. Finally! She'd been looking for other witches in San Francisco ever since she moved to the city, without success.

Unfortunately, she couldn't tell what type of power Lucy had simply by looking. She only knew that whatever it was, the old woman had it in spades.

As she swung her gaze around, she was surprised to discover the rest of the shantytown was full of hot spots. Tents and shacks shone with wards. Power swirled like mist around people dressed in rags. Magic seeped in through the cracks in the world.

"I suppose that makes sense," Val muttered. "The people here are living on the fringes. Some of them have a tenuous grasp on reality. Of course they would be in touch with forces beyond most people's understanding."

"Madness and genius often overlap," Mister E agreed. *"It takes a certain kind of mind to work with the forces of the mystic and occult."*

"Are you saying I'm crazy?" Val shot back.

The floating cat grinned. *"I'm not NOT saying it."*

"Thanks a lot."

"To be clear, I said 'madness and genius.' It's interesting that you fixed on the first word and not the second."

Val snorted. "I'm no genius. If I was, I wouldn't have sold my soul to you."

"You did not sell me your soul." Mister E sounded offended. *"Why would I want your soul? Souls are ratty, insubstantial things. I'd much rather have your body."* He waggled his eyebrows suggestively.

"Gross. I am ending this conversation right now."

The cat's hissing laughter followed her as Val hopped down from the rock and strode toward the shantytown.

9

V al explored the perimeter of the camp. A magical mist drifted around the shantytown in shades of purple, gold and pink. It flexed and bent like a living thing, gathering in odd corners, swirling around certain people and places. The magical energy thickened around the seaward side of the camp like fog. In one place it darkened to a deep navy blue, becoming so dense it almost completely obscured a round bald man hunched over a bubbling pot. His outline blurred and shifted, and Val was sure he was something other than human. He glanced up at Val with suspicious eyes as she passed.

"Does the thickening fog mean he has power?" Val asked Mister E in a low voice.

"Perhaps." The cat puffed on his candy cigarette, adding gold smoke rings to the haze. *"Or perhaps magic is simply drawn to him. Some creatures are magical lodestones. They draw power just by existing, though they themselves remain unaware of it. Haven't you ever known someone who was exceptionally lucky—or unlucky?"*

"Sure. But what does luck have to do with magic?"

"Nothing and everything. Magic warps probabilities, especially for those who aren't actively using it. It is like a set of weighted dice. Though if you aren't using the weight—that is to say, manipulating the magic yourself—

you can't be sure which side the dice will fall on. Magic is as likely to tip the outcome toward snake eyes as it is to give you a seven."

Val pursed her lips at this. "How is that different from random chance? If you can't predict the outcome, how is magic a factor at all?"

Mister E chuckled. *"For the uninitiated, it's not much different. Though with magic in play, more extreme outcomes become likely. A person may throw seven sevens in a row, for example, which would almost never happen with random chance."*

"So some people just seem lucky, when really they are unintentionally using magic?"

"Precisely. Magic is everywhere. And if something smells like fish, the odds are good it comes from the sea."

She gave the bald man a wide berth as she continued her search. She wasn't here to get tangled up with strange magic users. She was here to find Sandra.

Val had skirted nearly the entire camp now, and her frustration was building as she saw no signs of her former roommate. She was about to give up and burn another hair when she finally came upon a rusty old service door in the bridge's foundation.

"This door is in Sandra's sketches," she said, pulling out a few of the pages to double check.

Sure enough, the rusty door lurked in almost every one of them. Sometimes the door was hidden by hanging foliage or debris, but it was there.

"We should check it out."

The door was already cracked open, and the hinges squealed as Val pushed it fully open and stepped inside. Flecks of rust stuck to her fingers. The air inside smelled musty and damp.

Now that she was away from prying eyes, she burned another of Sandra's hairs. Her supply was limited, and Val was trying to parcel them out as best she could, but this seemed like a good time to check if she was on the right track. No sense wandering down this way if Sandra was somewhere else.

The smoke rose and lingered... then curled away down the passage. Val grinned. They were on Sandra's trail. Daylight faded out after a dozen feet, so she pulled out a flashlight, flicked it on, and pushed into the darkness.

The passage ended in the kind of spiral staircase you might find on a ship—diamond-tread metal steps winding around and around a red pole in a tight spiral. Val peered both up and down the steps but could see nothing to recommend either direction.

"Any suggestions?"

She could feel Mister E's shrug. *"One way is as good as another."*

"If I were Sandra, I'd be trying to hide. My guess is the stairs head up to the surface of the bridge, so I doubt she'd go up. Also, the smoke from the hair looked like it was sinking, not rising, don't you think?"

Mister E did not answer, which Val took for agreement. Down it was.

The metal echoed beneath her feet as she descended the staircase into the earth. It deposited Val on a walkway beside a rushing drainage channel. Dark water frothed and tumbled on its way out to the sea. Val wrinkled her nose at the familiar stench that came along with it.

"Why is it always sewer tunnels?"

"People do not go around digging tunnels on a whim," Mister E replied. *"Liquid waste removal is by far the most common reason. As long as you insist on spending time underground, you're going to continue to find yourself in sewage tunnels."*

"Lovely. Where are Malcolm and his magic nose plugs when you need them?"

She swung the flashlight up and down the tunnel. The bay was behind her, so she assumed the tunnel emptied out in that direction. Which meant they needed to go upstream.

Val had only taken two steps when a light flashed far down the tunnel ahead of them. She squinted in that direction.

"Sandra?"

There was no answer, and she clicked off her own flashlight so she could see the light better. The pinprick of light bobbed in the distance. It had a warm, yellow tint to it that felt almost organic. Could it be a candle? Why would someone have a candle down here?

Val squinted and watched as the light drifted up and down but didn't come any closer.

"Sandra?" she called.

Again, there was no answer.

"I guess we'll have to go to them," she said. "Lend me your eyes again."

The distant light didn't become any clearer through Mister E's eyes, but at least the cat's vision allowed her to see the walkway beneath her feet. The rushing water swallowed the sound of her footsteps.

The light started to drift away, as if the person holding it had decided Val was close enough. It looked like the light was floating out over the water, which had to be an optical illusion. Unless the tunnel turned just ahead, and she simply couldn't see it yet?

"What the hell is that thing?" she hissed. "A firefly?"

Mister E's crescent-moon smile shone in the darkness beside her. *"Close, but no cigar."*

"Gross. Why would I want a cigar?"

"I'm sure I don't know. I didn't create the expression."

"Are you going to answer my question?"

Mister E huffed. *"Has anyone ever told you how boring you are?"*

"You have. At least a hundred times. Answer the question."

"Fine." The cat pouted. *"I believe it is one of two things: A fairy or a will-o'-wisp."*

Val gaped at him. "Seriously? You're messing with me, right?"

"You asked for an answer, and I gave you one. Believe what you will." Mister E vanished with an annoyed flick of his tail.

"Flying toads." She stared at the little ball of light. Was there a tiny fairy in the center of that globe? A miniature human with dragonfly wings? Or was that cartoonish anthropomorphism?

"What's a will-o'-wisp? What do they do?"

Mister E refused to reappear, but his voice whispered in her ear.

"There are many versions of the story, but the most common is that the will-o'-wisp is a ghost light held by a wicked person who has been denied entrance into the afterlife and is doomed to walk the earth for eternity. The will-o'-wisp uses their light to lure unwary travelers off the path, often into bogs or marshes, which generally leads to the travelers' death."

"That's cheerful. So you're saying we shouldn't follow the light."

"I am saying nothing of the sort. You asked a question, and I answered. What you do with the information is entirely up to you."

Val glared at the little ball of light. It hung above the water, drifting slowly from side to side but maintaining the same distance from them. She felt sure the thing was mocking her.

10

Val followed the little ball of light deeper underground, pausing every so often to burn another of Sandra's hairs. Every time, the smoke drifted straight toward the light.

"Could it be leading us to Sandra?" she asked.

Mister E shrugged. *"Anything's possible."*

"But why would it help us?"

"The motivations of the fae are entirely their own. But you can be sure of one thing: It is not helping out of altruism. If it is taking us to Sandra, the creature has its own reasons for doing so."

As they traveled, the tunnels got older and narrower. Smooth concrete was replaced by stained brick, which in turn gave way to rough tunnels hewn out of bedrock. Still the light floated on, always staying fifty feet ahead.

Val paused to catch her breath. The tunnel had narrowed so much she could reach across and touch the dark, rough stone wall on the other side. Water trickled down the wall near her hand, joining a small stream running through the center of the cut. Mosses and fungi clung to the cracks and shelves.

"This can't still be part of the sewer."

"It's definitely not part of the modern sewer construction," Val agreed. "Maybe it's a sewer tunnel from one of the old Presidio mansions up on the cliff."

The demon-cat sniffed. *"If it was, they must have taken very small shits."*

The light disappeared around a bend in the tunnel. A breeze ruffled Val's hair. She smelled salt.

The tunnel opened into a vast cavern. Muted daylight filtered in through a crack in the wall, though most of the cavern was still in shadow. Distant waves boomed.

Val was so distracted by the cavern it took her a minute to realize what else had changed.

"The will-o'-wisp is gone."

"Curiouser and curiouser."

"Does that mean this is the place where it wanted to lead us?" She squinted into the gloom. "Do you think Sandra is in here somewhere?"

"Perhaps. Or perhaps it is simply an agent of chaos. Sound and fury, signifying nothing."

"I think you're projecting."

"Are you saying I'm an agent of chaos? Or that I signify nothing?"

"You're so smart, you figure it out."

Mister E gave a dry paper laugh. But before he could reply, a new voice hissed from the darkness to their left.

"Tressssspasser."

Val whirled to find red eyes staring back at her. At first the eyes were part of a looming shadow, but as Val's eyes adjusted, she saw they were actually attached to a reptilian man with scaly skin and a thick tail.

"Morlocks," Mister E hissed.

He was right. More glowing eyes appeared in the darkness. Many more.

Val tensed and drew her knife. "Not these guys again."

She'd tangled with the Morlocks once before. It hadn't been fun. The Morlocks were a tribe of misfit monsters that lived in the sewers. In battle, she'd discovered they were a tide of warriors that just kept coming. If Malcolm hadn't scared them off with his ridiculously bright spotlight, Val probably would have been overwhelmed by their sheer numbers.

Unfortunately, Malcolm wasn't with her this time. And judging by the eyes shining in the darkness, there was no shortage of Morlocks.

"Stay back. I don't want to hurt you," Val called out. Really, she didn't want *them* to hurt *her,* but it was better if the Morlocks didn't know that. You've got to project confidence if you don't want them to call your bluff.

The voice rasped a sound that might have been a laugh.

"Tressssspasser. It is you who should not be here. It is you who will be hurt. "

Val's eyes flicked back and forth, trying to size up the situation. Why had the light led her to this cavern only to abandon her? Had the Morlocks scared it off? Or had it meant to lead her to the Morlocks all along?

"I want to parlay," Val called out, her voice shaking only a little. "Take me to your leader."

Mister E's laughter rustled in her ear. *"Take me to your leader? Are you the hero of a B movie now?"*

"I don't hear you offering any suggestions," she growled under her breath. "I'm trying to get us out of here alive. If you've got nothing useful to add, shut your fluffy little mouth."

"Our leader?" the Morlock said. "Why would we take a tressspasser to our leader?"

Val bit back a grimace. She had no choice but to go all in with her bluff.

"Because I have information for him."

"Why doesss he want thisss information?"

"That's between me and him. I don't give my information to underlings."

The reptilian man considered this. Val held her breath. If the monster was going to attack, now was the time.

The moment stretched. Morlocks shifted in the dark. Waves boomed in the distance. Val gripped her knife so hard her hand ached.

The reptilian Morlock stepped forward.

"No. We think the tresspasser liessss." He bared his teeth in something that definitely wasn't a smile. "And a tresspasser that liesss, is a tresspasser that diesss."

11

The lizard-man shot forward. Sharp teeth bared. Clawed hands reaching out to tear Val's face off.

She was ready for it. Her previous experience with the Morlocks hadn't given her any reason to expect logic and decorum from them.

"Have low expectations and you'll never be disappointed," she growled, punching forward with a fist of wind. It deflected the charging Morlock, sending the creature reeling into a thick stalagmite.

Unfortunately, the other Morlocks in the cave took exception to that. They roared forward in a wave of scales, fur, and teeth.

"Flying toads. Just what I didn't want to happen."

"You can't always get what you want," Mister E said.

"Great, now I have the Stones in my head. You really know how to make a bad situation worse, don't you?"

She punched out with more wind, knocking a hairless, ratlike Morlock aside and flattening a pair covered in rust-orange fur.

Mister E's dry laugh filled her ears. *"Blasphemy. The Stones are one of the greatest bands of all time."*

"You're showing your age again," Val scoffed. She ducked away from a swiping claw and doubled the creature over with a kick to the ribs. "Only dinosaurs listen to that stuff."

"Those are fighting words," the floating cat hissed.

"Well, yeah." Val spun away from a long-armed Morlock and cleared a path with a funnel of wind. "What do you think I'm doing here? Picking flowers?"

She sprinted along the newly cleared ground, getting some distance between her tender flesh and the Morlocks' sharp claws. She had to keep the monsters from surrounding her.

Red eyes bobbed in the darkness in every direction, following her flight.

Flight.

Val cursed, "I'm such an idiot."

"Obviously. Your opinion of the Stones proved that."

"Not what I meant," she snapped. "Why am I standing here fighting when I can fly?"

And with a twist of her power, she did just that.

Wind roared through the cavern, curling beneath her and lifting her into the air. She didn't go far, mindful of the jagged ceiling lurking in the shadows above. Val let the updraft carry her just beyond the Morlocks' reach, where she hovered like a leaf caught in a dust devil. From her new vantage she could see through the crack in the wall to a sea cave beyond. Waves rushed in, churning up white foam.

"You're getting better at this," Mister E approved.

"Thanks. Practice makes perfect." Her words were light, but her tone was not. Keeping the wind under such tight control was difficult, and she ground her teeth against the strain. She wouldn't be able to keep this up for long. Better make it count.

"Now," she shouted over the roar of the wind, her voice echoing off the walls of the cavern,"are you going to take me to your leader, or do I have to sweep every one of you into the sea?"

To underline her point, she funneled another blast of wind beneath a Morlock who could almost pass for human—if you ignored his glowing green eyes. The creature yelped and thrashed as she plucked him up and carried him toward the sea cave.

Sweat trickled down the back of her neck. Her breath hissed between her teeth. Val wobbled and dropped a foot as she almost lost control of the updraft holding her.

"And I thought keeping myself in the air was difficult," she gasped.

"Hold it together for another few seconds," Mister E advised. *"They seem suitably impressed."*

It was true: The Morlocks gaped at her in amazement. A few cowered in terror.

Val found the reptile-man who had first confronted her. She glared down at him.

"Well? What's it going to be?"

He hesitated, and it seemed he might still defy her. Val's energy was flagging. She had only seconds left.

"All right," she snarled to herself. "One final demonstration."

As promised, she tossed the Morlock with the green eyes into the sea. The man wailed as he dropped, and several of his brethren dashed across the cavern to save him.

Val snarled down at the reptile-man. "Do you want to be next?"

The creature lowered his eyes. "You win. We will take you to our leader."

Val landed before him on the floor of the cavern. As she released her power, a wave of dizziness swept over her. Her knees started to buckle, but she snapped them back into place, just barely keeping it together.

It took every ounce of willpower she had left to smile at the reptile man.

"There. That wasn't so hard, was it?"

He glared a surly threat at her. "Come with usss."

The Morlock turned and headed back into the cavern. Val followed, her hair damp with sweat, legs rubbery. Still, she did her best to keep her head up, her swagger intact.

"Now I know how pop singers must feel," she murmured. "Singing and dancing for hours and smiling the whole time? They must be in amazing shape."

"Mick Jagger was still doing it in his sixties." Mister E gave his crescent grin.

Val rolled her eyes.

"Do you think we're still moving toward Sandra? I don't want to burn another hair with so many eyes on me."

Mister E laughed. *"You just flew for a solid minute, but you draw the line at burning a hair? You're a strange one, Valora Keri."*

"Well, when you put it that way..."

Val pulled a hair and a lighter out of her pocket. As she flicked the flame to life, the Morlocks around her hissed and drew back.

"No fire!" the reptile man barked.

"Relax, I'm just burning a hair. It'll only take a minute."

"No fire!" He slapped the lighter from her hand. It bounced down into a crevice and was swallowed up by darkness.

Val shoved him back. "I needed that, asshole." The knife was in her hand again, angry energy flooding through her.

The Morlock bared his teeth, but as wind started to swirl around Val, he flinched back. He hissed at her but didn't come any closer.

The standoff was broken by a slow clapping that echoed around the chamber. Val flinched as an enormous shadow detached itself from the darkness.

12

A deep voice rumbled, "Enough. The witch has proven herself."
Val gaped as the looming shadow stepped out into the dim light, revealing what could only be described as a giant. He was twelve feet tall, his skin covered in moss and slime. A ring of mushrooms sprouted around his neck and ferns grew where his hair should be. Beneath the foliage, his skin appeared to be made of stone, and a pair of yellow crystals gleamed in his eye sockets.

Val took an involuntary step back.

"What the?" she murmured. Mister E laughed. Aloud, she said, "Who are you?"

The giant smiled, exposing blocky gray teeth.

"I am the one you came to see. If the Morlocks have a leader, I am he. You may call me Stone Fist."

"That's your name?"

"I had another name once, long ago." The giant looked momentarily wistful. Then he shrugged his massive shoulders. "But now I am called Stone Fist. As they say, name follows form." He looked her over, his crystal eyes gleaming. "You have traveled far for this audience. What would you have of me, witch?"

Val straightened up, trying not seem overwhelmed by the giant's height. It was a futile attempt.

"I'm looking for a friend. Her trail led me here."

The giant's laughter boomed around the cavern. He spread his hands wide.

"Is your friend a Morlock? Only Morlocks are here."

"I don't know. She certainly wasn't the last time I saw her. But things change. All I know is that she survived a terrible tragedy and her trail brought me here. I just want to make sure she's safe."

"If she is with the Morlocks, she is safe. Morlocks protect their own."

Val bit her lip. She remembered the grafters in the market, transformed into monsters before her eyes. Had something similar happened at Zombie Coffee?

"Her name is Sandra. She disappeared yesterday. Can I cast my tracking spell to see if she's nearby? I only have to burn one hair."

"No." The giant folded his arms. "No fire here."

Val clenched her fists.

"Look. I didn't come all this way to give up now. I'm not leaving until I find my friend. I don't want to fight you, but I will if you leave me no choice."

"No fire." The giant set his jaw and squared his shoulders. Clearly, he wasn't going to be intimidated.

Val sighed. Why couldn't anything ever get done the easy way?

As she was gathering her power, a quiet voice spoke from the shadows. "It's all right, Stone Fist. You don't have to protect me."

A new Morlock stepped out of the shadows behind the giant. As the light fell across their features, Val took a shocked step back. The voice was Sandra's. The form most definitely was not.

The creature that stepped forward was human-shaped, with smudged overalls over a frayed hooded sweatshirt. Its hands were buried in the sweatshirt's pockets, and the hood was up. It kept its gaze on the floor, and Val could only see glimpses of a face and neck. Something moved beneath the hood.

"Sandra!" She stepped forward, but her former roommate did not come any closer. "Are you all right?"

Sandra made a sound that could have been a laugh or a cry.

"All right? Do I look all right to you?"

Val gasped as Sandra lifted her face to the light. Her ex-roommate refused to meet her eyes, keeping her gaze on the floor.

Sandra's skin was pebbled like snakeskin, her neck patterned in bands of yellowish green and black. The fabric of her hood writhed, as if something were struggling to break free.

But despite the changes, Val huffed in relief.

"You're alive. That's the only thing that matters in my book."

Sandra's face twisted, anger, grief, and despair flashing across her features in rapid succession.

"I'm a monster, Val. I... I hurt people." A tear rolled down her cheek. "I should be locked up."

"It's going to be all right," Val said, working to keep her voice calm. She had no idea how that statement could be true, but she knew Sandra needed to hear it. "We'll figure this out."

"The same way we figured things out when we lived together?" Sandra choked out a laugh that was half sob. "I don't think we're very good at figuring things out."

"You've got a valid point. I was a crappy roommate. Domestic situations are not my strong point. But you know what is my strong point? This right here. Weird stuff is my specialty. You're not alone. I'll help you, I promise."

Val stepped forward, bending to force Sandra to look her in the eye. As soon as their eyes met, the world reeled around her. Val staggered, reaching out to catch herself on a stalagmite. Her hand clicked clumsily against the rock. Her fingers refused to grip as she slipped down to one knee.

"Don't look at me!" Sandra reached up with both hands and tugged her hood down over her eyes.

Val tried to steady herself. "Flying toads. What was that?"

She felt like she'd been hit with a brick. She scrubbed her hands over her face... and stopped, her mouth dropping open as she stared at her hands.

Her left hand was normal, but her right hand was stiff and slow to respond. She tried to curl it into a fist but her last two fingers didn't move

Val looked closer. At the base of her ring and little fingers, the pink skin turned gray and rough, the change extending down the length of her fingers.

She felt the digits with her other hand. They were hard and inflexible.

Stone.

Her fingers had turned to stone.

13

Val jerked back, holding her hand out in front of her, trying to escape from her own body. But the gray fingers remained stubbornly attached.

Her mind turned that fact over and over, but no matter how she tried, she couldn't make sense of it.

Bodies didn't turn to stone.

Her body didn't turn to stone.

Distantly, she became aware that Sandra was muttering, "I'm sorry. I'm sorry." Over and over.

Val looked from her hand to the girl and back again.

"You did this?"

Sandra didn't answer, she just kept repeating her apology like a mantra, hugging herself with her arms, her face hidden beneath her hood.

Hot anger flooded Val.

"Did you do this?" She grabbed the girl by the shoulders. Sandra crumbled, her litany of apologies fading into a barely perceptible whisper.

Val shook the girl violently. "Answer me!"

"I'm sorry. I didn't mean to," Sandra moaned, her head bowed, face still hidden. Whatever was beneath her hood writhed in agitation.

Val hated that she couldn't see Sandra's face. She wanted to grab her ex-roommate by the chin and force her to look up. See if she was telling the truth.

But one look at her frozen fingers was enough to restrain the impulse. If meeting Sandra's eyes for half an instant had done that, what would longer eye contact do? Would her entire body turn to stone?

Suddenly, she realized what was moving beneath Sandra's hood.

"Snakes," she breathed. "You've got snakes for hair."

Val staggered back, her good hand covering her mouth.

"What are you?"

"She's a gorgon," Mister E supplied. *"The first I've ever seen in the flesh. How fascinating."*

"But... How?" Val asked.

Sandra answered, "I don't know. It happened at Zombie Coffee. One minute I was waiting for a bagel, and the next..." A choked sob escaped her. "I was a monster."

"A gorgon," Val whispered, staring at her gray fingers, "like Medusa."

She thought of the body bags she'd seen at Zombie Coffee. The ones Detective Chen had refused to let her look inside. Had they contained human statues? People turned to stone by Sandra's gaze?

"This doesn't make sense. People don't turn into gorgons. Flesh doesn't turn to stone." But her rough, gray fingers gave the lie to that statement.

"There was a Wild Storm," Mister E mused. *"We saw a storm transform those grafters at the market."*

Val started pacing. She had to move to keep her rising panic at bay. Focus her mind on answering questions so she didn't think about her fingers. She put her right hand behind her back, tucking it out of sight to keep from descending into numb shock.

A Wild Storm. It was true, they had seen a storm transform grafters into wild animals. Perhaps the same thing had happened to Sandra.

But that explanation felt too easy. Something nagged at the back of Val's mind. There was something she was missing.

"Tell me everything that happened before you changed," she said whirling on Sandra again. "Every detail. Don't leave anything out."

Sandra's voice was soft and halting. "I was standing at the counter waiting for a bagel. I was really hungry and my stomach was going crazy. Then the pain in my stomach got really intense, like something was trying to claw its way out from inside me. The world went black and... I'm not sure what happened after that. I heard people screaming. Windows breaking. When my sight came back, the cafe was empty. There were bodies on the floor..."

"Was there lightning?"

"What?"

"Lightning. Was there lightning when you were transformed?"

"No..." Sandra said slowly. Then with more conviction, "No, no lightning. There was some earlier though, when I went outside to cover my bike seat.

Val spun toward her. "You went outside? When?"

"A few minutes before. My bike seat was getting wet, and I went outside to cover it."

"And there was lightning? Were you struck by it?"

"What?" Sandra was dumbfounded. "No. Wouldn't I be dead if I was struck by lightning?"

"Not necessarily. People get struck by lightning all the time and survive."

"Really?"

"Yes." Val waved her hands in the air. "We're getting off track here. So you went outside. Did you get wet?"

"Yes. It was raining."

"Could it be the water and not the lightning?" Val mused.

"Possible, but unlikely. If it was the water, we'd have a whole city full of monsters," Mister E replied. He floated in the air behind her as she paced, toying with the chain on his monocle.

"Good point." To Sandra, Val said, "What else happened while you were outside? Tell me every detail."

"Um, OK. Let's see. I covered my bike seat with a plastic bag, even though it was already wet and I didn't know if the plastic would help anymore. Then I turned to go back inside, but I bumped into a man coming toward me. He fell down in a puddle. I felt bad and helped him up, then—"

"What did he look like?"

"The man? Um, I remember he had kind of a long face. I know it's not nice to say, but it was almost a dog face. He had really nice black curls, and a short beard. Sparkly eyes too. He had an electricity to him. It tingled all the way up my arm when I helped him up."

Val's head snapped around. "A dog face? With black hair and a beard? Are you sure?"

"Yes. Why, what's wrong?" Sandra sounded confused.

Val remembered the grafter who had followed her into the market. He'd had a long face too. Black hair and a beard.

"Would you recognize him if you saw him again?"

"I think so," Sandra started. Then she nodded more firmly. "Yes. Definitely."

"All right. It's not much, but we can start there." She'd need to go back to the market and get the security camera footage from Rosa.

She turned and found Sandra huddled on the floor, her knees drawn up to her chest. Val knelt beside her former roommate, being careful to stay out of her line of sight this time.

"First things first. Let's get you out of this sewer. I know better places we can go."

Sandra shook her head.

"No. I'm a monster. I have to stay down here with the other monsters."

"You're not a monster. You're a person who looks different. I know places full of people like you. People who can take care of you."

She extended her good hand, palm up. It hung there in the air between them, looking pale and soft and vulnerable. Val tried not to think about her other hand. The one tucked behind her back. The one with fingers cold and gray.

"Come on. What do you say?"

For a long moment, the only sound was the rumble of the waves rolling through the sea cave. The only movement the stirring of the ocean breeze.

Hesitantly, Sandra reached out and took her hand.

14

As she rode in Val's sidecar, Sandra kept one hand on her hood, holding the edge down over her eyes so the wind didn't lift it away. It was an unsettling way to travel, limiting her vision to the nose of the sidecar and the street directly in front of her.

It was intensely frustrating. As an artist, she usually swallowed the world with her gaze, letting her eyes wander, discovering angles that were unexpectedly pleasing.

That was the heart of being a good artist—for her, anyway. Finding unexpected beauty. The point of view that let your subject come alive.

Anyone could draw a picture of the Golden Gate Bridge, for example. But a true artist could capture the life inside the red girders. The breath of the workers who'd given their blood to its construction. The hard-working bolts and support cables. The flex and sway as the bridge strained under the weight of distracted commuters. The orange fog lights shining through from another world. That moment when the visitors' breath catches in their throat as they gaze out over the rail of the iconic span.

And it wasn't just famous landmarks. Everything was like that. Every corner. Every doorway.

Where a casual observer saw only surface details, Sandra saw hopes and dreams. The varnish that years of life left upon the world. Layers upon layers built up into a breathtaking patina.

But what she loved most was the secret things. The tiny, overlooked details. The flower sprouting through the sidewalk. The stubborn tree pushing through a crack in the wall. The patient spider building its perfectly symmetrical web. The beam of sunlight slanting beneath the stairs, falling on the blue eye of a doll hidden in a corner, lost by some child long ago. The tiny, perfect things people walked past a hundred times a day and didn't notice. The places where the magic lived.

But now if she accidentally caught someone's eyes, she would turn them to stone. Like she had Val's fingers.

She couldn't risk that.

So Sandra kept her hood up, and her eyes down. And her heart ached at all the beauty she was missing.

Val said she needed to stop by a corner market on the way to the apartment. As she pulled the Ural up to the curb, the door to the market was open. Racks of fruits and vegetables stood beneath a green awning out front.

Sandra wasn't sure if she could trust Val—the witch had evicted her from their apartment without warning, after all—but what choice did she have? Short of going back to the Morlocks, she didn't have anyone else to turn to. She'd just have to go along for the ride and see where it led.

"You can stay here, if you want," Val told Sandra, swinging her leg off the motorcycle.

"I'd rather stay with you, if that's all right." Sandra kept her eyes on the ground and her hood pulled low over her face as she climbed out of the sidecar.

"Suit yourself."

A Latina woman was mopping the floor when they walked in, her dark hair tied in a blue bandana. A parade of piercings circled her ears. Sandra kept the line of her hood at the level of the woman's nose, and she watched her smile as Val strode through the door. There was sunshine in that smile, and something else that made Sandra's breath catch in her throat.

"Hola, stranger. Back so soon?"

"No rest for the wicked." Val grinned in return. "It looks like everything cleaned up, OK?"

"Mostly. This blood stain is being stubborn, but I've just about got it." The woman leaned on the mop and turned toward the hooded figure standing behind Val. "This a friend of yours?"

"Old roommate. Rosa this is Sandra."

Without looking up, Sandra mumbled, "Nice to meet you."

"Don't mind her. She's shy," Val said.

"Whatever you say. What can I do for you?"

"This might be a strange question, but would you mind showing us the security footage from the incident? I need to check something."

Rosa shrugged. "Sure. No skin off my nose. Come in the back."

The back room smelled like old wood and cleaning products. Cardboard boxes full of back stock filled the ancient wooden shelves lining the walls. The open door to a small office revealed a desk littered with papers and a security monitor sitting on a milk crate.

Sandra resisted the urge to scratch her scalp. Her hair was restless, and the snakes were tickling her skin.

She shuddered.

Her hair was alive. Not just alive, but made of tiny snakes. Sandra kind of liked snakes, but even so, the thought was horrifying.

And how did they get so long, anyway? Her hair had been buzzed close to her scalp before her transformation. Now the snakes were a good six inches long.

Sandra scrubbed the tears from her cheeks. She didn't understand any of this. She didn't want any of this. She wanted to go back to her sketch pad and pencils. Sit in her corner and pretend to be invisible with her headphones on, watching the world go by.

Rosa sat at the desk and scrolled through a menu. She tapped a few keys. The picture on the monitor flickered and shifted. In it, Sandra saw Val entering the shop. Her hair was soaked and her boots left wet prints on the floor as she made her way to the counter.

Val's mouth soured. "I look like a drowned rat."

"Nah. More like a sea otter." Rosa's tone was playful. Flirtatious. "You're cute when you're wet."

Sandra saw a flush creep up her ex-roommate's neck. Val coughed and kept her eyes focused on the monitor.

On the screen, a lanky grafter came through the door behind Val. Sandra watched him saunter over and prop his elbow on the counter.

Sandra drew in a sharp breath and took a step back.

Val noticed her reaction. "Is that the guy?"

Sandra nodded.

"Why am I not surprised?"

He looked just as Sandra remembered. A three-day beard covered his long, droopy jaw. Dark hair curled over his ears. She recalled the feel of his hand in hers. The electric charge as she'd helped him up.

The monitor went white with static. Seconds ticked by, but the picture did not return.

"Is that it?" Val asked.

Rosa shook her head. "No. Keep watching."

After about thirty seconds, the picture returned. As it snapped back into focus, Sandra saw a tiger-girl stalk in through the entrance. She leaned forward, fascinated and horrified. The girl moved with a lethal grace, like a tiger in human form, deadly power barely contained, her skin furred and striped. Her snarling lips exposed sharp canines. There was blood around her mouth.

"It didn't record while they were changing," Val mused. "I guess that tracks. Technology and magic don't play well together."

Then she noticed something else that made her curse. "The guy is gone."

"Yeah, he disappeared." Rosa confirmed. "The cops noticed that too. They figured he must've slipped out while the camera was down." She cocked her face toward Val. "You don't think so?"

"No, I think so. But I think he might have been running for a different reason."

Sandra felt cold. She knew the reason the man had run. It was the same reason he'd run from Zombie Coffee. He had unleashed hell, and he wasn't sticking around to see the results.

The rest of the video cut in and out. Waves of static rose and ebbed over the screen.

Val turned to Rosa. "You didn't find any of that guy's hair lying around, did you? While you were cleaning up?"

Rosa puffed in disbelief. "Are you crazy? I had bigger things to focus on. Like the shelves you knocked over and the big puddle of blood in the middle of my floor. Of course I didn't notice some dude's random hairs."

Val held up her hands. "Relax. I figured it was a long shot, but I had to ask. If I had some of his hairs, he would be a lot easier to find."

Rosa made a strangled noise. "What happened to your hand?" She was staring at Val's gray fingers.

Val hid her hand in her jacket pocket. "It's a long story."

"But what happened? Why does your skin look all gray?" She took a step back. "It's not contagious, is it?"

Val scowled. "No, it's not contagious. It's a personal problem. Now, if you're done poking your nose into my business, we were talking about that guy's hair."

"Sure. The dumpster's out back." Rosa jerked her head toward a metal door on the far side of the storeroom. She remained where she was, giving Val plenty of space. "That's where I dumped the dustbin after I was done sweeping. Knock yourself out."

Sandra tugged her hood down and trailed after Val as she threaded her way through the storeroom. The dumpster in question turned out to be a rusty green rectangle squatting in the dim alley.

"Now I see why cops wear rubber gloves and dust masks when they investigate a crime scene." Val wrinkled her nose as she peered into the interior. Generations of garbage bags had spilled their guts over the years, and fungi of all shapes and colors speckled the interior. It smelled like stale piss and vomit. "This reeks even worse than the sewer."

She stared at the mess for a long moment, then sighed and turned away.

"No. Even if I could find something in there, crawling through that rot isn't worth it. I'll track down this guy some other way."

"How?" Sandra asked softly.

Val's smile was grim.

"I've got some ideas. But first, let's get you somewhere safe."

15

The sun had just dipped below the horizon, the undersides of the clouds glowing orange and pink when they pulled up outside the Mission District Shifter Settlement. The settlement had changed since the last time Val had seen it. The large block it occupied had been sparsely populated before, with lots of empty space between the small houses the shifters had built for themselves, filled with community gardens and sculptures.

Now those open spaces were stuffed with shacks and temporary structures made of plywood and blue tarps. Before, the settlement had been cute and cozy. Today it looked like a refugee camp.

A makeshift wall had been erected around the block, leaving a chain-link gate entrance.

"State your business." The smaller of a pair of guards challenged them as they approached. The stocky woman gripped a long spear in her hand, and while the guard didn't quite level the spear at them, she was clearly prepared to use it.

Val hesitated. What had happened here? Maybe bringing Sandra to the settlement wasn't such a good idea, after all.

But, they were here already. She might as well try to figure out what was going on before making any decisions.

"I'm here to see Alain," Val said.

"Regarding?" The guard's eyes flicked past Val, lingering on the hooded figure of Sandra.

The guard was squat and fidgety, her hands and arms compact and powerfully built. Val wondered what kind of shifter she was. She guessed maybe a badger or a mole. Something that liked to dig.

"Regarding sanctuary," Val said. She jerked a thumb at Sandra. "My friend needs help."

The guard's stance didn't relax. "Is she a shifter?"

"Not exactly."

"Only shifters allowed here."

"Can you just get Alain?" Val snapped. She was tired of this woman's suspicions. Since when did you have to play twenty questions to visit a friend?

Now the guard did level her spear, the metal tip glinting wickedly.

"I don't like your attitude," she growled.

"The feeling's mutual." Val started to gather her power. It had been a long day. She was tired and hungry. If this woman wanted a fight, Val would be happy to give it to her.

A familiar voice called out.

"Hey! Relax, you two!"

Alain came jogging up to the gate. The greyhound shifter was as lean as ever, sporting a scruffy black beard as he slid to a halt. "Gilda, put the spear down. Val, you don't have to fight your way in every time you come here, you know."

"I know that," Val growled. "You need to explain it to Officer Friendly here."

"You are not a resident of this community," Gilda hissed. "You don't get in unless I say you do."

Val shook her head in disgust. "Power drunk much? You give some people a little authority and they think they rule the world."

"That's it," Gilda stepped forward, pulling her spear back to stab the witch.

Alain dashed forward, putting his body between them, palms out.

"Peace! Peace! We're all friends here!"

Gilda was forced to halt her attack, the tip of her spear inches from his chest.

"Get out of the way, Alain," she growled.

Alain stared her down. "No. I vouch for this woman. She is my guest. Stop trying to stab my guest."

"Fine." The guard reluctantly lowered her spear. "But you are responsible for her. It's on you if she causes trouble."

"Of course it is. As it should be. Thank you for doing your job." Alain finally turned and grinned at Val. "Hello! Sorry about the hassle. Things have been a bit tense lately."

"So I gathered."

He peered past her and raised an eyebrow. "Who's your friend?"

"This is Sandra. She's the reason I needed to see you."

Alain's smile slipped. "I see. Please, come with me."

He led them toward a large tent near the center of the camp. The winding pathways through the settlement were cluttered with salvage. Rusty bicycles. Old car parts. Val even saw a free-standing fiberglass shower stall operated by a gravity feed.

"What happened here?" she asked quietly.

Alain sighed. "It's been a rough few months. A lot of new shifters have been appearing inside the city, most of them with no idea how they became shifters. We've tried to take in as many as we can." He gestured around at the cluttered camp. "As you can see, it's straining our resources."

"New shifters? You mean they just woke up one day and discovered they were were-creatures?"

"Shifters." Alain corrected sternly. "Please, Val. Names matter."

"Shifters, right. Sorry."

"And yes, that's exactly what happens. People are shifting who never have before. As you can imagine, most of them are terrified and traumatized."

"Do you know what's causing it?"

He shook his head grimly. "No idea."

"I've seen it happen," Val said. "I was in a market and a pair of grafters transformed during a lightning storm. I think the Wild Storms might have something to do with their transformation."

"Hmmm. Possible. I know a number of the new shifters said they transformed during storms." Alain pursed his lips. "Not all, though, so there's got to be some other factor at play as well."

"I've got some ideas on that."

"Really?" Alain looked at her appraisingly. "Do tell."

Val shook her head. "I'd rather not until I've investigated further. Right now it's just a guess. If it becomes more than a guess, I'll let you know."

"Fair enough. Come. Sit. Tell me how I can help you." Alain held the flap of the big tent aside and motioned them in.

Val smiled. That was one of the things she liked about Alain: He was always ready to help, and he didn't ask too many questions.

Inside the tent was a common area bigger than Val's entire apartment. A patchwork of rugs covered the ground, and threadbare couches and chairs of every description created a handful of small sitting areas. Almost a dozen people were in the tent, drinking various things and talking.

Off to one side, Val noticed a table with a camp stove and sink. A carafe sat on the counter beside a stack of mugs. Alain followed her gaze.

"Do you want some coffee?"

"No, thank you. I think there are others here who need it more."

Alain made a rude noise with his lips. "We have plenty of coffee. Living space might be getting tight, but the coffee supply is strong. Have a seat; I'll bring you some." He gestured to an empty circle of seats. "Would you like some coffee as well?" He asked Sandra.

She shook her head. "No. I can't. If I drink caffeine now, I'll be up all night."

"Beer? Water? Something else?"

"No, I'm fine."

Val studied the other people in the tent as they waited for Alain to return with the coffee. She assumed they were all shifters, though she didn't see anything that would give them away to a casual observer. She wondered how many of them were new arrivals. Many looked a bit threadbare, and the dark circles under their eyes told a tale of sleepless nights.

Val remembered the way the newly transformed grafters had attacked everything in sight. She wondered if that was common. Perhaps the insomniacs were new shifters, haunted by the memory of the things they'd done in those first panicked moments.

She found her fingers unconsciously tracing the lines of her memento mori tattoo, and she averted her eyes. Yes, well. A lot of people panicked and lost control when faced with new powers. Things got broken. People got hurt. She was in no position to judge anyone.

Alain returned and handed her a mug of creamy coffee. She tried to take it in her right hand, but cursed and almost dropped it as her stone fingers refused to close. She ended up having to cup it in both hands.

Alain frowned down at her. "What happened to your hand?"

Val grimaced.

"Well... that's kind of what we came here to talk to you about."

16

V al sighed and sipped her coffee. The corner of her mouth curled up in surprise. "You put butterscotch in it?"

The greyhound shifter smiled.

"Only for you, Val. I remember how much you like it."

Then he settled back into a worn armchair, his expression turning serious.

"Tell me how I can help."

"I hate to ask this. I can see you've already got too many displaced people here."

"But?" Alain prompted.

"But I don't know where else to turn. Sandra... she's not a shifter, exactly, but she's been transformed. She can't go home. She needs a safe place to stay. I was hoping you could take her in. Temporarily. Until I can find a better place for her."

Alain raised an eyebrow.

"Not a shifter, exactly? So what is she?"

Val ran a thumb over her stone fingers. They were hard and rough, but oddly warm, as if her blood still flowed through them unimpeded. Part of her was freaking out. The fingers felt wrong. Alien. Like some dead thing someone had attached to the end of her arm. Every time she saw them, she flinched as if she'd inadvertently picked up a large, hairy spider. She wanted to run around shaking her arms and screaming, "Get it off! Get it off!"

But she couldn't do that. At least, not in front of Sandra. The poor girl had suffered enough. Was suffering still. She didn't need Val adding to her trauma.

Besides, if Val hadn't kicked Sandra out of her apartment in the first place, maybe none of this would have happened. Or maybe her mistake had been letting Sandra move in with her at all. Perhaps she was a maelstrom of evil energy that infected everyone who got close to her. Maybe the world would be better off if she became a crazy old hermit living in a cave somewhere.

She shook her head. Enough with the self pity. She could cry herself to sleep later. Right now, Sandra needed her help. It was the least she could do.

She took a deep breath.

"Sandra has been transformed, but she's not a shifter. She seems to be stuck in her new form."

"And what form is that?" Alain looked curiously at Sandra, who remained hidden beneath her hood.

"You asked about my fingers? Let's just say you're better off not making eye contact with her."

Alain frowned. "I don't understand."

Val glanced at Sandra, hoping the girl would jump in and explain. She didn't.

Val sighed.

"She's become a gorgon."

"A gorgon?" Alain cocked his head to the side. "What is that?"

"Do you know the story of Medusa?"

"Ah, yes. She was said to have snakes for hair. Her gaze could turn men to stone..." He trailed off, his widening eyes returning to Val's fingers as it hit him. "You can't be serious."

"I'm afraid I am. I have proof." Val held her half-stone hand up to the light.

Alain scooted back in his seat. "That's impossible."

"Is it? Is it more impossible than the seraph that killed Ruby? Than shifters or witches or vampires?"

Alain tugged at his scruffy beard. His face was pale.

"But... how?"

Val studied Sandra. The girl's hood shifted slightly and the nose of a small yellow snake peeked out, forked tongue flickering as it tasted the air. Alain saw it too, and he sucked in a breath.

"My guess is, it happened the same way all of these new shifters were created," Val said, gesturing to the tired people in the tent. "If I can figure out what transformed one, I'll discover the reason for them all."

Alain chewed on that for a minute, regarding Sandra thoughtfully.

"No offense, but is it safe to have her here?" He finally asked. "What if she accidentally looks at someone? Stone fingers are a bad enough risk, but could she kill someone?"

"I'm not sure. Sandra? Can you help us out here?"

The girl shrank under their attention. Her voice came out so softly, Val had to lean forward to hear her.

"Yes. I could kill someone. It happened before..." Sandra choked. Her shoulders shook with silent sobs.

Val's heart ached for her. She wanted to give the girl time and space to grieve her lost humanity.

But they needed answers.

"In Zombie Coffee?" she prompted as gently as she could. "Can you tell us what happened?"

Sandra shook her head. "No. I don't remember what happened in Zombie Coffee. It was after that. I was running down the street, crying. Trying to get away. I don't know what I was running from. Myself, probably."

She took a shaky breath, and her hand darted beneath her hood. Wiping tears from her eyes.

"I came around a corner and an old man was there, walking his dog. He started to smile at me, then he noticed I was crying. His brow furrowed and he opened his mouth... he looked like he was going to ask me what was wrong... but the words never came out. His face turned gray and he just... he froze. Like a human statue. I was so shocked I stopped crying. I stepped forward, trying to figure out what happened. His dog barked at me, and I looked down at it... it was a white terrier, wearing a cute little red sweater... It looked at me, and it turned to stone too."

Sandra paused and took a shaky breath. Her voice had gotten firmer as she told the story. Harder. Like she was firming up her walls.

"I realized I had turned them to stone just by looking at them."

"How did you know?" Alain asked.

Sandra's shoulders rose and fell. "It suddenly seemed so logical. It was like when you're having a dream and you just *know* something. It doesn't matter how you know, you just do. I looked at this poor old man and his dog and I knew what I'd done."

17

S andra's words hung heavy in the air. In another part of the tent,
someone laughed. Sandra flinched. The sound grated against her
ears, with the image of the frozen old man and his dog fresh in her
mind. The man she had... Sandra bit her lip against the tears, her mind
shying away from the words.

"What happened after that?" Alain's tone was equal parts disgusted
and fascinated.

"I knew I couldn't look at people anymore. I had to get away. I was
just off Church and Market, where the old MUNI line comes out above
ground. The mouth of the tunnel was right there. I didn't even think
about it. I just went underground."

"And that's how you found the Morlocks," Val guessed.

"They found me, really."

"And they didn't attack you?" Alain sounded surprised.

Sandra shook her head.

"Why not?" Val asked. "The Morlocks are famously territorial. You
saw me experience their lack of hospitality myself."

"I guess they recognized a fellow monster when they saw one."
Sandra felt the truth in the words as she spoke them. That's what she
was now. A monster. She belonged with the other monsters.

Alain and Val digested Sandra's story. Finally, Alain spoke.

"If we let you stay here, how do we know you won't turn anyone else to stone?"

Sandra made a sound that was part laugh and part sob.

"You don't. I can keep my hood up and try not to look at people, but..." She trailed off helplessly.

Val opened her mouth, but Alain held up his hand. "I've heard enough. Please, let me think."

The scruffy shifter remained silent for several minutes, fingers steepled beneath his chin, his soft eyes troubled. Val frowned into her coffee. Sandra toyed with the sleeve of her hoodie, running the fabric through her fingers again and again.

Sandra tried not to think about what was next for her. The shifter settlement might be more comfortable than living underground with the Morlocks, but the shifters were still monsters, just of a different kind.

But Sandra wasn't a shifter. She'd still be an outcast. Never fit in, no matter where she lived. Would she have to go the rest of her life without looking another living being in the eye? Could a person even do that?

The alienation of the thought was staggering. Humans were social creatures. How could you feel connected to your friends without being able to see their eyes? To say nothing of lovers. Could you fall in love with someone and not look them in the eye? How would that work?

Not that Sandra expected to ever fall in love again. Who could love someone capable of turning them to stone with a glance?

At least she was alive, she reminded herself. Compared to those people in Zombie Coffee? Or the old man and his dog she'd turned into statues? Her complaints were trivial.

Maybe if she repeated that enough, she'd start to believe it.

Finally, Alain sighed. Sandra's heart fell. She could see the answer in the twist of his mouth before he even said a word.

"I'm sorry. I want to help, but I simply cannot let her stay here. It's too dangerous. We're already overflowing with nervous new shifters. If something happened, we'd have a panic on our hands. My first responsibility is to this community."

"I understand. Thanks, anyway." Val pushed herself to her feet, and Sandra followed.

"If there's anything else I can do, please let me know. I want to figure out what's causing these transformations as much as you do." Alain's brow was creased with guilt. "I'm happy to help in any other way I can. I simply cannot in this particular way. I hope you understand."

"I get it, Alain. I do. Thanks anyway. I'll let you know if you can help some other way." Val tried to summon up a smile for him. She was only partially successful. "Come on, Sandra. We'll find somewhere else for you that's safe."

As they left the camp, Sandra said, "You should have left me with the Morlocks."

"In the sewer tunnels? Seems like a pretty foul existence."

Sandra ignored Val's sad attempt at humor.

"At least they accepted me there. They didn't care what I was. All that mattered was that I was a freak. A monster like them."

"You're not a monster, Sandra. You're just a girl who's—"

"I am a monster!" Sandra screamed.

"Maybe you don't have to be," Val stammered. "Maybe we can find some way to reverse this. Once we figure out what happened—"

"I am a monster," Sandra repeated firmly, feeling the truth in the words. "And nothing you say is going to change it. The sooner we accept that, the better off we'll be."

Sandra's fists were clenched, her shoulders heaving with anger, fear and self-loathing. She wanted to scream and cry and hit things. Run and run and run and never stop. Find some way to escape from herself.

Val held out her hands as if trying to calm a wild animal.

"Sandra, I don't know your personal pain. No one can. But I do know what it feels like to be a monster. I've been a monster most of my life. I've hurt people with my power. Killed people. Not on purpose, but I still did it, and I have to live with my actions."

Val reached up and pulled the collar of her jacket down toward her shoulder, exposing part of a large mosaic tattoo.

"Do you see this? It's a memento mori. A memorial for the dead.

Everyone that has died because of me is represented here. My best friend in New York. Even my own mother. Believe me, I know what it feels like to not recognize yourself. To be afraid of yourself. To hate yourself. To think you're going to be alone for the rest of your life."

Val ran out of words and stood there, her hands opening and closing, groping for something only she could see. Sandra ran her eyes over the tattoo. She'd seen it poking out around the edges of Val's clothes when they lived together, but she'd never known what it was.

Now she knew. It was a memorial to the dead. She thought of the old man and his dog and wondered if she'd have to make a memento mori of her own someday.

She shivered as the icy wind caressed her exposed skin. Despite its reputation for being temperate, San Francisco really was a cold city. Chill breezes blew in off the Pacific every evening, and wet fog rose from the bay. No matter how sunny and warm the afternoon, you'd regret it if you left home without a jacket.

That was one good thing about having to wear her hood up all the time, she thought sourly. At least it kept the back of her neck warm.

"I don't pretend to have the answers. I'm too broken. Cracked at the core." Val's words spilled out of her like a confession. Her voice groaned under the weight of old pain. "No matter how hard I try to plaster them over, my faults remain. My sins. They're never going away."

She took a shaky breath. Ran her hands over her face. Grimaced at the rough touch of her stone fingers.

"I'm no savior. I'm definitely not a role model. I don't know the right thing to do. I don't know what tomorrow will bring. I just..."

Sandra reached out and closed her fingers around Val's hand. Val jerked back, but Sandra's grip was strong and she refused to let go. Val's muscles stayed tense, but she stopped pulling away. Sandra knew Val didn't like to be touched, but sometimes human contact was important.

"Thank you," Sandra said softly.

"For what?"

"For telling me that. For opening up to me. I never knew any of that. You always seemed so strong. So together. Like nothing could touch you. You're like some amazon warrior or something."

A startled laugh burst out of Val's throat.

"Strong and together? Me?"

Sandra's hood bobbed up and down. "Yes, you. I feel like nothing ever gets to you."

"Except when my roommate runs the vacuum early in the morning."

"Except for that." Sandra smiled, but her voice was solemn. "But seriously. Knowing you feel that way about yourself, it gives me... not hope, exactly. Maybe courage. If you can feel that way on the inside and still do all the things that you do. Maybe I can learn how to be a... I don't know... a good monster?"

Sandra gave a final squeeze and released Val's hand. From the corner of her eye, she saw a tiny snake peeking out of the shadows beneath her hood, tongue flicking as it tasted the air. The movement felt strange. Not in her control, but not entirely out of it either. Like the unconscious tapping of a finger when you were lost in thought.

She sucked in a breath and let it out. Life was weird. And getting weirder by the day.

Still, who knew what tomorrow would bring? Hadn't she always wanted to escape from reality? Wake up in some fantasy land far away?

This might not be quite what she'd imagined, but two days ago she would never have guessed she'd end up here. Surrounded by monsters and magic. Two days from now she might be somewhere else unimaginable.

All she could do was keep putting one foot in front of the other.

"So," she said. "Where do we go from here?"

18

V al swung the Ural away from the curb, the big motorcycle grumbling as it accelerated.

"Where are we going now?" Sandra sat in the sidecar, one hand holding her hood down over her eyes.

Val shrugged. "Home, I guess."

"Home? Like, your home? The same home you recently kicked me out of? Are you sure that's a good idea?"

"No, I'm sure that's a bad idea. But don't worry, I've got a backup plan."

They stopped at the light at Mission Street and waited while a man with a cat sitting on his shoulder crossed in front of them.

"Is that a cat?" Sandra asked. "I didn't know cats would do that."

"Humans make unreliable perches." Mister E appeared on Val's left shoulder, his striped tail wrapped around the back of her neck. *"It's a rare cat that will deign to sit on a human. Only the most trusting of us do."*

"Trusting? You?" Val scoffed.

Mister E looked offended. *"Of course I am trusting. I housed my essence inside your frail human shell, didn't I? If that's not trust, I don't know what is."*

The light turned green, and Val rolled her eyes as she twisted the throttle. As they reached the far side of the street, a dark shape vaulted onto the seat behind her.

"Flying toads!" Val cursed as the intruder clamped its arms around her shoulders.

"You'll be flying momentarily," the figure said into her ear. "Hold on tight now."

A chill went down her spine. Val recognized that voice.

"It's him," Sandra yelled from the sidecar. "The guy!"

Val didn't need to ask which guy she meant. It was the dark-haired grafter from the market.

Before she could throw an elbow back into his ribcage, the Ural began to change beneath her. The gas tank grew a black coat of hair. It expanded between her legs, while the gooseneck grew into a real neck, heaving with muscle. Instead of handlebars, Val found herself gripping a fluttering black mane.

A horse. She was straddling a galloping horse. With no saddle.

The hands released her as Val yelped and threw her arms around the horse's neck. Her heart was in her throat. She'd never been on a horse in her life. She had no idea how to ride a horse.

The first thing she noticed was that it was big. Really big. Much larger than horses looked when other people sat on them. The sleek back was twice as wide as she was, and the neck she clung to was a heaving column of muscle.

The black mane whipped in the wind, snapping her in the face. She winced and turned away... and that's when she got her second shock. The horse was much taller than the Ural had been. The street was a good six feet down. If she fell from this height and speed, she'd probably break her neck.

Sandra had it even worse than she did. The girl hung off the side of the horse, her arms wrapped around Val's waist, her feet dangling as she tried to keep them clear of the flashing hooves. Her hood had fallen off and her snake hair seemed as panicked as she was. The snakes were all colors and patterns, writhing and straining toward Val, coiling around her arms and legs.

Fortunately, Val didn't mind snakes. Having dozens of tiny snakes wrapping themselves around her wouldn't be her first choice, but things could be worse.

"At least they're not spiders," she muttered.

"Help," Sandra squealed, nearly losing her grip as the horse veered sharply.

One of the snakes panicked and sank tiny fangs into Val's thigh. She hissed with pain.

"Don't look up!" she snapped. "The last thing I need is more stone body parts."

Sandra nodded, her face buried in the side of the horse.

Just to be safe, Val kept her own face turned away as she reached one arm down toward Sandra, hooking it under the girl's armpit by feel. She tried to heave Sandra onto the horse behind her, but quickly realized the girl was too heavy for that, and she had very little leverage. She might be able to pull Sandra up if she turned and used both hands, but that would require letting go of the horse, and they'd both be eating asphalt if she did that.

"Use your magic," Mister E hissed.

"I don't have any horse magic!" she snapped.

"Not on the horse. On your gorgon friend."

"How would that work? Do you want me to charm the snakes? Don't I need a flute for that?"

"You're overthinking this. Use my strength the way you do when you're fighting. Extra strength is good for more things than simply throwing punches."

Val scrunched up her face. She'd never consciously thought about the fact that she was using Mister E's strength when she fought. She just reacted by instinct. Of course, she'd known she was tapping into his power, but could she do the same thing intentionally?

"Only one way to find out." She reached deep and felt power flood through her limbs. She shouted out to Sandra. "Get ready to swing your legs up behind me on three. One. Two."

On three, she heaved with all the power infusing her muscles. To her surprise, Sandra's body felt no heavier than a desk chair as she swung smoothly onto the horse behind her.

Sandra squeezed Val's waist and buried her face in Val's back. Val could feel her shuddering.

"What is happening?" Sandra had to shout over the wind and the thunder of hooves.

"Apparently, that guy can transform more than just people," Val called back.

"What do we do?"

"I don't know. Hold on until the horse gets tired?"

"What if it never gets tired?"

Val ground her teeth. She didn't want to say it aloud, but she was afraid that might turn out to be the case. The beast was magical, after all.

"Then we'll have to find a way to make it stop."

19

N ight had covered the city, and the black horse was still running. They'd been up and down so many streets, Val had lost track of where they were exactly. Somewhere in the hills above Noe Valley, she thought. It was hard to get a good look around with the drifting fog banks and the horse's mane whipping her in the face every time she opened her eyes.

Clinging to the back of a runaway horse in San Francisco was an awful experience. Her legs hurt. Her ass hurt. Her arms and back hurt from holding onto the beast's neck. She was wet and cold from riding through the fog.

"I don't think I can hold on much longer," Sandra yelled. "My arms feel like pudding."

"Me either," Val admitted. "My whole body feels like hammered tin. I'm not going to be able to walk for a week."

"Have you figured out how to stop the horse?"

"No. I think we're going to have to jump off."

"Seriously?" Sandra's grip tightened around her waist. "Won't we break our necks?"

"We might," Val conceded.

The Ural-horse was moving with frightening speed, running as fast as it would have gone if it were still a motorcycle. She didn't know if the beast's speed and stamina were due to its mechanical origin, or if they came with the spell that had transformed it. Either way, there was no denying the thing was running faster and farther than any horse had a right to.

"I don't want to die," Sandra said. "I may be a monster, but I'd rather be a live monster than a dead one."

"Same," Val called back.

They both yelped as the horse flashed across an intersection, hurdling the hood of a white car in the process.

"So how do we get off this thing without dying?" Sandra asked.

Val almost laughed. "It's cute that you think I have the answers."

"You're Val Keri. Of course you have the answers."

The faith in Sandra's voice made Val feel ill. She didn't deserve that trust. Didn't want it. She was just a messed-up witch muddling through as best she could. She made mistakes. A lot of them. Sometimes people got hurt. People died.

But it didn't look like anyone else was going to save them. And if she didn't do something soon, they'd eventually drop off from exhaustion. Better to try and fail than to do nothing.

She sighed and set her jaw, squinting against the whipping mane as she scanned the street ahead of them. They were moving through a small pocket between fog banks, and she could see almost two whole blocks ahead. This part of the city was steep, full of dramatic peaks and valleys. Several times the road had run along a cliff face on one side or the other. She watched until she saw what she was looking for. There. Halfway down the next block was a dark gap in the houses where the hillside fell away. She could see city lights sparkling in the distance.

"Get ready to jump off when I say," she called over her shoulder.

"Which side?"

"The right side."

"OK." Sandra peered ahead over her shoulder. Her grip on Val tightened. "Um. You're aware there's a cliff there, right?"

"That's where we're jumping off."

"We're jumping off the cliff?" Sandra's voice squeaked. "Are you crazy?"

"I thought you said you trusted me."

"Maybe I underestimated how insane you are."

"Don't worry, I'll catch you." The gap in the houses was approaching fast. Val tensed, getting ready to jump.

"Off the edge of a cliff? Who's going to catch you?"

"No time to explain. Don't worry, I've got this. Just hold on tight to my waist, like you're doing now."

"While jumping?"

"While jumping. And afterward. Don't let go."

The speeding horse drew even with the gap. Through it, the fog bank had swallowed up the night. The clouds below looked thick and soft, like a down pillow waiting to catch them.

Val wished that were the case.

"Jump!" she yelled, matching action to word.

Or she tried to, at least.

Jumping off a moving horse is not as easy as one might think. With one leg on either side of a very large animal, Val found that jumping at all was almost impossible. Also, her legs were sore and tired from clinging to the beast's back. When she tried to gather them and jump, all she managed was a kind of butt-hop, followed by an awkward slide down the side of the animal. Sandra came along with her, squeezing so tight Val thought she might break a rib.

This put them on a collision course with the street. And the black horse's flashing hooves.

They were about to either break their necks falling or have their spines snapped from being trampled. Not the most appealing options.

Sandra screamed in her ear, and Val winced. If she wasn't about to die, she'd be very annoyed by that.

Her plan had been to leap off the edge of the cliff and catch them both with an updraft. The extra distance between the horse and the base of the cliff would provide a margin of error and give her time to catch their falling bodies. Risky, but Val thought it was doable.

Their failure to jump complicated things.

Now, instead of having a couple of seconds of free fall to work her magic, Val had only an instant before they hit the asphalt. Which would probably be followed by a thorough trampling. Not a double whammy they were likely to walk away from.

She reacted instinctively.

Val yanked at the air with all the desperation and force she could muster. A fierce gust rushed beneath the horse, punching them sideways, knocking them away from the flashing hooves and sending them tumbling over the edge of the cliff.

There was no time to congratulate herself. Now they were falling properly, and Val knew there were jagged rocks lurking below.

The problem was, she already had the air pushing them to the side. Releasing that wind and creating an updraft from another direction would take time. Time they didn't have.

So she did the only thing she could. Val poured more power into the wind, and it flung them further away from the face of the cliff, shooting them out into the fog like autumn leaves caught in a storm.

Sandra squawked and squeezed so hard Val couldn't breathe. There was no time to complain, though. The wind might have been carrying them away from the cliff face, but gravity was still working, and Val knew they were arcing downward through the mist. With visibility limited to about five feet, there was no telling how close the ground was.

She encouraged the side wind, curling it beneath them like a giant hand. Then she began to rise.

The gust transitioned into a fierce updraft, carrying the two women with it. A few seconds later, they shot out the top of the fog bank.

Sandra gasped.

Below their feet, fog covered the city in a rolling silver blanket. Yellow streetlights winked in and out as the fog swirled. Above them, the night was dark and clear. A Cheshire Cat moon grinned above the dark silhouette of the mountains across the bay. Hundreds of stars shone overhead. In the distance, the lights of the bay bridge swooped over the water like a graceful string of pearls. A chill wind from the Pacific stirred and tore at the silvery fog, carrying the scent of brine.

They hung there, held aloft by Val's magic, taking it all in as their panicked heartbeats slowly returned to normal. Sandra's arms were warm around Val's waist, her head pressed against her back.

"Not a bad view, huh?" Val finally broke the silence.

"No. Not bad at all," Sandra agreed softly. "So, uh, you can fly?"

"Something like that."

"Very cool."

"It is, isn't it?" Val grinned. She'd never shared this with anyone outside of Mister E, and he didn't count. It felt nice.

The moment stretched as they hung there, taking it all in. The tongue of one of Sandra's snakes tickled Val's ear. The girl pressed against her back so close it felt like she was being hugged. It was a long time since Val had been hugged. She didn't hate the feeling.

Finally, Val cleared her throat.

"We should probably get home."

"Are we going to fly there?"

"Well, we kind of lost the motorcycle."

Sandra laughed. "Yeah, I suppose we did."

"It's nice and foggy, so we don't have to worry about people spotting us."

"Right." Val felt Sandra nod against her back. "So, flying?"

"Flying."

"Cool."

With a crook of her finger, Val directed the wind to carry them home.

20

"I'm going to have a sign made that says: *Val Keri's Home for Magical Misfits*," Malcolm announced.

They were sitting in the living room, warm cups of coffee firmly in hand. It might have been a beautiful night for flying, but it was also cold and damp, and Val and Sandra were both chilled to the bone.

They'd stripped off their wet clothes and now Val was perched in the window seat, wrapped in her fuzzy green bathrobe, while Malcolm had dug up an oversized animal onesie for Sandra. She sat in a battered recliner with the hood up over her face, looking like a cosplay orange fox. Malcolm had his legs stretched out on the couch, feet wrapped in rainbow socks, a delighted grin on his face. Hillary was out somewhere—Val didn't want to think about what she might be doing—so it was just the three of them.

"No, even better: *Val Keri's Magical Menagerie*," Malcolm amended.

Val made a face and slurped her coffee. Malcolm was having entirely too much fun with this.

"*Val Keri's Magnificent Magical Misfit Menagerie*." This time he drew his hands through the air like a ringmaster announcing a show.

"Enough, Malcolm," Val snapped. "It's not funny."

"*I think it's hilarious,*" Mister E chimed in. He was reclining on the back of the couch, laughing up at the ceiling. *"Send all of your unwanted creatures to Val Keri's Magical Misfit Menagerie. It's got a nice ring to it."*

"Sandra is not staying here, so you can wipe that ridiculous idea right out of your mind," Val said. "We tried being roommates once, and it didn't work. We're not going down that road again."

Malcolm drew an exaggerated frown in the air with his fingers. "Hashtag sad face. Just because you didn't get along with her doesn't mean I didn't. I thought Sandra was a lovely housemate." He reached over and patted Sandra's fox-knee.

"Even if we got along, there's no room for her. All our bedrooms are full. Unless you want to share a room with her?" Val asked pointedly.

Malcolm paled a little at that, his eyes going from Val's frozen fingers to the little snakes sticking their noses out from under Sandra's hood. The thought of sharing a room with someone who could accidentally turn you to stone was enough to make anyone blanch.

Sandra's quiet voice emerged from the depths of her fox hood. "Why did you bring me back here then?"

"I brought you back here because we were cold and exhausted and I needed to find somewhere safe," Val said. "It wasn't a permanent invitation. I was hoping the shifters would take you in, but obviously that didn't work out."

"So where do I go?" Sandra pulled her feet up onto the armchair and hugged her knees to her chest. "I can't imagine anyone would want a roommate who can turn them to stone."

"Anything's possible," Malcolm said. "I know people who are into some freaky shit. In a town as weird as this one, plenty of people would get off on having a roommate who can petrify them."

"We are not turning Sandra's... condition... into some new fetish," Val said. "She's looking for safety, not exploitation."

"Unless she wants to be exploited," Malcolm amended. "Maybe Sandra has always wanted to be a dominatrix. People would jump to obey your commands if you threatened to turn them to stone. It's all about consent, Val. Don't make assumptions."

Val groaned and pinched the bridge of her nose. She could feel a headache building.

"Sandra, is that something you want?" she asked.

Sandra's hood shook from side to side. "Definitely not."

"OK, I'm glad we cleared that up. Now, can we please have a constructive conversation about this?" Val glared at Malcolm.

"Oh! What about the basement?" Malcom said.

"The basement?"

"Sure. Didn't you stash Hillary down there for a while?"

"Yes, but Hillary is undead and doesn't need plush accommodations."

"Sandra is pretty low maintenance," Malcolm insisted.

"Have you been down in the basement lately?" Val asked.

"Well, no, but I'm sure—"

"It's a basement, Malcolm. It's full of cobwebs and broken furniture."

"We can clean it up!" he insisted. "You said yourself nobody ever goes down there. That's why you hid Hillary there. It'd be perfect for Sandra."

Val sighed. Once Malcolm got going, he was hard to derail. She could feel his enthusiasm overriding her objections.

"OK, let's say, for the sake of argument, that we could make the basement livable. Would Sandra even want to live in a dingy old basement?"

"What do you say, Sandra?" Malcolm turned expectant eyes to the girl. "Instead of roommates, we'll be neighbors. It'll be great!"

Sandra froze like a rabbit pinned by the gaze of a hawk. Val could feel the discomfort radiating from her. She opened her mouth to rescue the poor girl, but to her surprise, Sandra spoke first.

"I think that might be OK."

Val looked dubious. "Are you sure? Don't let Malcolm's enthusiasm make decisions for you. It's a basement, Sandra. Even if we clean it up, it's not going to be comfortable."

"Don't listen to her," Malcolm interrupted. "We'll put some shag carpet on the floor, drape some tapestries across the ceiling, get you a waterbed. I can see it now: It'll be like a 1970s love nest."

A laugh burst from Val's lips. Malcom's vision was so ridiculous, and suggested with such earnestness, that she couldn't help herself.

"I don't know about all that, but we'll figure something out," she said. "For now, there's a couch down there that's serviceable. We can post a sign on the door saying the basement is flooded or something to keep anyone from accidentally wandering in on you."

She shook her head as she took a sip of her coffee, collecting her thoughts.

"Now that we've got that sorted, we've got a bigger problem on our hands."

"That fucking guy," Sandra snarled.

Val was startled by Sandra's vehemence, but she supposed it was warranted. The guy had turned her into a gorgon, after all. If Val were in Sandra's shoes, she'd be on the bloody warpath.

"That fucking guy," Val agreed. "We need to figure out who he is, and how to track him down. Then I'm going to nail his ass to the wall."

21

The entrance to the Metropolis looked like it had been transported straight out of the classic Fritz Lang film whose name it bore, with an intricate art déco arch framing the door. Inside, it felt like a classic 1920s speakeasy interior. Gilt-framed mirrors hung over intricately patterned wallpaper. Stained glass shades cast colored light over tabletops, while crystal chandeliers dangled from graceful chains overhead.

Looking for a lead on her mysterious attacker, Val had contacted Padraig O'Ceallaigh. Padraig had helped her out in the past and, more importantly, he was at least part fae, and the scion of an ancient and affluent Irish family that imported illegal magical artifacts. Padraig had suggested she might find a lead at The Metropolis. He'd been cryptic about why he thought she should go there, exactly, as if something prevented him from giving her a straight answer.

"Just go see for yourself," he'd told her. "I can't give you the name of the fellow you're looking for, but there might be someone there who can. Or who can at least point you in the right direction."

"Do you know who he is?" Val had snapped. "And you're not going to tell me?"

"It's more a matter of 'can't' than 'won't'," he said.

"What does that even mean?"

"I'm sorry, but I can't be more specific. Just go. Trust me."

Val had thought long and hard, wondering who or what was preventing him from answering her questions. If someone could pull his strings, that someone had to be extremely powerful. Despite her burning curiosity, Val thought she might be better off not knowing who that someone was. Still, she couldn't help but wonder, and the question nagged at her like a sore tooth.

In the end, she'd decided to take Padraig's advice. What other choice did she have?

She'd sent Malcolm and Sandra to the Library to see if they could dig up any information on a dog-faced man who transformed motorcycles into horses and people into monsters, but other than the hope that they'd find something, she didn't have any leads to go on.

So. The Metropolis.

The night was young and sparsely populated, but the early-evening clientele matched what Padraig had told her to expect. The men wore sharp suits with rakishly angled hats and suspenders, while the women favored beaded dresses and stockings. A few even posed with long cigarette holders, which they expertly clamped between their teeth without smearing their lipstick.

Val had made an effort, but she still felt severely underdressed. For one thing, she never wore dresses—in fact, she hardly owned any. Hillary had offered to let her borrow a dress, but Val had refused. She was working, and she needed to be able to move freely if things went sideways.

After much debate, they'd finally decided to go in the other direction. Val was now dressed in a pin-striped suit she'd borrowed from Malcolm. It was a little loose in the shoulders and tight in the hips, but a surprisingly good fit, all things considered. Most importantly, she could move in it, and her knife was close at hand in the breast pocket. Malcolm had offered her the use of a fedora as well, but Val had declined. There were limits.

"Do you see anything unusual?" she murmured under her breath.

She sat at a high table against the wall, nursing a ginger beer in a highball glass while she carefully took in every detail. A couple of the men had given her and her suit double takes, but most of the patrons accepted her cross-dressing without a blink. This was San Francisco, after all.

"Aside from the fact that this place is a century out of date?" Mister E replied.

Val gave him the side eye. "You're one to talk."

Mister E had donned his top hat for the occasion and mounted his candy cigarette on the end of an ivory cigarette holder. A monocle on a gold chain circled his left eye.

The demon-cat blew smoke rings at the ceiling and grinned at her. *"Yes, but I was alive when these things were originally in style. The humans in this bar cannot say the same thing."*

"Are you, though?"

"Am I what?"

"Really alive?"

Mister E looked offended. *"Of course I'm alive."*

"I'm just saying. You don't have a body of your own. An argument could be made that you are actually a ghost."

"Spirits are still alive."

Val raised an eyebrow. "I thought ghosts were the definition of dead."

"I am not a ghost. Spirits and ghosts are not the same thing."

"What's the difference?"

Mister E gave a long-suffering sigh. *"A ghost is a spirit that remains after a physical body has died. They are lost souls who either refuse or are unable to move on to the next realm. A spirit is the energetic force that animates a body. A spirit may sometimes move about independently of its body. For example, the way your spirit did when you journeyed to the pocket realm of that dead girl in the Queen Anne Hotel. But that does not make your spirit a ghost."*

Val narrowed her eyes at him. "Wait a minute. Are you saying you still have a physical body somewhere? I thought the whole reason you were trapped inside my body was because your spirit had nowhere else to go."

"The answer to that is complicated, and not something you need to concern yourself with."

"I disagree. I think your presence inside my body is absolutely something I should concern myself with. What do you..."

Mister E interrupted, pointing across the room with his cigarette holder. *"That gentleman over there is watching you. You might want to stop arguing with yourself so vociferously."*

Val followed his gaze and found that, sure enough, her mutterings had drawn eyes. So much for being inconspicuous.

The gentleman in question wore a mint-colored suit over a black shirt. There was something familiar about him... though he was all the way across the room and it was too dark to get a good look at him from where she sat.

Val blinked. Did his face look furry?

She blinked again. No, it must have been a trick of the light.

The man smiled, exposing teeth that shone like the moon. Val looked away lest he think she was trying to make eye contact with him. She sipped her drink and studied him surreptitiously through her eyelashes instead.

"Does that guy look strange to you?" she muttered around the cocktail straw.

"He's wearing a glamour."

Val stiffened. "A glamour? Like one of the fae?"

"Perhaps. He could be any number of things. Many creatures wear glamours around humans for their own safety. Life would be rather difficult if you got attacked by an angry mob every time you tried to buy some bread."

Val stared at him. "Are you saying there are creatures wearing glamours around me all the time? And you never mentioned it before now?"

"What is there to say? Should I point it out every time someone walks by wearing a pair of designer shoes? To each their own."

"Wearing designer shoes is hardly the same thing as wearing a glamour."

"Isn't it? They're both just coverings one places over oneself to change one's appearance. Some wear glamours for style, some for protection. Either way, it's no business of mine."

Val eyed the man in the mint suit again. If he was wearing a glamour, he could be literally anything beneath his magical disguise. A seraph. A vampire. A faerie. Or something much worse.

She stiffened as a thought occurred to her. "Are there other creatures wearing glamours in this room right now?"

"Naturally. Weren't you listening?"

"Let me borrow your eyes for a minute."

The room blurred. Colors melted and ran like watercolor as she looked through the eyes of Mister E.

Magic was always around, but it was only observable on another spectrum—the same way some things were only apparent under infrared or ultraviolet light. The magical spectrum was outside the normal way we experienced the world. Looking through Mister E's eyes was akin to someone turning on several strings of colored lights. She saw the same world, plus something extra. Energy that had been there all along became visible and shining.

Val gasped as the club snapped back into sharp focus.

It wasn't just the man in the mint suit. Everywhere she looked, different colors of energy swirled and shone. The interior of The Metropolis was bursting with magic.

ower swirled around the bar, wisps of color drifting like mist.
The Metropolis was stuffed with magic: the walls, the chandeliers, the candles on the tables—everything shone before Val's altered
sight.

But the patrons shone brightest of all.

The guy in the mint suit was definitely wearing a glamour, but he
was far from the only one. Nearly half the patrons glowed in Val's
shifted vision.

"Flying toads. What is this place?" she whispered, her hand sliding
to grip the handle of her knife.

"It's a bar, obviously," Mister E said.

She glared at her companion. "Don't try to be clever. Nobody likes a
clever cat."

"I disagree. In fact...."

"Not now! I'm serious. What am I looking at here?"

Mister E rolled his golden eyes. *"Spoilsport."*

He took a maddeningly long drag on his candy cigarette, and Val
ground her teeth while he blew three smoke rings before answering.

*"The Metropolis is clearly a speakeasy for the magical community. I
thought you'd be pleased,"* he said. *"These are your people, after all."*

"They're not my people."

Val observed the glamoured creatures in the room through narrowed eyes. She'd never seen so many magical beings in one place in her life. Fortunately, other than the man in the mint suit, none of them seemed to be paying her the slightest attention. Still, she kept her hand on the hilt of her knife, ready in case one of them decided to attack.

"My people are witches. Humans who use magic. These are magical creatures hiding behind glamours."

"Potayto, potahto," the cat said lazily. *"Your friend Padraig hides behind a glamour, yet you don't seem distrustful of him."*

"That's different."

"Is it?" He smirked. *"It must be his bedroom eyes."*

Val scowled, but she had to admit he had a point. Padraig had proven that not all magical creatures were hostile. Some could even be helpful in the right circumstances.

She scanned the room again. The people wearing glamours were chatting, drinking, dancing. Enjoying their night and paying her no mind at all. In short, they weren't behaving any differently than the non-magical patrons.

Except for the man in the mint suit. His dark eyes smoldered when he looked at her.

As she watched, he got up and crossed the room. When he passed close to her table, his face blurred, wavered and re-formed. The dog-faced man winked at her, then he turned and vanished into the crowd.

"That's the guy," Val sputtered, bolting to her feet. Her knife was in her hand as she scanned the crowd.

The man had disappeared.

"He's taunting me," she growled.

Around her, the dancers swirled and came together. Broke apart and regrouped like leaves in the wind. There was no sign of the mint-suited man.

"Flying toads," she cursed. "He was right there. Do you think it's a coincidence he's here?"

"I don't believe in coincidence."

"Neither do I."

She started as she saw the man emerge from the crowd near an inconspicuous door across the room. Well, inconspicuous if you paid no attention to the security guard posted outside it.

The mint-suited man exchanged a few words with the guard. Arcane sigils in the doorframe flared as he put his hand on the doorknob. The door swung open and Val got a glimpse of a descending staircase as he stepped through and was gone.

"I'm guessing that's not the little boys' room," she muttered.

"That would not be my first guess either."

Val kept one eye on the door, but the man did not come back out.

Over the next half hour, she saw several other people disappear through the door. The pattern was always the same: they would exchange a few words with the security guard, put their hand on the door, the sigils would flare, and the door would swing open.

"What do you think it takes to get down there? A secret password?"

"Perhaps. Or a spell to activate the sigils. I can't tell from here. We'd have to get closer."

"Hmmm."

Val watched the room for another half hour, considering. In that time, three more people passed through the magic door. None of the people returned.

She watched the rest of the club too, but aside from the unusual number of people wearing glamours, nothing out of the ordinary caught her eye. As far as she could tell, The Metropolis was the speakeasy it presented itself to be.

Finally, Val pushed away from the table and got to her feet. "I guess there's only one way to find out."

She meandered across the room, observing the door from several angles while trying not to make the direction she was heading obvious. Still, the security guard picked up on her trajectory, and he watched her with flat eyes as she approached.

He was what you'd expect from a security guard at a nightclub—a hulking, unsmiling man dressed in black. But Val's enhanced sight told her that was merely a facade. The edges of his body glowed with the telltale signs of glamour. She had no idea what lurked beneath his disguise, but it was a safe bet he wasn't human.

She tried on a smile as she stopped in front of him. The security guard didn't return it. Up close, he was even bigger than he'd looked from across the room, towering head and shoulders above her. The shoulders in question were nearly twice as wide as her own.

Val swallowed and cleared her throat. "Good crowd tonight, eh?"

The man didn't so much as blink. If it weren't for his eyes watching her, he might have been carved from stone.

"So, can I go in the back room?"

His expression didn't change, but the man's mouth opened long enough to allow a single word to escape.

"Password."

"Ah. Right." She racked her brain for inspiration. "Um... moonlight?"

The guard's expression darkened. Beads of sweat dotted Val's forehead.

"Any ideas?" she muttered under her breath.

"I suggest you examine the sigils while we're close, then beat a hasty retreat so we can consider them."

"That's actually reasonable advice," she said, surprised. "What happened to the cat who wanted to bite everyone's face off?"

"We can bite his face off, if you'd prefer. I just thought you might like to try something else for a change." Mister E chuckled. *"Whatever you do, I suggest you do it quickly, before the security guard chooses for you."*

To the guard, Val said, "Wait, that's not it. Give me a minute." She studied the sigils while pretending to rack her brain.

There were only five primary symbols, traced in a repeating pattern all around the doorframe. A couple of them looked familiar, but she had no idea how to activate the sigils at a glance. Fortunately, she had an oracle thousands of years old living in her head, so Val concentrated on memorizing the pattern of the sigils, not understanding them.

When she had them firmly in mind, she said, "Sorry, today's password must have slipped my mind. I'll be back when I've got it."

She retreated into the crowd before the guard had a chance to object, but she could feel his eyes boring into her back all the way across the room.

Back at the table, Val dumped salt upon the dark wood and traced the sigils while they were still fresh in her mind. They glittered like constellations in the low light.

"Do you recognize any of these?" she whispered. "Can you tell me how to activate them?"

"Hmmmm, they're a pretty standard arcane alphabet, based upon ancient Sumerian. Yes, I see. I believe you need to activate them in this order," Mister E said, indicating the correct sigils one at a time.

"And that spells 'open sesame?'"

"Something like that, yes."

She peered across the room at the enormous bouncer. "Now we just need to get past the incredible Hulk over there."

"Perhaps a distraction is in order?" Mister E smiled wickedly.

"What kind of distraction?"

"Something that will draw him away from the door, obviously."

Val scanned the room, tapping her fingernail against her lips. "You know what? I think I've got just the thing."

As a bartender, Val had a good internal barometer for the energy of a crowd. She'd been watching this particular crowd all night and had noticed some people were having more fun than others. In particular, she'd noticed a heavily glamoured party crammed into a booth near the magic door. She didn't know what kind of beings they were beneath their glamours, or what kind of substances they were on, but the five of them were very loud and very energetic—bouncing around the club like a troop of over-caffeinated lemurs.

They'd annoyed many people with their jostling and shouting, but one offended group in particular looked ready to explode. They were the type to take themselves far too seriously, dressed to impress without a hair out of place, staring down their noses at everyone and everything. They also had a dangerous look that reminded Val of Vasilevski's crew, which used to hang out at the Alley Cat. She thought it would only take a small push to send them over the edge.

She waited until one of the bouncing party—a man wearing a yellow silk shirt with lace at the collar—was passing by the serious party. She used a small puff of air to tangle the man's feet, causing him to stumble into a sour-faced man in a sharp suit.

Val couldn't have drawn it up any better. The dandy's drink spilled all over the sharp-suited man's chest. Voices were raised. There was pushing and shoving. Both groups swarmed around them like bees to honey.

The bouncers moved in, converging from all sides of the room in a coordinated pincer action. The arcane door stood unguarded.

"Now's our chance," Val whispered.

She scampered across the floor. A quick glance over her shoulder showed her the fight was in full swing. A crowd had gathered, and the groups were laying into each other with wild abandon.

Val smirked. Nothing drew people's attention faster than blood in the water. The security guard would be distracted for a few minutes at least.

She laid her hand on the doorknob and focused. She trickled energy into the sigils carved into the doorframe one by one, until the entire border abruptly flared to life. The lock clicked open.

With a final furtive glance over her shoulder, Val slipped through and onto the staircase. The magic door clicked shut behind her.

23

A single lightbulb hung at the top of narrow wooden stairs leading down. Ancient boards creaked under Val's weight, each stair protesting so much she was afraid she'd crash through the rotting wood and break her ankle. The light from the hanging bulb didn't quite reach the bottom of the staircase, and as she felt her way down the last few stairs, she clutched the banister like a lifeline.

The instant Val's foot touched the bottom step, everything changed. Her ears popped as she felt herself pass through some kind of magical membrane. The barrier was tight over her skin, like she was sliding into a spandex bodysuit. It tingled slightly and squeezed, then she slipped out the other side and into another realm entirely.

She stumbled to a halt and stood blinking, trying to understand what her eyes were showing her.

Val wasn't in the basement she'd expected. She wasn't in a basement at all.

A dim glade opened before her: a twilight glow of indefinite source revealed heavy-limbed trees with round tables scattered beneath the boughs. Shadowy figures slouched in heavy wooden chairs.

"Things just got weird. Why does this look like a beer garden?" Val whispered.

"A beer garden populated by the rejects of every realm from here to Valhalla," Mister E snorted. *"This must be where the creatures upstairs come to let their hair down."*

"Let their glamours down, you mean."

"Precisely."

At first glance, the beings lounging at the nearby tables didn't seem to have much in common. There was a small, dark-skinned creature whose limbs were as twisted and gnarled as the roots of the oak under which he sat. A punk kid with a red hat on backwards sat across from the creature, carving something into the surface of the table with the tip of his knife. A long-limbed pair of fashion models lounged at the next table. Their ears were long and tapered, their high cheekbones so sharp they made Val flinch. Beyond them was a table occupied by a solitary bear of a man in a flannel shirt with the sleeves rolled up. His bushy beard and furry arms hinted that he might, in fact, be more bear than man. There was no sign of the man in the mint suit.

"Are you meeting someone?"

Val jumped as a stocky server with serious biceps appeared at her elbow. The top of the woman's head only came up to Val's shoulder, and a fiery braided beard hung to her belt.

"No. I mean, no one in particular," Val stammered.

The server pursed her lips in disapproval as she led Val to an empty table and took her order.

Now that she was seated, Val could observe the other patrons more closely. Her eyes bulged as she took in the scene. Tonight was definitely one to remember. First the club full of glamoured beings upstairs and now this. She'd never seen so many types of supernatural creatures in one place in her life. She'd never imagined there could be so many inside the city.

"Are we still underneath The Metropolis?"

Mister E laughed. *"I highly doubt it."*

"Where are we then?"

"It's impossible to say. The portal we passed through at the bottom of the stairs could have sent us anywhere. We could be on the other side of the city. Or in a different town altogether. Even another realm."

Val felt the blood drain from her face.

"We might not be in San Francisco anymore?"

The cat grinned and stretched, clearly enjoying Val's discomfort.

"We might not be on earth anymore."

Val gripped the edge of the table so hard her knuckles went white. "How do we get back?"

"What's the rush? We came here for a reason, did we not?"

She leaned forward and hissed, "But how do we get back?"

Mister E rolled his golden eyes. *"No doubt there's a portal that leads back to The Metropolis. A place this stable always has easy entrances and exits. Enjoy the ambiance, squalid though it may be."*

Val forced herself to breathe. Mister E had a point. They'd come here for a reason. It would be foolish to freak out and leave before they had even learned anything.

Examining her new companions, she decided the demon-cat might be onto something with his "rejects" comment as well. Though they came in all shapes and sizes, the creatures in the beer garden shared a disreputable air. The tall ones with the cheekbones had cold eyes. The jaw of the kid with the red hat was belligerent. The bear-man had a shabby look to him, as if he'd hit rock bottom a long time ago and had been dragging along it ever since.

"It looks like we've come to the right place," Val muttered.

"If by 'right place' you mean the bottom of the barrel." Mister E blew a trio of candy smoke rings. *"Do you see the man in the mint suit?"*

"No, but that doesn't mean anything. There are plenty of tables beneath the trees we can't see clearly. Also, that suit was probably part of his glamour. Down here, he could be anyone."

"So now what?"

Val eyed the beings around her as she sipped her ginger beer. Many of them looked dangerous, as if they wouldn't hesitate to knife you in the back and leave you to bleed out in an alley.

She swallowed, unclenched her fingers from the edge of the table and sat back in her chair with exaggerated casualness.

"Now we wait, and see if any of our fellow bottom-dwellers want to talk."

24

A tall creature that looked like a bundle of animated sticks approached Val's table. It had knobby elbows and twigs reaching upward in a wild approximation of hair. It bobbed its wooden face at her.

"May we sit down?" The creature's voice creaked like branches in the wind.

Val gave it a cautious nod, and the thing folded itself onto the chair across from her. It regarded her with leaf-green eyes for a long moment. Gazing into those eyes, Val was transported to a tranquil glade. A breeze rustled through the canopy, dappling the ground in moving shadows. It felt peaceful, and very, very old. As if human feet had not trod this ground in a long time. Perhaps ever.

The creature's voice broke the spell, "You are Valora Keri."

It wasn't a question, but Val answered anyway. "I am. Who are you?"

"We have many names. We do not attach importance to them. Some call us the Green One. We ourselves have always been partial to the name given to us by the playwright: Peaseblossom."

"The Green One? I've heard of the Green Man and Gaia, the Earth Mother. Are you related to them?"

Peaseblossom's expression did not change. "If you like. We are all part of the natural cycle. We are all related to the Green Man and the Earth Mother."

Val felt uneasy. The Green Man and Earth Mother were names for Mother Nature. From what Val had read, the powerful natural god was essentially a chaotic being. Constantly building up and tearing down. Mother Nature had no concept of good and evil. Birth, death, and rebirth were all equal parts of the natural cycle. If this being embodied that, she needed to be on her guard.

Still, the creature did not feel dangerous. On the contrary, the stick-figure felt peaceful and serene. Val doubted such a being would be able to help her track down the dog-faced man, but perhaps they could be helpful in other ways.

"How do you know who I am?" she asked.

Peaseblossom creaked with amusement. "All know who you are, Valora Keri. This realm is reawakening. You are a light that calls us from our dream."

"Reawakening? What do you mean?"

"We have been sleeping for a long time. Frozen in the permafrost. Now the world is thawing. Wild storms are spreading magic across the globe once again. Opening cracks in this reality. Breathing life into the in-between places where our kind once flourished."

"And I am contributing to this somehow?"

"You are a shooting star, Valora Keri. As we open our eyes once again, there are lights that draw our attention. People and places where magic burns bright. You are one such being. You call to us like moths to a flame."

Val's brow crinkled. That was a lot to wrap her head around.

"Are you saying that I attract magical beings? I'm some kind of magical magnet?" She felt a chill. For years, she'd suspected she was unwittingly summoning monsters.

Her fingers traced the memento mori tattoo over her heart as she thought of all the dead people in her life. She'd always suspected the death that followed her was her fault. Had Peaseblossom just confirmed that?

The being creaked again. "Not exactly. You are but one of many lights in this world. Unlike a magnet, your presence does not physically pull magical beings. But we can see your light from afar, and those who are curious may come closer in order to see you better. As we have just done."

This was all a bit much for Val. She needed to focus on what had brought her here.

"I'm trying to find someone. Or something. Can you answer some questions for me?"

A crown of little pink flowers bloomed as Peaseblossom bobbed their head agreeably. "We will try."

Val considered how to phrase her question. She knew the fae could be tricky.

"Have you seen a dog-faced man?"

"Of course."

"Can you tell me who he is?"

"If there were but one, we could. But there are many of that description."

Val frowned. Many of that description? She'd thought she was trying to find a single person. If more than one were running around, her task had become a lot more difficult. And dangerous.

"Who is this person, or persons? What do they want?"

Peaseblossom pondered this for a moment. "A being's motivations may be multi-faceted. Some beings produce facets exponentially. A single being may want many things. Many beings may want a single thing. It is impossible to say with certainty."

Val scowled and tried another direction.

"Do you know why humans have been transforming into monsters?"

"Certainly." The being did not elaborate.

She set her jaw and tried again.

"Can you tell me why humans have been transforming into monsters?"

"Certainly." Peaseblossom again said no more.

Val ground her teeth as Mister E's laughter rang in her ears.

"You are very bad at this."

"It's my first time questioning a faerie," Val hissed under her breath. "Cut me some slack."

The demon cat yawned and stretched, baring sharp teeth. *"Take your time. It's not as if I have anywhere else to be. I do wish there was a warm sunbeam I could curl up in. This magical light is no good for napping."*

"I apologize for the inconvenience," she growled.

Val turned her attention back to the faerie. Her error, she thought, was in the first word of the question. She tried a different tack.

"Will you tell me why humans have been transforming into monsters?"

"Perhaps," Peaseblossom said.

Val took a deep breath. In through the nose, out through the mouth. Stay calm.

"Are the wild storms transforming people into monsters?" she asked.

"Yes and no."

"What does that mean?" Val snapped. Fighting to control her temper, she bit the inside of her cheek so hard she tasted blood.

Peaseblossom looked nonplussed by her outburst, but gamely gathered themselves before continuing.

"Wild storms do many things. As I have said, they are redistributing magic throughout the world. One of the things they may do is, as you say, 'turn people into monsters.' Though they may just as easily not do so."

"So, some storms turn people into monsters and some don't?"

"That may be an accurate statement."

"May be?"

"It depends on your definition of 'monsters.'"

Floating above the chair to her left, Mister E blew candy smoke rings and laughed. Val ground her fists into her eye sockets and did her best to ignore him.

She'd heard that dealing with the fae could be difficult, but this was ridiculous.

"What I meant to say was—" She paused to consider her phrasing before continuing. "Please tell me how you would define 'monsters.'"

Peaseblossom considered this. The branches of their hair rustled as if they were being stirred by a summer breeze.

"It is my understanding that the Mirriam-Webster Dictionary is an oracle of great repute in the human realm. This oracle defines the word 'monster' as..."

Val buried her face in her hands.

25

T he exit from the garden turned out to be another portal that dumped Val into a narrow brick alley. She hoped the alley was located behind The Metropolis. You could never be sure with magic portals. She might find herself in an alley on another continent entirely.

Trying to get useful information from Peaseblossom had been like trying to pull teeth. Her own teeth. With a pair of rusty pliers and no anesthetic. After nearly an hour of Peaseblossom talking in circles, her head was pounding, and she was mentally and physically exhausted. She'd been too tired to even think about questioning the other beings in the glade.

Still, she'd worked hard to get down there, so she'd forced herself to walk a circuit of the garden, searching for the dog-faced man. Perhaps predictably, her search had come up empty.

Even worse, she still didn't know who the dog-faced man was, or have any clarity on why people were turning into monsters. She was no closer to answers than when she'd begun.

She sighed and turned toward the light at the end of the alley. Val stopped short. A large figure was leaning against the wall, silhouetted against the light. She tensed, but after a few seconds she realized the figure wasn't waiting for her. In fact, the figure seemed to be...

"Is that guy peeing?" She wrinkled her nose at the stench.

Val hesitated. The peeing figure was between her and the exit. It was too dark to tell who—or what—they were. All she could tell was that the person had a very large silhouette. Tall and broad as a bear. Maybe she should wait and let them clear out before she went anywhere.

As she stood frozen with indecision, someone behind her spoke: "I haven't seen you in here before."

She whirled to find the kid with the red hat boldly running his eyes up and down Val's body. He looked like he was maybe seventeen.

He toyed with a switchblade as he spoke, clicking the blade in and out. Up close, his eyes were flat and dangerous. "This isn't a place a girl should go on her own. A sweet thing like you... Who knows what could happen?"

"Red cap," Mister E hissed.

Val stiffened. Red caps were wicked fae, notorious for torturing people and dyeing their caps in the blood of their victims. The kid put out a sick energy that made her skin crawl. She forced herself to hold his gaze. If she backed down, she would immediately be classified as prey.

"I can take care of myself."

The fact that her voice didn't shake impressed her. All the stories she'd heard about red caps painted them as psychopaths. Now that she was staring one in the eyes, she could tell the stories were not exaggerations. The kid had a mad-dog light in his eyes, like he wanted nothing more than to bite her face off, chew it like bubble gum, and blow bubbles with the meat.

"Can you now?" The red cap leaned against the dirty brick wall, his blade going click-snick, never taking his eyes off her.

"Did you come out here to have a staring contest?" Val snorted and deliberately looked away from him. She kept the red cap in her peripheral vision, though. She wasn't stupid.

The kid went still at her words. Val held her power ready. She could feel him teetering on the edge. Any moment, the kid might launch himself at her.

"Can I buy you a drink?" She didn't really want to go back into the glade, but offering the red cap a gift seemed like a good way to diffuse the situation. If he accepted, he would at least have to refrain from killing her until the drink was finished.

He curled his lip at her. "Are you trying to put me in your debt?"

"No. Just being friendly."

"Friendly." He bared his sharp teeth and leered. "I know a place we can go to get friendly."

Val schooled herself not to react, even though she was on the verge of panic. She was walking a delicate line. If she insulted the red cap, she'd be in trouble, and she couldn't simply blow him off without insulting him. So she had to rebuff his advances in a way that didn't feel like she was rejecting him.

Fortunately, she had a lot of practice at this sort of thing. She got hit on every day working behind the bar at the Alley Cat, and it was astounding how many men had fragile egos. She'd gotten very good at being non-committal, neither confirming nor denying any interest. Distraction was the key. You had to get them talking about something else.

She quirked a lip at him.

"I'm still fairly new to town and learning the lay of the land. I'm sure someone like you knows all the heavy hitters around these parts. Maybe you can tell me who I should watch out for?"

"That's easy. You should watch out for me."

She forced a little laugh. "That goes without saying. But I know the city is full of creatures and organizations I know nothing about. Most of my contacts are human, and their knowledge is limited to the gangs that run the human side of the city."

The red cap sneered. "Humans are a bunch of cockroaches living off crumbs. They don't control shit. We just let them think they do."

"We?"

"The Fae Courts. We've been here for centuries. You think some human gang can challenge us?" He laughed, the sound like nails on a chalkboard. "We can take them out anytime. They're still alive because we let them be."

Val fought to control her racing heart. There were Fae Courts in San Francisco? As if cabals of vampires and gangs of seraphim weren't bad enough, now she had to watch out for fairies too? Wonderful.

"Does that mean a human gang would have to ask your court for permission to kill a rival?"

"They can kill each other all they like." He pinched the brim of his hat, the wet fabric squishing between his fingers. "The more blood, the better."

Val fought back a shudder.

"What about something that would shift the balance of power in the city? One gang trying to eliminate another. The Fae Courts wouldn't care about things like that?"

The red cap shrugged one shoulder. "Maybe. Maybe not. Big picture, balance of power stuff isn't really my department. I'm more of a hands-on type."

"Violence runs through this one's veins. He is not a creature of subterfuge. If you want him to talk, you have to speak of violent subjects," Mister E hissed. The demon-cat's energy buzzed, as if the red cap had put him on high alert. If the red cap made Mister E nervous, that was a very, very bad sign.

Val considered that. The red cap clearly liked to talk; she'd already learned more from him in two minutes than she had from Pease-blossom in an entire hour.

She decided to take a chance.

"Hands-on like the dog-faced man that's been turning people into monsters?"

"The Puca? That mutt's nothing compared to me."

Val's heart leaped. The Puca! She had a name!

"You didn't know that, did you?" The red cap's eyes narrowed, and her blood ran cold. Fairies didn't like giving out information uninten-tionally. His tone went flat and malevolent. "Does that make you feel good, Valora Keri? Does that make you feel smart? Tricking me into giving you a name?"

The red cap stepped toward her, flicking his blade open. Light glinted along its edge.

"You've reached the end of your credit, witch. Time to pay the piper."

Val backed away, trying to figure out what to do, but her brain was caught in a panicked mantra of *oh shit oh shit oh shit*. She'd faced down a lot of monsters in her day, but red caps were one thing she'd never wanted to tangle with.

Desperately, she drew in her power as he stepped towards her. A sharp smile pushed at the corners of his mouth. There was murder in his eyes.

26

"Valora Keri?"

She and the red cap both froze. Val cautiously turned her eyes towards the deep, slightly slurred voice.

The big male figure had finished draining his bladder, and he belched as he pushed away from the wall. He stood upright, his massive outline nearly filling the alley from side to side before he lurched unsteadily toward her.

More trouble? The figure didn't seem hostile, but he knew who she was, and she didn't know him, which was disconcerting. She was getting tired of everyone knowing her name before she knew theirs. It put her at a disadvantage. And she needed every advantage she could get dealing with these creatures.

"Who wants to know?" Val gripped the hilt of her knife.

The bear shifter in the flannel shirt stepped into the light and stood swaying, peering unsteadily over his bushy beard. Val wrinkled her nose. He smelled like a distillery.

"I thought that was you." He grinned, and to Val's relief, his smile was nothing like the red cap's. There was no sinister gleam in his eye. No teeth filed to sharp points. In fact, he seemed happy to see her.

She squinted at him. "Do I know you?"

The bear-man shook his head. "Nope. Never met. But Alain has told me a lot about you."

Val relaxed. Despite turning Sandra away from the settlement, Alain was still a good friend. A friend of Alain's was someone she could count on.

"Move along, fluffy," the red cap hissed.

The big man seemed to notice the red cap for the first time. He swelled a little, his massive silhouette growing even larger.

"You take that knife somewhere else, shorty. Valora Keri is under my protection," he rumbled.

The red cap's eyes narrowed. The bear man growled. The alley crackled with tension.

Val tried to step back and clear the way between them, but there was nowhere for her to go. The walls were too close. If push came to shove, she'd be caught in the middle.

For several heartbeats, nobody moved.

Then the red cap laughed. "Hunting is more fun anyway." He snicked his blade closed and winked at Val. "I'll be seeing you soon."

Val sagged as the red cap turned and sauntered away.

"That was close," she whispered.

"Don't worry about him," the big man said. "Those little fuckers get off on fear. He just wanted to scare you."

"So he won't be stalking me?"

"No, he'll probably stalk you. It's what they do."

"Great. Just what I always wanted: a psychopathic fae stalker," she muttered. "Not my idea of a good time."

He shrugged. "Not anyone's idea of a good time. But the red caps are like mosquitos."

"Mosquitos?"

"They're always around, always annoying, and there's not much you can do about them."

"And they like blood."

He chuckled. "Oh yeah. They definitely like blood."

Val sighed.

"Thank you for getting rid of him. Do you live in the Mission District Shifter Settlement?"

The big man shook his head. "No. We've got a community out by the old zoo."

Val waited for him to go on, but he just stood there, swaying.

"OK... Well, it was nice meeting you. I've got to run, so." She started to edge past him.

"No." He stretched out a hand as big as a dinner plate. "I've got something to tell you."

Again Val waited, and again the bear simply stood there, staring at her. She sighed. Drunks could be as thick as a tree trunk.

"Are we going to stand here all day? Or are you going to tell me whatever it is you've got to tell me?"

He leaned toward her, lost his balance, and just caught himself on the edge of a battered dumpster. The man's breath reeked of stale beer and garlic, and Val tried not to cringe as he whispered softly, "The weather."

"The weather?"

"The weather," he repeated solemnly..

Val was growing impatient. "What about it?"

"The Wild Storms are getting worse." He waggled his bushy eyebrows in a significant way.

"Yes, I know they are. Does that mean something?"

He leaned in close and lowered his voice. Val almost choked on the stench of his beer breath.

"They're doing it on purpose."

"Doing it on purpose?" she repeated.

"Exactly." He smiled and nodded his big, shaggy head sagely. "Alain told me you were smart."

With that, the big shifter lurched past her and stepped through the portal back into the beer garden. Val stood gaping at the empty space where he had been.

"What was that about?" she wondered.

"The weather, obviously," Mister E said. *"He must be an amateur meteorologist."*

Val snorted. "Maybe. Or maybe he's a drunk wasting my time."

"At least he chased the red cap away."

"For now," she agreed.

Shaking her head, Val pushed the thought aside as she moved down the alley. She didn't have time for drunk bears. Or red caps.

Now she had a name. She knew who she was hunting.

But the Puca was still out there, turning people into monsters.

Val needed to find him before he found her.

27

Malcolm and Hillary were eating pasta in the living room when Val got back to the apartment. Her stomach growled at the scent of parmesan cheese, and she eyed their bowls hungrily.

"Don't stand there looking at me like Oliver Twist. There's more on the stove," Malcolm said, pointing a finger toward the kitchen.

Val grinned. "Thanks, Malcolm. You're a lifesaver."

"That's what they tell me."

Moments later she joined them, steaming bowl in hand.

"Homemade pesto?" Val mumbled around a mouthful of noodles. "You really outdid yourself, Malcolm."

"I outdo myself all the time. Somebody had to raise the bar around here, and it certainly wasn't going to be either of you." He looked at them askance.

Val ignored the dig. She was too busy stuffing her face to be offended, and besides he was right. She rarely made anything more complicated than toast.

"Where's Sandra?" she asked.

"Sleeping in the basement. She's an early bird, remember?" Malcolm said. "She turned into a pumpkin hours ago."

"Oh, right," Val said. Then she quirked an eyebrow at Hillary. "I thought you didn't eat gluten?"

Hillary looked at her like she was an idiot. "They're rice noodles."

"Ah. Right."

Val decided to concentrate on eating. Low blood sugar was obviously making her slow.

But Malcolm was eyeing her expectantly.

"So, did you find out who or what is responsible for Sandra's new form?"

"New form?" Hillary gave him the side eye. "Are you training to be a politician?"

Malcolm looked offended. "Of course not. Why, what would you call it?"

"Just call it like it is. She's a monster. Like me." The vampire demonstrated by exposing her fangs

"A gorgon, to be precise," Val corrected.

"Yes, a gorgon." Hillary nodded, then she looked puzzled. "I'm not sure how that's different from Medusa. I mean, she turns people to stone with her gaze. Doesn't that make her Medusa?"

"That's like saying every vampire is Dracula," Malcolm said. "Medusa is the most famous gorgon, but she is only a single member of the species."

"Are they a species?" Hillary asked.

Malcolm sat up and assumed his professor voice. "In the Medusa myth, there were three gorgons, and she was their Queen. Some stories say the gorgons were the children of the sea god, and others say they were created by Gaea to aid her children in their battle against the gods. Perseus was able to defeat her by using his shield as a mirror so he didn't have to look directly at her. He decapitated Medusa, and her severed head could turn anyone who looked at it to stone."

"Do you sit around memorizing obscure facts all day, or what?" Hillary asked.

"No. Sandra and I went to the Library today, remember? She was naturally curious about what she'd become, so we did some research on gorgons."

"How did you get into the Library, anyway?" Hillary asked. "I thought the Librarian only allows magical creatures in there."

"I am a magical creature, thank you very much." Malcolm stuck his tongue out at her.

Hillary rolled her eyes. "I'm pretty sure you're the wrong kind of fairy."

"How little you know. There is no wrong kind of fairy," he said archly. "The Librarian loves me, for your information. We go way back."

"Back a whole month, at least," Val snorted. "Since I'm pretty sure you didn't even know the Library existed before that."

"A month is plenty of time to become friends. I've made lifelong friends overnight."

"How many drugs were involved?" Hillary deadpanned.

"I do not need drugs to make friends," Malcolm insisted. Then he winked at her. "But there may have been a few."

"Did you learn anything else useful at the Library?" Val asked.

"Ah-ah-ah!" Malcolm shook his fork at her. "I asked you first. What did you find out at The Metropolis? Spill."

Val gave him a sour look. "Fine. Well, first of all, I learned that there are a lot more supernatural creatures walking around this town than I thought."

"I could have told you that," Hillary said.

"No, I mean walking around in plain sight," Val said. "Half the people in that club were wearing glamours."

Malcolm scrunched up his face. "Like makeup and fake eyelashes?"

"No, glamours are magical disguises," Val explained. "The fae like to put on glamours to appear human. That way they can go out in public without being noticed."

"So you're saying the fae are like movie stars."

Val shrugged. "Sort of."

"Don't they also use their glamours to appear beautiful?" Malcolm mused. "Maybe that's where our modern interpretation of the word comes from."

"Could be. Anyway, The Metropolis was full of creatures wearing glamours. There were more magical creatures in that building than I knew existed in the entire city."

"I'm guessing that's a bad thing?"

"You're the history buff, you tell me." Val said. "What have you read about the fae? As far as I know, they generally don't play well with humans."

Malcolm nodded slowly, his gaze becoming introspective. "I wish I'd known about this before I went to the Library... but from what I recall, the fae are crafty and arrogant and they look down on humans. In many stories they treat us like playthings. They hate cold iron and they steal children and leave changelings in their place, though I've never been sure why they do that.

"They are chaotic creatures but strangely lawful: If you can get them to agree to something, they always keep their word. But they will follow the letter of the law, not the spirit, so you'd better be sure of exactly what you're agreeing to." His eyes focused on Val again. "That's all I remember."

She nodded. "That's pretty much what I've got, too."

"This is all very interesting," Hillary interrupted. "But what does this have to do with Sandra? Are you saying she was transformed by fairies?"

"That's exactly what I'm saying," Val confirmed. "The dog-faced guy that turned the Ural into a horse was at The Metropolis. The little shit dropped his glamour and winked at me. I'm sure I don't have to remind you that he's the same guy that was at the market when the grafters were transformed. Sandra also saw him at Zombie Coffee right before all hell broke loose."

"Oh, I just remembered some more things about the fae!" Malcolm exclaimed. "Certain flowers are supposed to protect you from them: Daisies and primroses and marsh marigolds. Also red berries from rowan, holly, or ash trees. And walking sticks made of ash or rowan wood."

"Anyway," Val continued, annoyed at the interruption, "I followed the dog-faced guy into a secret basement that turned out to be this magical beer garden or something. He gave me the slip, but as I was leaving, I talked to a red cap, and—"

Malcolm spit his wine across the room. "A red cap? And you're still walking around?"

Val gave him a weak smile. "For now, yeah. I'll be looking over my shoulder for a while, though."

Malcom shuddered. "I should hope so. I've read horrible things about red caps. Did you know they dye their hats with the blood of their victims?"

"Yes, I know. Can I continue?"

"Sorry, that was just shocking. Go on."

"Anyway," Val continued, "The red cap gave me a name. He said the dog-faced guy's name is Puca."

Malcolm's eyes lit up. "Puca! That fits. I read about them in a book on Irish Mythology. Puca are shapeshifters who have been known to transform people into animals. They also like to put people on the backs of runaway horses and send them on wild rides."

"It sounds like we've found our culprit." Val gave him a predatory smile. "Now we just have to catch the wicked thing."

Malcolm clapped his hands in excitement. "I think I might know how to do that too."

28

———

Val awoke in a cold sweat. Something was gnawing on her arm, sharp pains shooting from her fingers up past her elbow. She sat up in a panic, gathering power to defend herself while instinctively grabbing Mister E's sight so she could see in the dark.

There was nothing there.

She sat alone in her bedroom, chest heaving, breath coming in short gasps. The house was still and quiet around her.

"Was that a nightmare?" she mumbled. It had felt so real. Like someone was sinking sharp fangs into her right hand.

She shook her head. "I guess that's what I get for eating pasta right before bed." She started to scrub her hands over her face—and groaned as the pain came back.

Val fell on her side and curled around her right hand. The feeling was excruciating, burning and sharp, like someone was peeling off her skin with red-hot knives. She could only whimper as agony pulsed through her.

The pain finally ebbed away after a few minutes, leaving her wrung out and soaked in sweat. She lay there, limp as a noodle, panting as her heartbeat thudded in her ears.

Eventually, she was able to sit up again.

"What just happened?" She cradled her right hand in her left, feeling the roughness of her stone fingers. Her breath caught in her throat. "What the...?"

Even with Mister E's eyes, it was hard to make out her fingers in the dark bedroom, but touch confirmed what she thought she was seeing. The petrification had spread. Her middle finger had turned to stone as well.

She reached over and flicked on the lamp. Three gray fingers stared back at her. Over half her hand.

"Is this going to keep spreading?" she croaked. Her heart was in her throat. "Mister E?"

"I'm afraid I don't know," the demon-cat said.

"What do you mean, you don't know? You're supposed to know these things! Am I going to turn into a statue? Why is this happening?" She was hyperventilating and quickly approaching a full-blown panic attack.

"I repeat: I don't know. However, if it will make you feel better, I can make an educated guess."

"Yes. Please guess. Tell me something. Anything."

The demon-cat examined her hand, his golden eyes glowing like lanterns. When he spoke, his voice was calm and almost soothing—a far cry from his usual mocking tones.

"I was wondering why only two of your fingers had been petrified, when the gorgon clearly has the power to turn entire bodies to stone. My first guess was that you had been affected in proportion to the amount of time you maintained eye contact with her. You only made eye contact for an instant, ergo only two of your fingers were petrified."

He stopped and puffed thoughtfully on his candy cigarette.

"Get to the point," Val snapped. She had to bite her tongue to keep from screaming.

The cat ignored her outburst and continued in the same clinical manner: *"My second theory is that the magic already inside you has given you some kind of immunity. Your power is fighting off the infection, as it were. So, where a normal person would have been entirely petrified, only two of your fingers were affected."*

"So why is it spreading now?"

"Well, this is where it gets interesting." He paused to blow a pair of smoke rings at the ceiling.

Val wanted to shake him by his furry shoulders until his teeth rattled.

"My current hypothesis is that no matter which of these is true—whether it was the length of your exposure or your natural immunity that limited the infection to two fingers—it did not stop the infection entirely; it has only slowed it."

"So it's going to continue to spread?" she whispered.

"My best guess is that it will."

The room spun around Val. She felt like she was going to throw up.

"What do we do?"

Mister E narrowed his eyes.

"An excellent question. Normally, I would say you need to trace the infection back to its source and force them to reverse it. But Sandra has no idea how to control her powers—assuming they can be controlled at all. So that's out. Supposedly this Puca is responsible for turning Sandra into a gorgon in the first place. Perhaps he could reverse the process?" He paced across the bed, his tail twitching in agitation. *"Failing that, we would need to find a healing spring. Or appeal to a higher power."*

"A higher power?"

"Yes. The fae are famously hierarchical. I don't remember this Puca being particularly high in their power structure. If we could find a member of the Fae Court, they should be able to stop the infection."

"Could they also turn Sandra human again?"

"Perhaps. With the members of the Fae Court most things are not a question of can they, but rather will they."

"How do I find the Fae Court?"

He speared her with his golden gaze. *"I think we should exhaust all other possibilities first. One becomes entangled with the Fae Court at one's own peril. I would recommend it only as a last resort."*

Val didn't like it, but what he was saying made sense. She didn't know how long she had left or how quickly the infection was going to spread, and her every instinct screamed for her to stop it before pigeons started roosting on her head. Despite the risks, finding the Fae Court seemed like the quickest way to do that.

"Fine," she hissed. "We'll try to catch the Puca first. But we should at least figure out how to contact the Fae Court in case that falls through. Do you know how to do that?"

"No. But I'd wager your friend Padraig does."

Val considered this. Padraig's family made their living importing magical artifacts. Also, he was at least part fae himself.

She nodded. "You're right. If anyone would know how to contact the Fae Court, it would be him. First thing in the morning, we need to find a blacksmith to help us carry out Macolm's idea. After that, we're going to pay Padraig a visit."

29

Sandra was dusting the living room when she heard Val stumble out of bed. She'd been awake for hours and had gotten bored sitting in the basement alone. Also, she wanted to earn her keep somehow, so she'd come upstairs and done all the dishes. Then she'd cleaned the bathroom, swept and mopped the kitchen before moving on to the living room.

It had taken some serious willpower to not get out the vacuum—the hall carpet was filthy—but Sandra had learned her lesson on that one. She knew Val's idea of morning was radically different from her own, and she didn't want to get kicked out of the apartment again.

Sandra followed Val into the kitchen in her fox onesie, chattering while the witch poured herself coffee. Val responded to her queries with monosyllabic grunts while she stirred butterscotch and cream into her cup.

"Do you feel anything when your power activates?" Val surprised them both by asking a coherent question.

"My power?"

"You know, the stone gaze. When you make eye contact with someone, does something change inside you? Can you feel the power kick in?"

Sandra frowned, her mouth barely visible beneath the drooping edge of her fox hood.

"Now that you mention it, there is something. It's like... butterflies in my stomach. Not exactly like that, but something inside me goes all twisty."

"Do you think you could control it?"

"You mean, stop it?"

"Yeah. Or even reverse it."

Sandra tapped her lips as she thought, her gaze drifting to Val's petrified fingers. She gasped.

"You've got three frozen fingers now! Is it spreading?"

"It looks like it. Woke me up in the middle of the night last night. Hurt like hell." She held up her right hand for examination. Her middle, ring, and pinky fingers were all gray and unmoving.

Sandra's eyes filled with tears.

"I'm sorry, Val. I wish I could fix them. But I don't know how. I don't know anything about this curse. If I could take it back, I would. But I can't control it."

"It's OK; I didn't think you could. But if you can feel the power activate, that's a good sign. It means it's not a permanent thing. It turns on and off when you make eye contact with someone. That makes me think it might be an ability you can control with enough practice."

Sandra laughed bitterly. "Practice? Did you forget that it only activates when I make eye contact with someone? How do I practice without turning people into statues?"

"Valid point." Val sipped her coffee. "Hey, I want to try something. Wait here a minute."

She went into the bathroom and returned with a small hand mirror. She turned her back to Sandra and held up the mirror.

"I want you to lift your hood and look at my reflection in the mirror."

Sandra hesitated. "Do you think that's a good idea? What if my power still works?"

"I don't think it will. Do you remember the story of Perseus and Medusa? He looked at her reflection in a polished shield or something so her power wouldn't affect him."

"But what if it does?"

Val looked a little green at that, but she did her best to project confidence.

"Trust your gut. You said you can feel it when your power kicks in, right? If you feel it starting to work, drop your hood."

Sandra tugged at the sleeves of her onesie. She shuffled her feet.

"I don't think this is a good idea, Val. I don't want to turn you into a statue."

"I'm already infected, Sandra. I'm the perfect person to try it on. Come on. The only way to learn is to experiment."

Sandra shuffled her feet some more, but finally she nodded. "OK."

She took a deep breath and slowly lifted the edge of her hood. Her heart twisted as, bit by bit, Val's face was revealed. Her housemate's skin was puffy from lack of sleep, and there were bruised circles under her eyes.

Sandra thought she probably didn't look any better. Ever since she'd been transformed, all of her nights had been tearful and sleepless.

Maybe monsters never slept well. Maybe lack of sleep was one of the reasons they looked so terrible.

Then her hood lifted the final inch, and Sandra's eyes found Val's in the mirror.

She yelped and dropped her hood. "I'm sorry!"

Her stomach clenched as she waited to hear Val curse. Waited to see how much more of her would be frozen this time.

But nothing happened.

"Did you feel the power kick in?" Val asked.

Sandra bobbed her head. "Yes. My stomach went all twisty as soon as I saw your eyes. I'm sorry!"

"Don't be sorry. It's OK." Val checked her hands and arms. Her stone fingers were still petrified, but the rest of her flesh remained flesh. A smile stretched her face. "It worked! Your power didn't affect me!"

"It didn't?" Sandra was puzzled. "Are you sure? I felt it..."

"Yes, I'm sure. Don't you remember what happened last time? If it hit me, I'd be lying on the ground right now. Nothing happened! It worked!"

Val looked like she wanted to dance. Sandra was more restrained.

"Maybe it wasn't the mirror. Maybe it's because you're already infected. Maybe you can't get infected twice."

"I hadn't thought of that. You're right. I'm not the ideal test subject." Val frowned. "Flying toads. I thought we were getting somewhere. I guess I'm back to Plan A for today."

"What plan is that?" Sandra asked.

"I'm going to talk to a blacksmith about an idea Malcolm had for catching the Puca. After that, I'll meet with Padraig and see if I can get an introduction to the Fae Court."

30

The Imaginarium was a collective workspace housed in a repurposed paper factory. The open floor plan had been partitioned into dozens of workshops, which were filled with sculptors, ceramicists, welders, tailors, brewers, blacksmiths, and everything in between. The shared ceiling arched high overhead, and the partition walls barely reached eight feet, so a pleasant cacophony filled Val's ears as she stepped through the main entrance, sounds drifting freely above the partitions. Ethereal harp music played somewhere off to her left, making an odd counterpoint to the table saw screech to her right. The sound of hammering was abruptly cut off with a curse, followed by voices arguing. Elsewhere, someone with a beautiful voice was singing.

Many of the workshop doors were left open, allowing Val to peek inside as she passed. It always amazed her how differently creatives organized their workspaces. Or didn't organize, as was sometimes the case. A few of the workshops had spotless workbenches and pegboards on the wall, with every tool hung on its proper hook. In others, the tools lay in haphazard piles and the floor was lost under drifting waves of scraps.

If her roommates were here, Malcom would definitely have the former type of shop, and Hillary the latter. Val shook her head at the thought. How two such opposite people could get along as well as they did was a mystery to her. She wondered which end of the spectrum Sandra would settle on—would she be messy or neat? She thought neat, but she couldn't be sure. The last time they'd lived together, Sandra hadn't been around long enough for her to find out.

Val cut that thought at the root. It didn't matter whether Sandra was messy or neat, because Sandra would not be staying. Val was going to catch the Puca and force him to make her human again. Then Sandra could get out of the basement and go back to her old life.

She wandered down row after row of cubicles, passing dozens of workspaces. Just how big was this place, anyway?

She was starting to think she'd never find the shop she was looking for when a big guy stepped out into the hall in front of her, blocking her path. The word big didn't begin to do him justice. He was huge, even bigger than the bear shifter outside The Metropolis, the top of his head almost as high as the eight-foot partition walls. He had small, dark eyes and a generous mouth full of big, square teeth. Shaggy hair tumbled past his shoulders and an equally shaggy beard hung down the front of his unbuttoned plaid shirt. His sleeves rolled back over bulging forearms—also hairy—and the biggest workman's boots she'd ever seen covered his feet. Val gaped. Both her feet could fit inside one of his boots.

"Can I help you find something?" he rumbled. His voice was so low Val felt the vibrations in her sternum. It was like standing in front of a subwoofer.

"Uh, yes. I'm looking for the Dream Forge."

The guy huffed and narrowed his eyes. "Anything he can make, I can make better."

"Thank you, but a friend specifically sent me to the Dream Forge. I'm just following instructions."

He grunted and looked disgusted. For a moment, Val thought he was going to turn her away. Then he shook his head and hooked a thumb up over his shoulder.

"Back that way. In the corner. Careful you don't hit your head on the ceiling."

"Thank you."

"You want some real work done, you come see me," he called after her. "Gunter Gristle. I can make anything he can. Twice as good for half the price."

"OK. Thank you," Val waved awkwardly over her shoulder as she hurried away from the gigantic man.

"What was that all about?" she muttered under her breath.

Mister E's laughter rang in her ears.

"That, my child, was a troll."

Val was still processing the fact that she'd just interacted with a troll when she finally found the sign hanging on a rack of steel beams all the way at the back of the building. The sign was a polished plate with the words *Dream Forge* cut out of the metal in neat letters. Underneath the sign, rusty bits of scrap metal had been welded into a dark tunnel that disappeared beneath the rack.

"It looks like a hobbit hole," Val said, peering into the opening. "If hobbits made their holes out of rusty scrap metal instead of earth."

"Dwarves have always loved their tunnels," Mister E said. *"It looks like this one made his own."*

She cocked her head, listening. Deep inside the tunnel she could hear the ring of a hammer.

"I don't see a bell. I guess I just walk in? You'd better give me your eyes so I don't brain myself on the ceiling."

The inside of the tunnel glowed a warm yellow as Mister E's night vision layered over her own. The tunnel only came up to her shoulder, so Val had to hunch and shuffle awkwardly into the opening. Once inside, the tunnel was longer than she expected, and she had to shuffle that way for several minutes. Despite her caution, Val did bump her head—twice—and she was feeling very annoyed when she finally saw a light at the end of the tunnel.

"It's about time," she muttered. "My back is aching from being hunched over like this."

The tunnel had been sloping gently downward as she walked, and it now opened into an underground workshop. Val stepped into the larger space with a sigh of relief. She stood up, straightening her aching back—and promptly hit her head on the ceiling again.

"Flying toads!" she cursed, rubbing her head as she ducked. Closer examination showed her that the workshop ceiling was higher than the ceiling in the tunnel, but only by a few inches. She still couldn't stand up straight.

"My shop is not hospitable to intruders."

Val looked up to find a short, thickly built man regarding her from behind an anvil. He wore a leather apron and gloves, and held a heavy-looking hammer in his hand. A welder's mask was pushed back on his bald head. To Val's surprise, he was clean shaven.

"Aren't dwarves supposed to have beards?"

"Beards are flammable," the dwarf replied. "Hair as well. Obviously the humans who made up those stories never met a real dwarven smith."

He took a step towards her, brandishing his hammer.

"Now why don't you tell me what it is you're doing here?"

"I heard you were the best smith in the city."

"Flattery is always a good opening gambit." The dwarf broke out into a grin and gestured her towards a small table with two chairs. "Have a seat, I'll get you some ale."

"Water is fine." Val said, sliding gratefully into the seat. Her spine popped as it finally unbent.

"Water? Are you feeling all right?" He narrowed his eyes at her. "You're not sick, are you? I'm too busy to be laid out by some gods-cursed cold."

"I'm not sick. I just don't drink alcohol."

He huffed in disbelief before shaking his head and grumbling, "What's the world coming to?"

The dwarf poured himself a mug of thick ale and reluctantly placed a glass of water on the table in front of her. He sank into the other chair, took a long drink from his mug, belched contentedly, and grinned at her.

"Duncan Hammer at your service."

"Val Keri."

"What can I do for you, Miss Keri?"

She described to him the special chains Malcolm had told her she needed to catch the Puca. Duncan rubbed his chin and nodded.

"I can make chains like that. Once you get them locked, he won't be able to shape-shift out of them. The real challenge will be getting the beast into the trap, of course. I assume you've got some good bait?"

"I'm still working on that. But that's my concern, not yours. How soon can you have the chains ready?"

He thought for a minute, staring at the ceiling and muttering to himself.

"Two months," he finally said.

"Two months?" Val gaped at him. "I can't wait two months. This creep is turning people into monsters. I need to catch him now."

The dwarf shrugged. "That's what happens when you hire the best. There's a waiting list for my services."

"Isn't there any way you can do it faster? What if I paid you more?"

She winced as the words came out of her mouth. With the Alley Cat closed, she was currently unemployed and had a dwindling bank account. She didn't have extra money to throw around. But she had to catch the Puca, and she certainly couldn't wait two months to do it.

Duncan slammed his mug on the table.

"Do you think you can bribe me? I'm a craftsman. Every project on my list is important. I won't jump you up the line because you wave some money in my face. I stick to my word. I've got integrity."

Val held up her hands.

"I'm sorry, I didn't mean to insult you. But people are dying out there. I can't wait two months."

Duncan shrugged.

"Two months is my timeline. Take it or leave it." He waved a dismissive hand towards the tunnel. "There are other smiths out there. Maybe one of them can make it for you faster. Don't expect good work, though. Quality takes time."

Val chewed her lip. Duncan was supposed to be the best, and he was guaranteed to make the chains properly.

But she couldn't wait two months. Who knew how many people the Puca would transform in two months? How many innocent people would be killed by the fresh-made monsters?

Not to mention her own problem.

She ran a thumb over the rough surface of her stone fingers. She didn't know how fast the petrification was progressing, but in two months Val could be a statue. She couldn't wait that long.

"Thank you anyway," she said, rising to her feet.

Val heard the ring of the hammer start up again as she shuffled awkwardly down the tunnel, searching for a new plan.

31

G unter Gristle was bent over his workbench when Val stuck her head into his cubicle. The troll's bushy eyebrows were a wild tangle over the dark goggles protecting his eyes from the arcing line of sparks sent up by the grinder in his hands. With Mister E's sight layered over hers, Val could clearly see that he was a troll. The faint outline of his pointed ears shone beneath his shaggy hair, and his skin had a greenish tint. The hair on his arms and hands was so thick it could almost be called fur.

When he noticed Val standing there, Gunter stopped working and pushed the goggles to his forehead.

"Back so soon?" He grinned at her. "I guess the dwarf wasn't so impressive after all."

"He's too slow." Val stepped into the cubicle. The troll's workspace was organized, but not overly clean. His tools were mostly put away, but the drawers hung open, and the floor was covered in an inch of sawdust and metal shavings. "I was hoping you could make what I need faster."

"Depends on what you need."

Gunter nodded as Val told him about the chains.

"I can make that. What's it for?"

"Catching a troublemaker."

"Which troublemaker would that be?"

"That's my business."

The troll gave her a challenging look, baring his big, square teeth.

"There are plenty of troublemakers around. Some would say I'm one of them."

"What's that supposed to mean?" Though she had to crane her neck up to do it, Val met his gaze without blinking.

"It means I'm not sure I like making something like this without knowing who it's for. It could be meant for a friend of mine."

"And if it was? Does that mean you won't make it?"

The troll's grin exposed his big blocky teeth. "No. It just means the price goes up. A man needs a certain amount of compensation to betray his friends."

"If I give you a name, how do I know you won't claim they're your friend no matter who they are?"

His grin grew wider. "You don't."

Val scowled up at him. "So you're asking me to trust a troll."

"You were going to trust a dwarf," he pointed out. "Are you saying trusting a troll is different? Because that smells like racism where I'm standing."

Mister E's laughter rang in her ears. *"He's got you there. Outmaneuvered by a troll. I'm never letting you live this one down."*

She ground her teeth in frustration. Mister E was right, the troll had run rings around her.

If she refused to tell him who the chains were for, she would appear racist. Heck, forget appearances, she would actually be a racist. After all, she had told the dwarf who the chains were for. Denying the troll the same information simply because he was a troll would make her a racist.

"Flaming toads," she cursed. "Fine. The chains are for a Puca who's been running around town turning people into monsters." She glared up at him. "Now I suppose you're going to tell me the Puca is a good friend of yours and the price just doubled."

Gunter laughed. "Nah. Puca are all troublemakers. I can't stand the little buggers. If you're aiming to capture one, I say good riddance."

Val stared at him in surprise, her hands still clenched into fists. She'd been sure the troll was going to try to cheat her, and she'd been geared up to argue with him. Now that he hadn't, she was all wound up with nowhere to put her outrage.

"You're not going to charge me extra?"

"Are you deaf? I just said that, didn't I?"

With an effort, Val unclenched her fists. It was a weird feeling, being all geared up for a fight and not finding one. She needed to go run around the block to work off her adrenaline.

"OK. How soon can you have it ready?" Val braced for the answer, expecting the worst.

Gunter gazed at the ceiling for a moment, his jaw working in silent calculation.

"Two hours."

"Two hours?" Val gaped at him.

"That's the best I can do. Since the Puca's a shapeshifter, there's some tricky bits making a collar he can't shift out of. My apologies for the delay."

"No, that's fine," Val stammered. After the dwarf's quote of two months, she'd been prepared for the worst. Two hours was a faster turnaround than she'd dared hope for. "How much will it cost?"

"How about twenty pounds of rat meat, two boxes of wine, and three comic books."

"What?"

"Twenty pounds of rat meat, two boxes of wine, and three comic books."

"I heard you the first time. I was just surprised, is all. Um, any particular kind of wine?"

"A nice rosé would be my preference, but anything red will do in a pinch."

"And the comic books?"

"I've always been partial to mutants." He grinned. "They seem like my kind of people."

Val digested this. "OK. I can do that."

"Aren't you going to ask me about the rat meat?"

"No, I think I can handle that one. Unless you have something against kebabs?"

"Nope. Kebabs are my favorite. Make sure you get the sweet and sour sauce."

"Will do."

"A pleasure doing business with you. I'll see you in a couple of hours?" The troll held out a big hand.

Val shook it. "Yeah. Two hours."

She left the troll humming happily as she made her way back out to the street.

32

V al paused and mopped her brow, puffing as she topped another hill. Her legs and glutes were on fire, and she groaned as she tried to stretch out her lower back. Walking sucked, and she cursed the Puca for the hundredth time that day.

Getting around in San Francisco is never as simple as going from Point A to Point B. There are always several hills you have to climb over or go around, and choosing which path to take isn't an easy decision. Val didn't like going out of her way, so she generally took the most direct route. Which invariably took her over the crest of at least one massive hill.

"At least the view is nice," she grumbled.

There was a park on the crest of this particular hill, surrounded on three sides by the picturesque Victorian houses for which San Francisco was famous. A salty breeze cooled the sweat on her neck, while the bay sparkled in the distance. It was a beautiful sunny afternoon, the sky clear and cloudless above her. Which meant that flying was out of the question.

"I'm going to kill that Puca when I catch up to him," she promised. "I can't believe he turned my Ural into a horse. This city was not made for pedestrians."

"Walking is good for you." Mister E's head materialized, sans body. It floated in the air at eye level and grinned his smug crescent-moon smile at her. *"You don't get outside to exercise enough."*

"That's what the gym is for. I prefer to exercise indoors, like a civilized person."

"Civilized? You?"

Val shot him a dirty look. "You ever think about the pot calling the kettle black? My worst impulses all come from you."

Mister E chuckled. *"You keep telling yourself that if it helps you sleep at night. But we both know I never made you do anything. I only gave you the power to fulfill the desires of your secret heart."*

Val scowled as she started across the park. She didn't like to admit it, but she knew Mister E was right. Her secret heart was as black as sin. She could blame the demon-cat all she wanted, but she could never escape the truth.

Lost in dark thoughts, Val didn't pay much attention to where she was going, letting her feet guide her in the general direction of Padraig's mansion. It wasn't until a grating voice stopped her in the middle of an alley that she realized her mistake.

"Well, look who we have here."

Val froze, taking quick stock of her surroundings. She was in a dingy alley between two old buildings. The paint on the walls had become gray with age, and leaky bags of trash sagged beside overflowing garbage cans. The alley was so narrow she could touch both walls by stretching out her arms.

The end of the alley was only fifty feet ahead of her, but standing between her and the exit was a kid with a red baseball cap turned backwards on his head. A switchblade gleamed in his hand.

Val felt cold to her marrow. The red cap from the beer garden had found her. Even worse, he'd caught her in an alley when she was distracted. Not good.

"Valora Keri." The red cap flashed her an evil grin. His voice scraped like metal on concrete. "I told you we'd meet again."

Val stepped back and drew her own knife, grimacing as her petrified fingers refused to grip the hilt. She awkwardly switched the knife to her left hand.

"Stay back. I don't want to hurt you."

"Hurt me?" The red cap sneered at her. "You've got the situation all wrong. I'm not the one getting hurt."

"Tell me what you want and maybe nobody has to get hurt." Val worked to keep her voice firm. Never show a predator fear.

"What I want?" The red cap sauntered forward, forcing Val to scuttle back. His smile exposed sharp, yellow teeth. His voice lowered to a hiss. "What I want is blood."

The red cap shot forward with blinding speed. Val barely had time to flinch before she felt hot pain as his switchblade sank into her left forearm. Her knife clattered to the ground. Scarlet blood rained over the blade.

She clamped her right hand on the gash to staunch the bleeding. She lashed out with wind, trying to push the red cap away, but he was already gone.

Ugly laughter came from down the alley.

"There, that's what we needed. A little blood makes everything better."

She looked up to find the red cap leering at her. She shuddered as he ran his tongue over the blade of his knife, tasting her blood.

"Are you happy now?" she growled. "You've gotten your blood."

"Oh no, my cap is still dry. We're just getting started."

"You want a fight? I'll give you a fight," Val hissed between her teeth.

She filled the narrow alley with a whirlwind, plucking up a storm of debris. Most of the detritus were harmless things: bits of paper, plastic bottles and old coffee grounds. But other things lurked in there as well: crushed cans and jagged bits of tin, beer bottles and broken glass.

She caught snapshot glimpses of the red cap through the maelstrom. "Come and get it, you little shit."

His smile widened. "What fun. Now we get to play."

The red cap blurred into motion. To Val's shock, he didn't try to avoid her cyclone; he put his head down and barreled straight through it. Bits of glass and metal tore at him, flinging red spatter lines of blood along the dingy alley walls.

The red cap didn't even slow. He emerged from the whirlwind with several long gashes on his face bleeding, including a slice that had missed his eye by millimeters. His feral grin never wavered.

The switchblade flashed faster than Val could follow. She threw up her arms, trying to protect herself, but compared to the speed of the red cap it was as if she was swimming through honey. She felt her skin part, felt blood spurt, but the wounds were too numerous to count. Hot pain flared in her shoulder, her ribs, her stomach. Then something popped in the back of her knee and her leg folded, making her collapse to the filthy ground.

Val curled into a ball, waiting for the end. The red cap was too fast, too strong. She was hopelessly outclassed. She lay there, arms over her head, expecting a killing blow that never came.

Instead, soft cloth dabbed at her blood. Was the red cap cleaning her wounds?

Confused, she peered up to find the red cap squatting down beside her. His hat was off, and his hair was as wild and coarse as crab grass.

His hat. That was what she'd felt. The red cap was soaking his hat in her blood.

He grinned down at her. "There, now. That's better. I was feeling a bit parched."

"Just finish it, you freak," she growled. She was bleeding from too many wounds to count. Everything hurt. She'd lost. She just wanted this to be over.

"Finish it? What do you think I'm doing? Blood was needed to balance the scales. It's blood I'm collecting."

"You aren't going to kill me?"

His grating laughter echoed off the walls.

"Why would I do that? If I killed you, we wouldn't be able to play anymore, would we?" He put his soaked hat back on his head. It squelched softly, and a little rivulet of red ran down his temple. He winked at her. "Until we meet again, Valora Keri."

Pain hazed her vision as Val watched the red cap walk away. She tried to get up, to hit him with a tornado, to do... anything.

But she'd lost too much blood. Her head swam when she tried to lift it off the ground.

The last thing she heard was the red cap's laughter as darkness closed in.

———————

33

V al surfaced in a sea of white. A soft comforter lay over her like a blanket of fresh snow, and a thick down pillow swallowed her head. A white canopy draped overhead. Something warm curled beside her, and her questing fingers found a small bundle of fur. The cat started rumbling as soon as she touched it, its entire body vibrating against her ribs.

"I don't know whether to feel flattered or appalled," a familiar voice said from nearby.

Val lifted her head out of the pillow enough to make out Padraig O' Ceallaigh, scion of the O'Ceallaigh family, sitting in the chair beside the bed. He was immaculately dressed, with the light blue collar of his shirt creased down over the lapel of his dark jacket. His gold earrings were set off by his artfully mussed auburn hair.

His smile exposed perfect teeth. "We have to stop meeting like this, Valora Keri."

She let her head flop back down with a groan of relief.

"Padraig. You have no idea how happy I am to see you." The little calico cat gave an offended yowl. Val scratched its back as she amended, "You too, Fiona. Of course. I'm always happy to see you."

Padraig chuckled. "I think I've got a pretty good idea, actually.

When we found you, you looked like you'd taken a bath at the local blood bank."

"How did you find me?" Val asked.

"Fiona gets all the credit for that," he said. "Want to tell me what happened?"

"I ran into a red cap."

Padraig sucked in a breath. "Ah. That'll do it. How did you run afoul of one of those creatures?"

"It's kind of a long story."

"It's a good thing I've got time then. Let's have some tea and you can fill me in."

Padraig helped her sit up and poured her a cup of tea, adding a generous dollop of honey and cream without having to be asked. He listened patiently while Val told him the events of the past few days, starting with the Wild Storms and the Puca, and ending with the red cap in the alley. Padraig winced when she got to the part about Sandra becoming a gorgon, but he didn't interrupt until her tale was complete.

"That's a fine kettle of fish, Valora Keri," he said at last. "I can't say I'm surprised. You always did have a nose for trouble."

"Thanks?" Val replied. "I'm not sure if that's a good thing or a bad thing."

"Neither am I, to be honest. It's just the hand you've been dealt, isn't it?" He leaned forward, his hazel eyes catching hers. "I want you to be careful, though. These are deep waters you're swimming in. It would be dead simple for a person to drown."

Val sighed. "If you think the waters are deep now, you're really not going to like the next favor I have to ask you. Can you introduce me to the Fae Court?"

Padraig choked on his tea.

"The Fae Court? Are you mad? It's admirable that you want to help your friend, but you need to stay as far away from that den of wolves as you can."

"I wish I could. But this has gone farther than just Sandra."

Padraig's lips tightened as Val held up her petrified fingers.

"I noticed those when we put you to bed," he admitted. "It's unfortunate, but believe me, it's not worth risking your life for."

"It's spreading, Padraig. It's only a matter of time until I become a statue."

Padraig chewed his lip as he digested this new information. Finally, he sighed.

"Fine. But only as a last resort. First, we find this Puca and see what he's got to say about it. If he can't undo what he's done..." He paused, his face puckering like he'd swallowed something sour. "I'll introduce you to the court. But you'd best pray it doesn't come to that. I know you're tough, Val. But the Fae Court will eat you alive."

Val nodded wearily. "Agreed. We only go to the court as a last resort. Believe me, I don't want to get mixed up with them any more than you do. I may not have a choice, though." She sipped her tea and tried to put on a positive tone. "But first, we've got a Puca to catch, right?"

"Right," Padraig agreed. "That'll be no easy task either. Pucas are shape changers and mischief makers. They're shifty little bastards."

"I think I've got a solution to that." Val filled him in on the special chains Gunter Gristle was forging for her.

Padraig pursed his lips. "That might work."

"The biggest problem is finding him. How do we track him down?"

"Our best bet is to go fishing and lure him into a trap. Bait the hook with something he can't refuse."

"Such as?"

"That's the easy part. This Puca's clearly infatuated with you. He's already taken you for one wild ride. I doubt he could pass up the chance for another."

"I was afraid you were going to say something like that," Val groaned. "There's only one problem."

"What's that?"

"The last time I saw the Ural, it was galloping off to parts unknown. I don't have another motorcycle."

"Well, it's a good thing I'm rich then, isn't it?" Padraig grinned and winked at her. "I happen to have the solution to your problem sitting in my garage right now."

Val gave him the side eye. "And what will I owe you for this, Padraig O'Ceallaigh? I know you don't do these things for free."

His grin got bigger.

"I'll put it on your tab. When this is all over, you're going to owe me the mother of all favors."

Padraig's laughter rang in her ears as Val groaned and buried her face in the pillow.

34

Val twisted the throttle on the little loaner motorcycle Padraig had given her. The electric motor wheezed like an ancient grandmother. She scowled. Motorcycles were not supposed to sound like tiny farts.

The thing was so light it felt like a stiff breeze would blow it over, and it made almost no noise at all. Every time Val saw pedestrians, she was afraid they'd step out into the street right in front of her without even looking her way. Perhaps it was strange that she should feel relaxed hurtling down the street on a tank like the Ural, but tense as a mouse in a barnful of owls when riding this little bike, but that was just the way it was.

Also, she felt ridiculous. Her battered leather jacket and boots didn't exactly match the aesthetic of the sleek electric cycle. Not to mention the bandages she still sported from the red cap's attack. She could feel eyes judging her as she passed.

Her scowl became fierce. Let them judge. She wasn't trying to impress anyone.

She parked the bike in a public charging station beneath a rusty turbine tower. That was one good thing about riding an electric bike, at least. Wind-powered charging stations were everywhere. Some were owned and maintained by private companies and individuals, and those you had to pay for, but there were plenty of alternative stations erected by DIY do-gooders and collectives. Some of them were held together with aluminum foil and bubble gum, but they got the job done. A few even had bike-powered generators you could ride to charge up your vehicle when the wind wasn't blowing. Which seemed counter-intuitive to Val. If you were going to pedal the damn thing, why not just get a bicycle and skip the electricity altogether?

She carefully pulled the chain out of the lockbox. True to Gunter Gristle's word, the chains were ready when she went to pick them up. Val had given him his rat meat, wine, and comic books, and he had delivered a fine length of chain no thicker than her finger.

She frowned as she examined the links. The chain was so thin it seemed the Puca would be able to snap it like a thread. But Gunter had assured her it was a lot stronger than it looked.

"Also, it's cold iron," he'd said. "The fae are powerless against that stuff. Be sure you get it fastened, though. If you leave that shapeshifter any wiggle room, he'll slip out of it like a greased pig."

Val carefully stored the chain in an inside pocket of her leather jacket. The weight was comforting.

From the outside, Rosa's market looked like it had fully recovered from the grafter's attack. Sunlight sparkled off the green awning. The produce bins lining the front walk were colorful and full. Val breathed in the scents of oranges and fresh basil.

Inside the market, the scars still showed, if you knew where to look for them. Right in the center of the floor, half hidden by a display stand full of gummi bears, Val could make out the bloodstain left by the tiger-girl she'd killed. It was barely there, almost impossible to find if you didn't know what you were looking for.

But to Val, it was plain as day. And from the guilt on Rosa's face, Val knew the blood was obvious to her as well.

"Back again?" Rosa asked. Her smile was strained around the edges. "You're becoming a regular."

"A regular pain in the ass," Val quipped.

Rosa laughed, her smile becoming more genuine. "You said it, not me."

"Oh, I know what I am. I'm not denying it." Val's answering smile came to her easily. Something about Rosa made her lower her guard. Despite the traumatic experience they'd shared—or perhaps because of it—they connected on an unspoken level. She felt like she'd known the woman for years. Being around Rosa felt comfortable.

"So, what can I do for you? More tamales? Or do you need to see the security tape again?"

"Neither." Val glanced around and lowered her voice. "This might sound weird, but what time do you close?"

Rosa glanced up at the clock over the door. It read 2:10. "I take a siesta break around 2:30. I go home to eat and put my feet up, then I open up again around 4:30. Why?"

"This is going to sound weird, but do you mind if I stay in here while you're gone?"

Rosa squinted at her. "You want to stay in my shop while it's closed? Why?"

"I need to track down the monster that attacked us, and I need some time alone in here to do that."

"You're not going to do a seance, are you? I don't need any bad spirit energy in here."

"No, nothing like that," Val lied.

Actually, the ritual she wanted to conduct could easily be mistaken for a seance by a casual observer. But it wasn't the same thing. Not even close. She could honestly tell Rosa that her ritual wouldn't result in her market being haunted.

At least, she hoped it wouldn't.

Magic was a tricky thing. There were no absolutes or 100% certainties.

Rosa studied her through narrowed eyes. "You ask a lot of favors for a girl I just met."

"Favors are kind of par for the course with me. I owe a lot of people favors. One day they'll all come to collect at once and the house of cards of my existence will come crashing down." Val shrugged. "Until then, I'll keep doing what I've got to do."

Rosa chewed her bottom lip while she thought. The shopkeeper's lips were full and juicy, and Val found herself wondering what that pink flesh would feel like between her own teeth. Warmth crept up the back of her neck and she averted her eyes. She was here on business. Even if she was in the market—which she was not—that sort of thing was definitely not on the agenda.

Finally, Rosa said, "OK. You can stay and do"—she wiggled her fingers at the air—"whatever it is you're going to do. But if my market ends up haunted, you're paying for the exorcist."

Val laughed. "Fair enough."

Twenty minutes later, Rosa was gone, and the market was locked up tight. Val had pushed the gummi-bear display aside and drawn a chalk pentagram over the faint bloodstain.

"I don't see how this is going to help you track down the Puca," Mister E observed. He was lounging on the counter, idly batting at a keychain display with one paw while he watched her. *"That blood belonged to the tiger girl, and she's dead. The only place you'll track her to is the city morgue. And you know what happened the last time we broke into the morgue."*

"There's more than one way to skin a cat," she said, carefully setting a candle on each corner of the pentagram.

"I find that expression offensive."

"It's a good thing you're not a real cat then, isn't it?" Val said as she went around the pentagram lighting the candles one by one.

"It doesn't even make any sense. Why would you skin a cat at all? Let alone think up multiple ways to do it."

"Maybe someone wanted fur-lined boots? Or cat kebabs?" Val folded her legs and settled down in the center of the pentagram.

Mister E shuddered. *"Barbaric. Cats have been worshipped for centuries. Anyone who would skin a cat is a savage."*

"If you don't shut up and let me concentrate, you're going to find out what one of those ways to skin a cat is."

"Rude." Mister E stuck out his tongue at her, then pointedly rolled over on the counter, putting his back to her. *"If you need me, I'll be over here napping."*

Val ignored him and focused on her breathing. She let her eyes drift shut, the candlelight an orange glow through her eyelids. She rested her fingertips on the stained linoleum floor.

As her consciousness sank, Val's power began to stir.

35

M agic has a certain taste, and every spell is subtly different. To call it a taste is oversimplifying, of course. Magic affects us in ways beyond the scope of our base five senses, and the practitioner experiences its effects in ways that are impossible to describe with traditional sensory metaphors. However, without direct experience, words, metaphors, and the five senses are all we have to work with in our attempts to describe the indescribable. So we'll stick with the metaphor of taste, for now.

If you think thirty-two flavors of ice cream is a lot, you've obviously never tried magic in its infinite variety. Some magic is sweet, some spicy. Other spells leave a smoky residue in the nostrils, or a sour tang on the tongue.

No two spells are exactly alike. Every caster has a base flavor that dominates every working—you can think of this as the basic sauce or bouillon the recipe rests upon—but each individual spell cast is flavored slightly differently. A dash of rosemary here, a pinch of pepper there. A delicate hint of saffron.

In the same way that a gourmand can detect fine differences of flavor in every bite, the experienced tracker can detect faint variations distinguishing one spell from another. Detecting the strong base flavor that reveals the identity of the caster is relatively easy. Recognizing and individualizing the subtle gradations that separate one spell from another takes practice, experience, and a discerning palate.

Val, unfortunately, did not have a gourmand's palate. As she reached down into the traces of blood still staining the floor, Val recognized the flavor of the Puca's magic at once. She'd gotten a strong taste of it when he transformed the Ural into a stallion beneath her. It tasted like fennel and black licorice pickled in vinegar.

Fairly disgusting, in other words.

But the strong base flavor of the Puca's magic was all she could detect. Thanks to her limited palate, she couldn't tell how the spell that had transformed the grafters was different from the working that had brought the Ural to life. She only knew that it was definitely the Puca's doing.

That confirmation was all she needed.

"Got you, you little prick," she muttered.

In magic, a powerful connection is formed between the caster and the object of the spell. A binding. Like footprints in the sand, this connection fades over time. But despite Rosa's attempts to eradicate the physical stains, the Puca had changed the grafters fairly recently, so the lingering flavor of the creature's magic was still strong.

Val could taste the magic permeating the blood that had been spilled on the floor, and she could feel traces of the Puca's magic spreading into the city from this spot. These traces would lead to the other grafters who had been transformed, and to the Puca himself. She just had to follow them before the traces faded away.

The bell above the market's door chimed, pulling her from her trance. She looked up to find Rosa silhouetted in the doorway, one hand still on the door handle, staring down at her. The market owner was backlit, so Val couldn't see her expression, but she had a pretty good idea of what it was. She'd had people walk in on her sitting in the middle of a pentagram before, and they all looked at her with the same mixture of horror and curiosity. It was like finding an unusual spider occupying the corner of your room. Fascination and revulsion in equal measures.

"Are you sure you're not making my market haunted?" Rosa

stepped inside and shut the door behind her. "Because sitting in a pentagram on a bloodstain seems like a pretty good way to end up with a haunted market."

Val uncrossed her legs with a groan. Sitting in the same position for hours was definitely not good for the circulation.

"I know what this looks like, but believe me, I wasn't talking to ghosts or trying to summon a demon."

"What were you doing then?" Rosa cocked her head at Val. She didn't sound upset, just curious.

"You're handling this whole thing pretty well." Val got to her feet and stretched. Her spine popped like a string of firecrackers. "People usually freak out when they catch me sitting in the middle of a pentagram."

Rosa shrugged. "I told you, magic runs in my family. My aunt tells fortunes with chicken bones and entrails. I know real magic is weird and messy. Clean boarding-school kids with robes and wands are only in the movies."

The corner of Val's mouth quirked. "True. Well, to answer your question, I was trying to track the other transformed creatures and the Puca who caused them to transform in the first place."

"You can do that?"

"Sure, though certain things make it easier. Blood, for example, maintains a very strong resonance. The blood that's in your linoleum is still connected to the other transformed grafter and the Puca."

Rosa whistled. "So you can tell where they are just by communing with the blood? Impressive. So where are they?"

Val shook her head. "It doesn't work like that. I don't have some GPS map in my head that pinpoints their location. It's more like a scent trail. I've got their scent now and I can follow the trail. I don't know where it will lead until I get there."

"Very cool." Rosa went behind the counter and started flipping on lights, preparing to open the market again. "What is this Puca anyway? Some kind of nasty spirit?"

Val got the hint and started gathering up her candles.

"No, he's not a spirit. He's a faerie. A shapeshifter and a trickster.

He likes turning people into animals and sending them on wild rides. Have you got a mop?"

Rosa showed Val where the mop and bucket were stored in the back room. Val continued explaining while she mopped up the pentagram.

"Tricksters tend to be morally gray. They like to stir up trouble for its own sake. Sometimes the outcomes are bad, sometimes they're good. I don't think the tricksters really care either way. I think they just want to cause chaos."

"That sounds pretty evil to me," Rosa said.

"It can be," Val acknowledged. She thought of Sandra's transformation into a gorgon and her lips tightened. "It definitely can be."

Rosa eyed the faded bloodstain as Val positioned the gummi bears back into place.

"When people die, that's evil in my book," Rosa said. "I don't care what your intentions are. That's crossing the line."

"That's fair. And I agree. That's why I'm going to stop the little prick before any more people get hurt."

Rosa gave her a big smile. "Glad we got that sorted out. You want something to eat before you go hunting? You don't want to try to catch a Puca on an empty stomach."

Val returned her smile.

"Thank you. Don't mind if I do."

36

V al's stomach was full and warm when she finally pulled
    Padraig's electric motorcycle away from the curb. Which was
good, because the San Francisco air most definitely was not. She
shivered and pulled the collar of her leather jacket closed against the
chill Pacific wind. Tendrils of fog licked the streets, leaving her face
damp.

"I swear this city switches from summer to winter every day at five
o'clock," she complained.

*"With the fae moving in, I hope that doesn't mean it switches from the
Summer Court to the Winter Court,"* Mister E commented.

"What's the difference?"

*"The fae of the Summer Court can be whimsical and tricky, but they
generally mean no harm. The fae of the Winter Court are another matter altogether. Your friend the red cap belongs to the Winter Court. I advise you to
steer clear of them."*

An image of the red cap soaking his hat in her blood came to Val's
mind unbidden, and she shivered again.

"Noted. I'll do my best to stay away from Winter Fae."

She pulled over to the curb and took in a deep breath, smelling for
traces of the Puca's power. The trail split, with one part leading down

toward Mission Bay and the other heading in the direction of Bernal Heights, uphill and away from the heart of the city.

"Which trail belongs to the Puca and which is the shifter?" Val wondered.

"The stronger trail probably belongs to the Puca," Mister E advised. *"His entire being reeks of his magic, while the new shifter has only been affected by it."*

"That makes sense." Val closed her eyes and focused. Sure enough, the trail leading towards Mission Bay was noticeably weaker than the one running uphill. As she pulled back into traffic, she asked, "Which court does the Puca belong to? He doesn't seem like he fits into either one."

"You're right, he doesn't. The Puca is most often associated with harvest time. One of his favorite tricks is to turn an entire crop rotten if it isn't harvested by the night of Samhain. On that night, farmers are supposed to leave a part of their crop out for him so that he will be in a good mood on November 1st. That day is the one day of the year he will supposedly be benevolent, and the Puca gives advice or speaks prophecies to any who find him. I believe he is technically a creature of the Winter Court, though he is relatively harmless compared to most creatures of that ilk."

"So he's an autumn faerie."

"You could say that, yes."

Val frowned. "Why are there only Winter and Summer Courts? What happened to Spring and Autumn?"

"It is my understanding that Spring and Autumn are turbulent, transitional seasons, and the fae that belong to them are too quixotic to maintain any kind of organized court. The fae who would belong to these courts have been forced to bow to the power of either Summer or Winter, though they remain chaotic and unpredictable. In the frequent power struggles between the Summer and Winter Courts, these fae are the ones whose allegiances may change. They are often the ones who tip the balance and ultimately determine the winner on any given day."

"So when you say the Puca belongs to the Winter Court..."

"I'm saying he is most often associated with that court. His true allegiance may change with the wind."

Val mulled this over as she followed the trail of the Puca's magic into Bernal Heights. The trail led south off Cortland, and she eventually parked the motorcycle beside Holly Park.

It was a small, round park, not much more than a pocket park, really. But as she gazed into its untended depths, dread crept into the pit of her stomach. Holly Park had clearly been left to its own devices for a long time. The little circle was completely overgrown, with a bushy hedge and snaking vines forming a tangled wall around the border. A single path led into the interior of the park, and it snaked around a wall of honeysuckle and disappeared from view after only a few feet.

Birds called and insects thrummed with the vigor of a rainforest, but when Val put her foot on the path every one of them fell silent, as if turned off by a switch.

"That doesn't seem good," she whispered.

"At the very least, it means they know we're here," Mister E confirmed. *"I hope you weren't planning on taking them by surprise."*

Val checked the Puca's trail. Sure enough, it lead directly into the heart of the park.

"Maybe this is far enough for today," she whispered. "We can come back with reinforcements."

"But you've come so far already. ," a new voice said from right behind her. "It'd be rude to stay out on the doorstep."

Val whirled. Facing her, a wicked smile stretching his long face, was the Puca.

37

S andra had officially run out of things to do. She'd spent the past two days cleaning the basement from top to bottom, until it hardly resembled a basement at all. First, she'd stacked all the old furniture and boxes in the corners and swept the cobwebs out of the rafters. Next, she wiped down the walls, polished the cast-off furniture, and hunted the enormous dust bunnies lurking in the corners to extinction. Finally, she mopped the cement floor and covered it with a spiral scrap rug.

A trunk full of old sheets gave her an idea, and she nailed them across the ceiling, creating a colorful, patchwork mosaic that made the entire space feel like a festival tent. Sandra lay on the battered blue couch and gazed up at it, imagining where each sheet had come from, and whose bed it had once graced.

This made her happy, which in turn made her fingers itch for a pencil and her sketchbook. But the only sketchbook she had was the green one she'd abandoned at Zombie Coffee. Val had returned it to her after bringing her back from the Morlock tunnels, but Sandra hadn't been able to draw in it. Just touching its cover made her chest seize up and her hands go cold with memory.

So she'd abandoned the basement and gone upstairs to the apartment, only to find herself stymied there as well. She'd already cleaned everything there was to clean, Malcolm and Val weren't home, and Hillary was sleeping the sleep of the undead.

Sandra paced the living room for a while, doodling on scraps of paper and wishing she could go out and get a new sketchbook. But it wasn't safe for her to go out into the world. She could hurt someone. Turn them to stone. That was the entire reason she was staying in the basement, after all. To prevent deadly accidents.

So she sat in the window seat and stared out at the sunset, pining away like some Victorian spinster. She was in this position when a voice behind her nearly made her leap out of her skin.

"Just go out, already. Your sad puppy face is making me nauseous."

Sandra saw a dark silhouette reflected in the window. She whirled around to see who it was, and a muffled curse made her drop her gaze just in time.

"Watch it!" Hillary shielded her eyes with a raised arm, turning her pale face away. "Be careful where you point those things."

Shame flooded Sandra as she jerked her hood down over her eyes.

"Sorry. I didn't know anyone was here."

"Just us monsters," Hillary quipped. At the hangdog look on Sandra's face, she continued, "That's a joke. If you can't laugh at yourself, who can you laugh at, right?"

"I don't think I'm ready to laugh about this." Sandra stared at the floor. To her horror, her eyes filled with tears. She turned back to the window, sniffling.

She heard Hillary sigh. The recliner squeaked as the vampire lowered herself into it.

Sandra tensed. She hardly knew Hillary. The vampire had moved into Sandra's vacated room after she moved out of the flat, and the two of them had just been introduced when Sandra took refuge in the basement. Sandra knew she should be more open-minded about monsters —especially considering she was one now—but the knowledge that she was a few feet from a vampire made every muscle in her body tense.

Would Hillary want to feed on her the way she fed on Malcolm? Did Sandra still have normal human blood now that she was a gorgon? Would her blood smell tasty to Hillary, or were monsters unappetizing? Or—even worse—were monsters delicacies?

That thought made her breath catch in her throat. Maybe she smelled like truffles to Hillary. Truffles and bacon. Maple bacon truffle bars.

She couldn't bring herself to look at the vampire's reflection in the window, lest she catch Hillary inhaling Sandra's scent, her fangs bared...

"Relax. I'm not going to eat you," Hillary said.

Sandra jumped and her cheeks flushed with embarrassment. Had the vampire read her mind? Was that a thing vampires could do?

She peeked from under her hood, surreptitiously checking Hillary's reflection in the window. To her relief, the pale woman appeared to be leaning back in the armchair, one leg crossed over the other.

Sandra's eyes widened as realization hit her.

"I can see your reflection! I thought vampires didn't have reflections."

"I'll take *Things the Stories Got Wrong About Vampires* for $200," Hillary said wearily.

"What?"

"Never mind. It was an old game show." Hillary waved the thought away with a flick of her wrist. "Yes, we have reflections. Trust me, most of what you think you know about my kind is wrong."

"Like what?" Sandra said, curiosity overriding her fear.

"Well, for starters, I love garlic."

Sandra blew a raspberry between her lips. "That's not surprising. I always thought that was the least believable myth about vampires."

"I also will not burst into flames if I go out in the sunshine."

"Really?" That one gave Sandra pause. "Then why do you sleep during the day?"

It was Hillary's turn to make a rude noise. "I have sensitive skin. Just because I won't burst into flames doesn't mean sunlight feels good. I get a raging sunburn in about thirty seconds and sun poisoning in a couple of minutes. It's not as dramatic as bursting into flames, but it'll still get the job done. Ten minutes in the sun and I'd be as dried out as an eighty-year-old swimsuit model in Arizona. Being nocturnal is much easier."

"But you could go out during the day if you wanted to?"

"Sure. Wrap me in bandages like the invisible man or put me in a cloak with big sunglasses and gloves and I'd be fine. But who wants to live like Audrey Hepburn? Which brings me back to my original point. If you want to go outside, go outside. You can't spend the rest of your life holed up in here. That's a good way to go stark raving."

Sandra dropped her gaze. "I can't. I don't want to hurt anyone."

"News flash. People accidentally hurt each other all the time. They break each other's hearts, they trip each other down flights of stairs, they bonk heads bending down to pick up keys, they knock each other into traffic. Shit happens."

"But not like me! I could turn someone into a statue. I can kill them just by looking at them!"

"It's true, you have more of a challenge. All that means is you need to be more careful than most people."

"You don't understand," Sandra huffed. "I'm a monster."

Hillary laughed. "It takes one to know one. Believe me, I understand better than you think. This body is ridiculously fast and strong. I have to treat people like they're made of eggshells. If I accidentally shook someone's hand at full strength, I'd crush every bone in their fingers."

"But you wouldn't kill them just by looking at them. It's not the same."

"No, but I know a thing or two about having to adjust to new powers and a new body. It's like anything else. It just takes practice."

"But my 'practice' could kill someone."

"Stop being so dramatic. That's true of every student driver who ever got behind the wheel. Our lives are literally in the hands of hundreds of individuals every day. You are trusting that every person you walk past on the street won't turn and stab you in the throat. That every cab driver won't crush you against the side of a building. Some person in a third floor apartment won't drop a fifty-pound weight on your head. Every person is responsible for the lives of every other person they meet. It's no different for you and me."

Sandra didn't know what to say to that, so she kept staring at the floor in silence.

When Hillary spoke again, her voice was softer.

"Instead of focusing on what you can't do, you need to focus on what you can. I understand your power doesn't affect people if you look at their reflection in a mirror. What if the opposite is true?"

"What do you mean?"

"What if you cover your eyes so people can't see them?"

"I'm doing that already," Sandra pointed out. "That's what the hood is for."

"I mean something more direct. What if you covered your eyes with mirrored sunglasses? Then people would only see their own eyes reflected back at them when they looked at you."

Sandra chewed on that idea.

"How would I test it?"

"Don't look at me." Hillary got up and padded toward her bedroom. Her voice came floating down the hall. "I've got an extra pair of mirrored sunglasses you can borrow, but I'm not going to play guinea pig for you. I'd rather not end up petrified if my hypothesis turns out to be wrong. You'll have to wait for Val to test it out. She's more comfortable risking her life than the rest of us."

Hillary returned and pressed a pair of aviator glasses into Sandra's hand.

"The bottom line is, no matter how low you feel right now, your life isn't over. Your circumstances have changed. Drastically. All that means is you've got a new set of challenges to overcome. If you put your mind to it, you can get through this. Trust me, from one monster to another: I've been there."

Sandra turned the glasses over, looking at her reflection in the mirrored surface. Her eyes looked the same as they always had, their soft brown surface giving no hint of the deadly power they contained.

Could Hillary's idea work? It seemed too simple. Then again, looking at someone's reflection in a mirror was simple too, and that worked just fine.

She tried to clamp down on the feeling building inside her, but despite her best efforts, the corner of her mouth curled into a hint of a smile. For the first time in days, a spark of hope kindled within Sandra's heart.

38

Val tensed, drawing in her power, waiting to see what the Puca would do next. Her hand slid into her pocket, fingers on the cold links of the chain. The dog-faced fae gave her a sly smile.

"It won't do to have guests standing out on my stoop," he said.

"I was just passing by," Val lied. "I don't have time to come in right now."

"Oh, I must insist. Let me give you a little tour."

Val gripped the chain as the Puca's smile continued to grow, his face becoming longer and longer. In a blink, the faerie was a man no more. Instead, a black stallion stood facing her, pawing at the ground with a foreleg.

"Not this again," Val backed away, but that just took her deeper onto the narrow path. Honeysuckle brushed her shoulder on one side, while the hedge wall blocked the other. She squeezed the chain in her pocket, but the collar had been fashioned for a human-sized neck. It would never snare the Puca in his horse form. "Stay away from me, you creep."

A root caught her heel as she stepped back and Val stumbled, dropping her guard for a second as she flailed her arms, trying to catch herself.

She never hit the ground.

The Puca flowed beneath her, and she found herself astride a black horse once again.

There were two important differences this time. First, she was seated backwards, facing the rear of the horse. Instead of a mane to hold onto, there was nothing before her but a long black tail.

Second, and more importantly, instead of a transformed motorcycle, this time the horse was the Puca himself.

"Hold on tight," he giggled. "You wouldn't want to fall off in the twilight realms. You might never be heard from again."

"Twilight realms?" Val wondered.

"The transitional realms between our world and the fae lands," Mister E supplied. *"You can think of them as pocket dimensions."*

"Thanks. That clears everything up," Val huffed.

The Puca started to move, and she clamped onto his back as best she could with her legs and hands. She thought about turning around, but as she twisted to look behind her, she started to slip sideways off his back. Heart in her throat, she aborted the movement and threw herself down flat, wrapping her arms around the Puca's rump.

Since she was facing backwards, the passing foliage whipped at her legs and ass as the Puca gained speed. It felt like she'd been a bad girl and someone had gotten out a switch.

"Not funny," she snarled.

The Puca giggled. "That depends entirely on your perspective, doesn't it?"

The horse came to a burbling stream and Val yelped as he leapt over the channel. When they landed on the other side, everything had changed.

Gone were the trees and vines whipping at her backside. In fact, all the greenery was gone. Now the walls surrounding the path were stone. Val risked a glance ahead and saw they were galloping through a maze of boulders, each towering twenty feet over their heads. The boulders were made from every kind of rock she could imagine: gleaming ebony and quartz, striated granite and marble, red sculpted sandstone and chalk-white walls of lime. A sliver of sky snaked above the path, and it shone with a gold richer than any sunset Val had ever seen.

"What is this place?" she breathed.

"One of the twilight realms." Mister E sounded grim. *"Don't be fooled by the beauty. And whatever you do, don't fall off the Puca's back. If we get lost here, we may never find our way back to mortal lands again."*

The path turned at that moment and the Puca pivoted sharply. Despite Mister E's warning, Val started to slide. She desperately threw her arms across the Puca's back while her legs slid off the opposite side. She found herself lying sideways on her stomach, legs dangling off one side of the broad back as her arms and head pressed against the other. This position felt even more precarious than straddling the horse backwards, and she fought to pull herself up. As she grabbed a fistful of horse hair and yanked, the Puca turned again...

... and everything changed.

Val gagged as the stench of vomit filled her nostrils. Now they rode across a swamp, the Puca's hooves dancing along a narrow path between black pools of fetid slime. The reek was unbelievable, and it was all Val could do to not lose her lunch all over the Puca's legs.

"This is even worse than the sewers," she croaked. "What is this place?"

"I've heard it called many things," Mister E hissed, his fur standing in disapproval as he floated along beside her. *"But I think the one who came closest to the mark is the person who dubbed it the Bog of Eternal Stench."*

"Wasn't that in a movie?" Val asked.

"Indeed it was. Though the Hollywood version pales in comparison to the real thing."

"You can say that again."

The Puca weaved between the stagnant pools at breakneck speed, sending Val sliding from one side to the other. He never stayed on a steady path long enough for her to gain a proper seat, and she was forced to claw at his back desperately, always inches away from losing her grip and tumbling into the reeking bog.

Finally, the Puca rounded a dead tree, jumped into the air, and turned a complete one hundred and eighty degrees, landing with his nose pointing back the way they'd just come.

This about-face was almost Val's undoing. The Puca's back spun so fast beneath her that it was impossible to keep her grip. As the black horse completed his rotation, Val started to fall.

She did the only thing she could think of to anchor herself. She stabbed her knife into his back.

This proved to be a mistake.

39

The Puca screamed and bucked, and Val found herself airborne, surrounded by stinking bog on all sides. Time slowed. She saw everything in crystal detail: the mist rising off the bog to her left, the orange sludge swirling through the bog to her right, the sad mangrove tree drooping listlessly behind her, the endless swamp stretching past the horizon in every direction.

Then time lurched again, and she was falling. The stinking brown mud reached up to grab her and never let go.

Only one thing could save her: the knife, still embedded in the Puca's back. She clung to the handle with all her strength, desperately twisting her body away from the thick muck. Her feet danced across the path, her body jerking up and down, hanging from the knife like a marionette on strings. The Puca's flank heaved against her, sharp hooves flashing like broken glass.

She tried to lift herself, but the jarring of the Puca's gallop was too violent. She couldn't get any leverage; there was nothing stationary to push against. One of the black hooves caught her in the ribs and Val almost lost her grip as she felt something give inside her.

She gathered her power, trying to get onto the Puca's back with a gust of wind, but sharp pain sawed through her with every jolt, breaking her concentration. The best she could do was push up with little puffs that were never quite enough, like an adult boosting a child up onto a slide but leaving them to climb the last few feet alone.

Between one step and the next, the world around her blurred and shifted. Now they ran through an English garden, the path straight as an arrow, surrounded by flowers planted in neat rectangular rows. They circled a wide fountain. A bronze boy blowing on a pipe stood upon a shifting mound in the center of the pool, children and fairies and a solitary rabbit swirling around him as if entranced.

The Puca was shifting as well, his body stretching and changing as he tried to dislodge the cold metal embedded in his back. Smoke rose from the skin around the blade as it burned and bubbled. His furred flank turned to smooth black scales, his feet sprouting hooked claws, legs retracting into a gigantic, serpentine body. He bared wicked fangs, hissing in pain and rage....

"It burns," he shrieked. "Get it out..."

Then the fountain was gone, replaced by a whirling dervish of yellow dust. The sun was painfully bright, the hardpan land bleached and cracked as far as the eye could see. A trio of vultures tore at the carcass of a dead thing, then rose into the air with great flaps of their wings as the writhing Puca flashed past, quickly becoming black specks that circled and circled and circled. Waiting for their next meal to fall.

The world changed again. The starlit darkness was so crisp and cold it stole Val's breath from her lips. The Puca sprouted a thick lion's mane, his body covered in golden fur, his feet the cruel claws of an eagle.

Another blink. Another world, another shape. And another. And another. And another.

Val's strength was flagging, her injured ribs tearing at her with every breath.

"I don't know how much more of this I can take," she whispered.

"Hold on," Mister E hissed. *"Just a bit longer. He's got to return to the park soon. All this skipping across worlds is wearing on him as much as it is you."*

Forcing her attention back to the Puca, Val could see that Mister E was right. The Puca had the head of a horse again, and white lather covered his neck. He was blowing hard, eyes rolling wildly in their sockets. A dark pool of blood spread around Val's knife, which was still planted in his back.

"Stay ready," Mister E advised. *"When you see the park, jump."*

Val nodded, too exhausted to even reply.

The world changed, and they were in a vast garden of roses. Another step and the Puca danced across a rushing stream, his sure feet finding purchase on slick, moss-covered rocks. Another blink and they crossed a stone aqueduct, towering fifty feet over the land. A breath after that, the Puca steamed over a starlit field of snow.

Once more the world blurred, and tangled greenery came into focus. Honeysuckle and ivy, pressing close on every side.

The park!

Val yanked the knife free and tumbled away into the undergrowth.

She lay still, her eyes pressed tight against the pain. Tumbling with broken ribs was even less fun than it sounded. Her insides were a mill of pain, grinding against her nerves with every breath. She lay curled on the ground, teeth clenched, hissing as she tried to breathe as shallowly as possible.

After what felt like hours, the pain receded a tiny fraction. Enough so that pain wasn't her entire universe anymore. Merely a gas giant dominating her view.

Val cracked her eyes open and found herself lying in a small clearing in a dark forest. Brave daisies pushed through mossy green inches from her nose. Beyond them she saw clover, and beyond that lay the body of the Puca.

The fairie had reverted to his human form, though his face looked even more bestial than usual. He lay whimpering, smoke still rising from the wound in his back.

Val instinctively reached out to help him, unsure how but wanting to alleviate the suffering of her fellow being.

Mister E hissed at her, *"Stop! Foolish girl. Now is the time to bargain with the fae. Now, while he is weak and you have him in your power. In a few minutes, he will heal and disappear, and you will be left with nothing. Put the chain on him."*

She stopped her outstretched fingers. It hurt her to let the Puca suffer. He looked so pathetic, his dog eyes liquid and sad. Like a child who has dropped an ice cream cone.

Val steeled herself, hardening her heart. She thought of the grafters he'd transformed in Rosa's market. Of Sandra. This was her chance to help them.

Pulling out the chain, she held it close to the downed creature. The Puca hissed and shied away from the cold iron.

"I could capture you with this chain right now. I could bind you and force you to do my bidding. Instead, I would strike a bargain with you," she said. "I will not use this chain on one condition. You must undo the mischief you have caused in the mortal realm. Allow all of those you have changed to return to their natural forms."

"Yes," the Puca gasped. "All of those I have changed."

Val narrowed her eyes at him. It felt like the Puca was agreeing to her terms too readily. Was she missing something?

"I will not bind you with this chain. In exchange for this, you will immediately return all the mortals you have changed to their natural forms," she stated, trying to be as precise with the terms as she could. "Do we have a bargain?"

"Yes," the Puca hissed. "We have a bargain."

Hesitantly, Val returned the chain to her jacket pocket.

The Puca shuddered with relief as the cold iron moved away from his body. His coloring slowly became healthy again, the wound on his back mending with every breath. In less than a minute, the creature sat up, looking whole once more.

"Now you will undo the changes you have wrought," Val commanded.

The Puca gave her a sly smile. "Nothing could be simpler, mistress. 'Tis already done."

Val frowned down at her half-petrified hand. She lifted it for the Puca to see. "It would appear you have not undone everything."

"Oh, I did not make that change to you, Valora Keri. That falls outside of our bargain. In fact, 'twas the Wild Storm that wrought all of the changes in the mortal realm. My hand merely helped to shape the clay. Therefore, there are no changes for me to undo, for none were made by my hand." He rose to his feet, his movement liquid as a cat's. He gave her a mocking bow. "Our bargain is complete."

"You tricky little—" Val lunged at him, but the creature was too fast.

The Puca skipped away into the undergrowth, his wicked laughter ringing in her ears.

40

V al struggled to get to her feet.

"I'm going to cut that guy's liver out and feed it to him."

Then she groaned and sank back to her knees as the ends of her broken rib ground inside her.

"Just as soon as I can walk again," she amended weakly.

"Now you know why the fae are such notorious bargainers," Mister E commiserated. *"You never get the deal you think you are getting."*

"How was I supposed to know it was the Wild Storms that were changing people? The Puca was there every time!" Val slammed her fist against her knee, then groaned at the pain that accompanied the movement. "He admitted he was helping to choose the forms the storms changed people into. That should still count."

"It is a fine distinction, to be sure. The fae have always twisted their bargains around such fine distinctions."

"Now what do we do?" Val blinked at the forest surrounding the clearing. "And where are we? This isn't the park."

She knelt in a small clearing, surrounded by a dense forest of autumnal trees. The trees were smallish, their lowest branches no higher than Val's head. Their trunks were ash white and gnarled, as if they could not grow straight up, but had to contort themselves around invisible obstacles in their quest for sunlight. Their leaves were vaguely maple-shaped, but different in some subtle way Val could not identify. They blazed with color, flaring a golden yellow at their tips which faded down through vibrant orange and red, until finally becoming a deep, sullen plum at the stem. Little underbrush grew beneath the trees, only an occasional fern or fanlike mushroom.

A soft breeze whispered though the branches, carrying with it a sweet, spicy smell that called to mind mulled cider and gingerbread. It brought a breath of oncoming winter, crisp and cold against her flushed cheeks.

"I would guess we are close to the realms of faerie." Mister E bobbed thoughtfully upon the air, his golden eyes a reflection of the forest. *"Judging from the breeze, I'd say we are not too far from winter."*

Ice crept down Val's spine.

"That's a bad thing, right?"

"Most certainly. The winter realms are safe for neither man nor beast."

"So what do we do?"

The cat shrugged. *"Pick a direction and start walking. There must be a path back to the mortal realm somewhere. All we have to do is find it."*

"What if we find winter instead?"

"My advice would be: Don't."

"But what if we do?"

"Then I suggest you be prepared to run."

Val hissed as she pushed to her feet, sagging over the stabbing pain in her ribs.

"Can I learn some healing magic next? The way I keep getting wounded, I think that would be really useful."

Mister E frowned. *"Healing is a magic all its own. Great healers are prized specialists. I can't teach you something I don't know. Be thankful the magic circulating through your system helps you heal quickly on its own. Beyond that, I can't help you."*

"Wonderful. Thanks for nothing." Val took a labored step, grinding her teeth against the pain. "Walking like this is not going to be easy. I wonder if I can... Hmmm."

She unzipped her jacket and slipped it from her shoulder. Then she pulled up her shirt to expose an ugly, hoof-shaped bruise over her ribs.

"X marks the spot."

"It looks more like a U to me."

"Funny. Now shut up so I can concentrate."

She called up a small breeze and focused on making it very cold. The icy wind caressed her exposed skin, pimpling her flesh with goosebumps.

"That's not a bad idea."

Val grinned. "Better than an ice pack."

She closed her eyes and leaned into it, letting the frosty breeze numb the area. The breeze grew stronger, and the temperature plummeted. Snowflakes swirled around her. In a heartbeat, the wind had grown from a tiny breeze numbing her side to a howling winter gale.

Val cowered against stinging sleet, covering her face with her arms. She released her power, letting the wind dissipate. But nothing happened. The storm continued to rage.

"What is this?" She had to yell to hear herself over the howl of the storm. "Why won't it stop?"

"We are in the twilight realms," Mister E yelled back. *"Magic can be unpredictable here."*

"You couldn't have told me that before I summoned a blizzard?"

"You didn't ask. Besides, I didn't know you would summon a blizzard. It was just as likely nothing would happen. As I said, these realms are unpredictable."

"So what do we do now?"

"Are your ribs numb?"

"Everything is numb!" she shouted back.

"Then I suggest you start walking. Hopefully, the storm is just a localized phenomenon."

"And if it's not?"

"I hear igloos are fairly easy to construct."

"Hilarious."

Val maneuvered her arm back inside her leather jacket and pulled it closed. The zipper was crusted with ice, and it took several tries before her numb fingers could get the teeth to work. Finally, she got the jacket zipped, buried her hands in her pockets, and started walking.

She didn't know which way to go, so she flipped her collar up, hunched her shoulders, and moved away from the wind. The sleet turned to hail, pelting her with stinging little balls of ice. Frozen ground crunched under her feet. She quickened her steps and hurried beneath the canopy.

The spreading leaves blocked the hail, and the wind mellowed until it was less of a gale and more of a steady breeze. It was quiet in the forest, with only gentle snowflakes drifting down. Val shook hail from her hair and stamped her feet.

"That was terrible. Is that going to happen every time I use magic here?"

"Perhaps. Perhaps not. It's impossible to say. It may be that particular type of magic has an affinity for the environment here."

Val squinted at him. "Say that again in English."

The demon-cat rolled his golden eyes. *"As I told you when we first arrived, this land borders on winter. By summoning cold, you may have inadvertently summoned the power of winter."*

"Ah." Val regarded the falling snow uneasily. "So by trying to numb my side, I may have taken us closer to winter?"

"It's possible. Perhaps the autumnal twilight realms are not the best place to summon cold winds."

"Now you tell me."

"It didn't occur to me until it happened. In hindsight, the possibility is obvious." Mister E shrugged and blew candy cigarette smoke rings. *"If we are lucky, we are now moving away from winter. Things should start to warm up soon."*

Val trudged through the snow muffled forest for several minutes. The only sounds were the rasp of her breath and the crackle of her footsteps. Her broken ribs were a dull, numb ache, which was a big improvement on the sharp stabbing pains she'd had before.

A distant howl ahead of her broke the silence. Val froze, listening. A second later, it was answered by another howl ahead and to her left. Then a third joined in.

"What are those?" she whispered.

"Winter wolves."

"Why are they ahead of us? I thought we were walking away from winter."

Mister E's expression was grim.

"It seems we've been walking in the wrong direction."

41

"What do you mean, we've been going the wrong way?" Val snapped. "I thought you said we were walking away from winter?"

"I was mistaken," Mister E replied coolly.

"But the wind is at our back. The winter wind. If we're walking away from it, we have to be walking away from winter," Val insisted.

Her hair prickled along her scalp as more howls sounded in the distance. The winter wolves were getting closer.

"If the wolves are ahead of us, that means the winter realm is ahead of us as well."

"What about the wind?"

Mister E looked like he'd swallowed something sour. *"The wind must have been intentionally deceiving us. It was herding us toward winter."*

"But why?"

"Why does any predator drive prey toward its lair?"

Val swallowed. "So what do we do now?"

"I suggest you stop talking and start running."

"Thanks for nothing. I could have figured that one out myself."

She lurched into a jog, wincing as each step jolted through her cracked ribs. The cold had numbed her ribs, but not deadened the pain completely. And jogging wasn't an activity she enjoyed under the best of circumstances.

With cracked ribs?

"One star. Would not recommend," she hissed.

The howls came again, the sound twisted and spun by the wind until it was impossible to tell which way the wolves were coming from.

"Where are they? Are we still running away from them?"

"Keep your nose to the wind and you'll be fine. That definitely takes us away from winter."

"Five minutes ago you said the same thing about the opposite direction. I think your fae GPS is broken."

"Not broken, just rerouting."

Running into the wind was a hundred times worse than running away from it. Going with the wind, Val had been able to let it carry her. She'd felt like a sailboat, pushed over the snow with almost no effort on her part. All she had to do was move her legs fast enough to stay upright and let the wind do all the work.

Now she had to lean forward like a mountain climber, squinting against the driving snow, every step an effort. Despite the frosty air, Val was sweating from the exertion.

"At least I'm not cold anymore."

"See? Silver linings are everywhere."

"You're like one of those bad life coaches with faded motivational posters on the wall."

"You should thank me."

"For what?"

"For taking your mind off the wolves."

Right on cue, the howls came again. They sounded close. Val squinted into the storm, but could see nothing through the swirling snow.

"I don't think we're going to make it," she said.

"I'd advise you to take defensive measures."

"But I can't even tell how close they are. How will I know..." Her words cut off in a cry as a furred shape came flying out of the murk.

Val reacted instinctively, twisting the storm gusts into a barrier of icy wind. It caught the wolf at the last second and punched its head to the side, its snapping jaws missing Val's face by inches. Unfortunately, the rest of the leaping wolf was too heavy to divert so easily, and its flank collided with Val's shoulder, sending her crashing down into the snow.

She cried out as the impact jarred her ribs. Pain so sharp she couldn't breathe stabbed through her. Tears sprang to her eyes. For a timeless moment, she lay there, immobilized by pain, completely helpless, praying that the wind would protect her.

After an eternity, the pain receded a notch. Sweet air crept back into her lungs.

One breath. Two.

She looked up, searching for the wolf, but the tears had frozen to an icy crust on her eyelashes, making the world a glistening smear. She scrubbed the back of her fist across her eyes.

When she looked up again, ice blue eyes were staring back at her.

Val flinched, but the wolf stayed where it was, hateful gaze locked on hers. The beast was white as the snow, with thick fur rippling in the wind. It stood just beyond the swirl of her defensive perimeter, as if it knew exactly how close it could come without hitting the barrier.

The wolf was huge, at least four feet high at the shoulder, its head massive. Its eyes shone blue and cold as the sun through a glacier. The wolf's lips pulled back from powerful jaws, baring fangs like icicles.

"Why isn't it attacking?" Val whispered.

"It knows it can't get through your barrier." Mister E replied. *"Either that, or it's waiting for the rest of the pack to catch up."*

"That's not reassuring." Val struggled back to her feet, keeping her eyes locked on the winter wolf. She wanted to be ready if it leapt at her again.

"Keep moving," Mister E advised.

She turned and lurched into motion, but she hadn't taken two steps before the wolf got in her path, head lowered, a low growl rumbling in its throat.

Val snarled right back at it. "You don't want me to go in that direction? Too bad."

She punched out with her power and was shocked when her fist of wind lifted the wolf ten feet off the ground and flung it howling into the storm. She stared down at her hand.

"That was more than I expected."

"I told you, this realm plays havoc with your power. Be glad it amplified your abilities instead of doing the opposite."

The blood drained from her face. "It could do that?"

"Of course. The twilight realms may amplify a breeze into a gale or reduce a hurricane to no more than a sneeze."

"Well," Val said, leaning into the headwind once again, "I'm glad it went the way it did."

"The next time it might not. You must hurry."

More howls sounded from somewhere nearby as Val pushed forward. The snow was piling up now, her boots crunching through the icy crust with each step. She squinted into the driving snow but found no blue eyes staring back at her.

The blizzard cut the visibility around her like a shroud. She saw nothing but white. Heard nothing but the roar of the wind. Felt nothing but the sting of the cold on her face.

Fangs flashed to her left, and Val flinched away, only to find the wolf had disappeared as quickly as it appeared.

Behind her, another snarl.

She whirled in time to see the tip of a white tail swallowed up by the storm.

To her right, blue eyes.

She moved left, only to have a different wolf come hurtling out of the storm in full leap, reaching for her throat. It bounced off her defensive wall of wind and spun away, yelping.

The wolves flashed in and out of the storm. Snarling and snapping. Leaping and disappearing.

Val pushed on. Flinching away from snapping teeth. Jaws that rend and tear.

It took her a long time to realize the wolves were forcing her to walk in a certain direction. Herding her. Toward what, she didn't want to find out.

"The hell with that." She turned at right angles to face the wind.

The wolves attacked immediately, barking and snarling. Snapping at her face. Trying to drive her back.

But now she saw what they were trying to do. And Val was having none of it.

"Get out of my way, you mutts." Val lashed out with a blast of wind, trying to clear the wolves from her path.

Nothing happened.

Well, that's not entirely true. Something did happen. But that something wasn't what Val had intended.

With a soft sigh, her defensive barrier collapsed.

The full force of the headwind hit her, knocking her back a step. As she fought to regain her balance, Val looked up. Her blood froze. Four pairs of cold blue eyes were staring back at her.

42

Val staggered under the force of the blizzard winds.

"I didn't realize my shield was blunting the force of the storm so much," she groaned. "I can't walk into this. I can barely stay on my feet."

"You must," Mister E hissed. *"The storm tries to blow you back into winter. If it succeeds, we may never win free again."*

"I don't think the winds are the worst of our problems."

The winter wolves had stopped their harassment, as if they understood that her shield was down. All four of them stood directly across her path now, gazes locked on her, blue eyes colder than the snow slanting down. Their bodies were thickly muscled, paws splayed wide like snow shoes. A thick ruff of fur encircled their necks. The wolves' jaws were as wide as Val's shoulders.

The largest of them stepped forward, lowering its head and baring its teeth. Val felt the low rumble of its growl in her bones. She raised her hands, palms out.

"Nice doggie. Easy there."

The wolf took another step forward and the other wolves followed it in a loose arc. Val retreated a step, considering her options. It was obvious that the wolves, like the blizzard, wanted to drive her back into the realm of winter. Why the Winter Fae wanted her there was anyone's guess, but she would rather not find out.

"How you feeling in there? Powerful?" she muttered under her breath. "You're a cat. I bet you'd like nothing better than to beat up on some dogs, eh?"

"Winter wolves are hardly dogs," Mister E corrected. *"And I resent your implication that I may not be able to take these mutts. If I had a body, I could scratch their eyes out with one paw tied behind my back."*

"Glad to hear it. So if I blast these puppies, it'll work?"

"I cannot guarantee that. Even my power is subject to the whims of the Twilight Realms."

"Wonderful. So, hypothetically if I go at these beasts and our power falls flat..."

"They'll rip your throat out."

Val swallowed. "That's what I thought."

As the wolves advanced again, she drew her knife, just in case. Not that she expected the knife to do much against the massive wolves. She doubted it would even get through their thick fur.

Still, if she was going down, she was going down swinging.

The lead wolf crouched, snarling, preparing to spring. Val gathered her power and raised her knife.

As the wolf leapt, Val blasted it with wind. Her power surged out of her, ready to bat the wolf out of the air like an insect.

Nothing happened.

She had half a second to feel dismay before the wolf was on her.

The weight of the wolf hit her chest like a bag of stones, knocking the breath from her lungs in a rush and bearing her to the ground. She threw an arm up, desperately trying to keep its teeth away from her throat. Fangs scraped against stone and for the first time she was thankful for her petrified fingers.

She stabbed with her other hand, but her blade was swallowed by the wolf's thick fur and she didn't feel it hit flesh. Val tried to roll away, but the wolf was too heavy, its weight pinning her to the ground. The rest of the pack came rushing in, fangs snapping. This time she felt them sink into flesh.

Val screamed and lashed out in desperation.

Something clicked.

Power burst out of her in a wave, sending wolves and snow exploding into the air. The ground shook, the backwash flinging Val away like a rag doll. She tumbled end over end as the wind howled and raged around her, the world obliterated in a whirl of white.

Finally, the surge ended and Val lay still, face down on the ground, bruised and battered, but intact.

She lifted her head.

The snow had been blown away from her in a star-shaped blast radius. The blizzard winds had let up too, and the world around her was now still and silent, with fat snowflakes drifting gently down.

"What the funk was that?" she asked weakly. Her voice sounded small and distant, her ears filled with a high-pitched ringing.

Mister E was amused. *"That is what happens when this realm boosts our power. Fairly impressive, don't you think?"*

"Yeah. Impressive." She looked unsteadily around at the blasted landscape. "Now what?"

"Now, I suggest we get moving before those wolves come back. You may have flung them into the next realm, but I doubt that will deter them for long. We should be gone when they get back."

"Right." Val agreed wearily. "Gone."

She managed to lever herself back to her feet. Everything hurt. She felt like she'd been through a tumble-dry cycle in a dryer full of hammers. She squinted around at the horizon.

"The wind stopped. Which way do we go?"

Mister E stretched out his nose and tail and spun in the air like a floating furry compass. He came to rest facing off to Val's left.

"The mortal realms are that way."

"Wonderful." Val stumbled into motion, legs moving mechanically beneath her. Her eyes drooped with weariness. "If I fall asleep on my feet, just wake me when we get there."

The demon-cat's soft laughter rang in Val's ears as she stumbled drunkenly into the twilight.

She hadn't taken five steps before the winter wolves' howls rose once again.

Val cursed and pushed herself to move faster, lurching into a half-run, pain stabbing through her injured ribs with every step. She was bleeding in several places, dark blood staining her clothes.

Out of the corner of her eye, she saw a flash of white fur and ice-blue eyes. Ahead of her she saw a small grove of trees with spiky leaves. Red berries covered their branches.

"Holly trees," she muttered. "What did Malcolm say about holly berries?"

"He said they can be used to keep the fae at bay," Mister E said. *"If you hurry, we can shelter beneath the holly branches."*

Val broke into a sprint. At least, as close to a sprint as she could come with her injuries. In truth, it looked more like the kind of lurching, rolling stagger a hunting zombie might use.

Val didn't care. She wasn't here to win style points. She just had to get to the holly grove before the wolves.

More wolves flashed into sight. Two on each side of her. They were trying to surround her again.

The lead wolf surged ahead of the others, trying to cut her off. Val put every ounce of energy she had into her legs, willing herself to run faster. Her heart pounded in her ears, breath rasping in her throat.

It wasn't enough.

The wolf easily outpaced her, planting itself directly in her path. This one was even bigger than the other wolves, its shoulders as high as her own, ice-blue eyes staring directly into hers. Its lips pulled back in a snarl.

To either side, the other wolves were angling toward her flanks. Closing the noose.

Val gritted her teeth. Her only hope was to get to the holly grove. She couldn't stop.

She put her head down and charged the lead wolf. The beast snarled, baring gleaming teeth as long as her fingers. It crouched, preparing to leap into her charge.

When she was only three steps away, Val whipped her knife at its face.

The wolf acted instinctively, dodging the knife by leaping aside.

But Val wasn't trying to hit the wolf. She was trying to get it to move.

Before the surprised beast could recover, her momentum had carried her past it. Ten steps after that, she was diving beneath the holly branches.

43

V al pressed her back to the tree trunk, huddling in her small circle of shelter. The bark was solid against her spine, the ground soft beneath her boots as she fought to get her panicked breath under control. The holly tree's branches spread over her head like a blessing, the spiky leaves and red berries forming a bristling barrier. Just beyond the circle of protection, the winter wolves watched her, fangs bared, calculation in their cold predator's eyes.

"I will never scoff at Malcolm for his esoteric knowledge again," she vowed.

"That's taking things a bit far, isn't it?" Mister E replied. *"Scoff all you want. Just remember to take note while you're doing it."*

"Noted."

"That's the spirit. Nothing is ever so serious that you can't have a little fun with it."

"Now that we've established that, do you have any ideas on how we're going to get out of this? I don't think we can hide under this tree forever."

Val stared out at the wolves. The wolves stared back.

Mister E perched primly on a branch over her head. *"I've already done my share. I remembered what Malcolm said about holly trees. It's your turn to contribute something useful."*

"Thanks a lot."

Val scooped up a handful of small red holly berries from the ground and rolled them between her fingertips. A memory flashed through her. A lone holly tree standing in a front yard just down the street from her house.

Her original house, where she'd lived with her original parents.

Val smiled, remembering the way she and the other kids used to pelt each other with the berries. She recalled the feel of her bare feet pounding the dirt while she shrieked with excitement. Such simple, happy times.

Girls against boys was their most common game, and she remembered hiding beneath an old woman's porch with Katrina, giggling and throwing berries at any boy who approached.

The happy memory soured and wilted at the thought of Katrina. It was replaced by an image of the girl as Val had last seen her: lying on the ground with a branch as big as a fist punched through her chest, choking on blood as the light slowly left her eyes. A branch Val had put there.

Val shuddered and pushed the memory away. Her childhood memories were poisoned. Her entire life was poisoned.

She flung a berry at the demon-cat, cursing as it passed harmlessly through his body. It was all his fault. Him and his stupid bargain.

She angrily threw the rest of the berries out into the snow. The winter wolves scattered to avoid them.

Val barely noticed. She pounded her fists on her thighs, her jaw clenched tight.

It wasn't Mister E's fault. It was hers. All the death and destruction stemming from the moment she had accepted his bargain was nobody's fault but her own.

She didn't know how long she sat there, stewing in self-hatred, but eventually something plucked at the corner of her mind. She shoved it aside with her black thoughts, but it kept coming back. Persistent and annoying.

"What?" she finally barked, giving the thought her attention at last.

Then she saw it, and felt stupid for ignoring the thought for so long.

"The berries," she whispered.

"What's that?" Mister E hung upside down from the branch, giving her a lopsided grin.

"The berries," she repeated. "The wolves shied away from them."

She picked up another berry and threw it at the nearest wolf. The animal danced aside.

She chucked another holly berry at a different wolf, and this one actually yelped as it dodged the tiny projectile.

"That's it." She rose to her feet triumphantly. "That's how we get out of here."

Val reached up and plucked a handful of berries from the tree. Then she cautiously summoned a small cyclone.

To her relief, her magic acted as she expected it to this time, and the wind scooped the berries from her palm, spinning them around her body. She plucked more berries, adding them by the bunch until a maelstrom of spinning berries surrounded her.

A flick of her wrist sent a few of them shooting toward the wolves. The pack barked and danced aside.

"That's what I'm talking about." She grinned and emerged from beneath the holly tree, hundreds of little red berries now whirling around her. The wolves snarled at her, but kept their distance.

Val oriented herself away from winter and started walking.

"Let's get out of here. I'm tired of my toes being frozen."

Val stumbled to a halt in the fog. She was surrounded by thick foliage. It was cold, dark and damp. But this was a familiar cold, not the bone-deep chill of the twilight realm on the edge of winter.

She breathed in, letting the soft air fill her lungs. Human smells came to her: baking bread, rusty metal, the faint tang of old urine. She winced as her cracked ribs protested the deep breath, but even that couldn't spoil the moment. She was back in San Francisco. She was home.

She followed a winding path to the edge of the green, beneath the yellow glow of a streetlight. Val stopped, her brow furrowing.

"This isn't the same park we left from."

"It appears not," Mister E agreed. *"The fae have always been drawn to green places. I would guess that many of the city's parks contain paths to the twilight realms."*

Val sighed.

"That's inconvenient. How am I supposed to—Wait. Is that Rosa's market?"

Across the street from the park, a familiar green awning bent. A young Latina woman had just scooped up a crate of cilantro and was turning to carry it inside the market.

Rosa saw Val in the same instant.

"Val?" she called out. Her welcoming grin faltered as Val swayed on her feet. "Are you all right?"

Rosa dropped the crate and hurried across the street. Her eyes widened as she took in Val's battered and bitten state.

"What happened to you? Come on, let's get you inside."

Val protested half-heartedly but allowed Rosa to pull her into the market. The shop keeper sat her down on a stool at the counter.

"You look like hell. You get mugged or something? Should I call the cops?"

"No, no cops. I'm fine. I just need to get some rest."

Rosa raised a skeptical eyebrow. "Three days of rest, maybe. After we soak you in antiseptic and get you some stitches."

Val shook her head. "I'm fine, really."

"You are definitely not fine." Rosa slid a cup of coffee under Val's nose. "Here, you sit and drink this while I close up. Then I'll get you taken care of."

Val was too tired to argue, so she nodded and took a grateful sip of the coffee. It tasted a little acrid—it had probably been sitting all day—but she sighed as the warmth spread down her throat and into her belly.

"I feel like I haven't been warm in years," she muttered.

"The Winter Realms will do that." Mister E perched primly upon the

counter and started cleaning himself. *"And we weren't even in winter proper. Believe me, it only gets worse from there."*

Val shuddered. "I'd rather not picture it."

In what felt like seconds, Rosa was back at her elbow, pulling her to her feet. She escorted Val outside, locked the shutters, and put a steadying arm under the witch's shoulders.

"Come on., let's go get you cleaned up."

"Go where?"

"My place. It's only a few blocks. Come on."

"I don't...."

Rosa put a finger to Val's lips. "Don't speak. No arguments. You're coming home with me."

She winked and Val felt something warm stir inside of her. She irritably pushed it down. She was frozen and bleeding and exhausted and her libido wanted to come out and play now? What was wrong with her?

Mister E smirked. *"That's what happens when you repress your sexuality for years. It turns into a desperate monster, starving for any scrap of affection."*

"I am not desperate," she growled under her breath. "And getting close to me is bad for people's health. I keep them at arm's length in order to keep them safe."

The demon-cat's laughter was her only reply.

Rosa occupied the ground floor of a three-story Victorian a few blocks from the market. Thick ivy climbed the front of the building and wound across the doorframe, forming a dark green archway. Tiny white flowers released a heady fragrance. As they passed through the door, the air became warm and moist. The scent of rich earth and growing things filled Val's nose.

"What...?" she began as Rosa led her into the front room. Her head felt wrapped in wool. Her eyes started drooping.

"Don't speak." Rosa's shushing finger was warm against Val's lips. It smelled like flowers.

She lowered Val onto a soft green couch.

"Rest here. Don't fight it. Relax."

"I don't..." Val said, but the thought dissolved half-formed.

The inside of Rosa's flat looked like a garden. Ivy, orchids, spider plants, violets, and dozens of growing things Val didn't recognize spilled from pots covering every surface. A gigantic rubber tree bent thick branches across the ceiling. The air was warm and humid. Somewhere, a stream gurgled.

"Sleep now." Rosa's voice whispered like wind in the leaves.

Val could hear Mister E shouting. But his voice was far away. Someone had put the cat out for the night and now he was outside the flat, yowling to be let in.

Rosa smoothed a soft hand over Val's fevered brow.

"Rest. I'll take care of everything. Sleep now."

Val was so, so tired. Exhausted from the cold and the constant pain of her cracked ribs and her desperate flight from the winter wolves. She'd been riding on adrenaline, and it all came crashing down at once.

She thought she heard Mister E again, far in the distance. Then the wind rose, covering the sound with its soothing whisper. The stream gurgled. Soft moss cushioned her back. Blossoms tickled her cheek. She breathed in, and her head was filled with the soft scent of flowers.

Val slept.

44

S andra was grateful for the fog and the darkness. They cut down visibility and made her feel slightly less dangerous. Like a short-range gun instead of a sniper rifle.

Not that she was taking any chances, either way. She walked with the hood over her face and her eyes focused on the sidewalk in front of her. As an extra precaution, she wore the mirrored aviator glasses Hillary had given her. She wasn't sure if they would block her power or not, but she wore them anyway, on the off-chance they would. Her power was as terrifying as a nuclear reactor, and she'd take as many layers of safety as she could get.

It was weird being out in the city and not being able to really see it, but it still felt good to be outside. She'd been cooped up in the apartment too long, like a caged animal. Out here there was fresh air and people. Even if she couldn't look at their faces, just having them around made her feel better. She was an introvert by nature, but she'd always enjoyed being alone in a crowd. She loved to sit in coffee shops and draw, feeling the buzz of humanity around her while she sat in the corner, lost in her imaginary worlds.

She wanted to buy a new notebook and a couple of pencils, but she hadn't been able to pluck up the courage to enter a shop yet. Going inside felt too risky: The thought of interacting with a clerk at checkout made her insides freeze up. So she'd been wandering the streets, quietly observing the world while she tried to pluck up the courage to join it.

Sandra rounded a corner, glanced up, and froze. Halfway down the block, a man with dark curly hair was walking away from her. She could only see his back, but recognition jolted through her. She knew this man.

A hundred feet further on, he turned his head toward a bicycle passing on his left and she saw his face in profile. Dreaded confirmation crept up her spine. It was him. The dog-faced man from Zombie Coffee. The man she'd accidentally knocked over and helped up.

She could still feel the electric charge that had run through her when he'd touched her skin. The sly smile that had spread across his face.

She knew with cold certainty that touch had been magic. This man had changed her. He was responsible for turning her into the monster she was now.

Sandra trailed after the man for blocks, wondering what she should do. Should she confront him? Call the police? Go home and get Val?

She decided to follow him and see where he was going. Then she could go home and tell Val where he'd gone. If she left now, she'd have no idea where to find him again.

The man ducked into a corner market.

Sandra stopped in the shadows across the street, her brow wrinkled. This was the same market Val had brought her to. What was the man doing in there?

She remembered seeing the dog-faced man on the security tape they'd watched. She shuddered as images flashed through her mind of the transformed tiger-girl with blood on her mouth.

But hadn't Val said the dog-faced man was responsible for the girl's transformation? Why would he return to the scene of the crime?

She stood there, watching from under her hood, trying to decide what she should do. Was the Latina girl who ran the market in danger? Should she run in and help?

That was what Val would do, certainly. Val would face down a big bad wolf without blinking.

But Sandra wasn't like that. Despite her bulky physique, she didn't like confrontation. She didn't run headlong into things. Sandra was a watcher. An observer.

Minutes crept by, and the dog-faced man did not come back out.

Sandra shuffled her feet in an agony of indecision. She crept a few steps to her left, trying to get a better angle on what was happening inside the market. All she saw through the open door was a shelf full of snacks and a circular rack of sunglasses. There was no sign of the dog-faced man or the woman who ran the market.

More time passed. Fog slowly seeped into her hoodie, the fabric becoming damp and cold. Sandra shivered and took a couple of hesitant steps toward the market. Maybe she should go in and get something. There would be warm food and drinks in there. They might even have a notebook and some pencils for her.

She had just about made up her mind to risk it when a dark figure emerged from the park to her right. Sandra froze and put her eyes on the ground, hardly daring to breathe, picturing herself small and invisible.

The figure was halfway across the street before Sandra glanced up and recognized Val. She opened her mouth to call out, to warn Val the dog-faced man was in the market. But she'd been standing still too long. Her mouth didn't want to open. Her limbs refused to move.

By the time she overcame her paralysis, Val had already disappeared inside the market.

Sandra waited, straining her ears, listening for the sounds of conflict. When Val saw the dog-faced man, sparks would fly. Sandra shivered as she remembered what had happened to the tiger-girl on the security tape. Maybe it would be better if she waited outside where it was safe.

Again, Sandra stood watching the doorway to the market. Again, all was quiet and still.

Eventually, the Latina girl came out and brought the produce boxes inside. What had her name been? Something with an R... Rachel? Ramona? No, Rosa.

Sandra watched Rosa carry the boxes in. She chewed her lip. Where was Val? Was she all right?

She watched the lights click off as Rosa shut down the market for the day. Sandra was trying to work up the courage to cross the street and confront her when Rosa emerged with Val in tow. A dark, curly-haired pointer dog followed at their heels. Val was unsteady on her feet, and Rosa slid an arm around her, supporting her as if she were drunk. They moved away down the street together.

Alarm made Sandra's breath catch. Beneath her hood, her snakes writhed in agitation. What had happened to the dog-faced man? What had happened to Val? And where was Rosa taking her?

45

Val woke with the taste of berries on her tongue. A quiet breeze murmured through the leaves. Humid air lay soft against her cheek. The scent of unfurling blossoms filled her nostrils.

She yawned and stretched, her pillow giving slightly beneath her head as her eyes drifted open. She felt deliciously rested, as if she'd slept for a week.

It took her a moment to understand where she was. It looked like a garden of some sort, with greenery and blossoms everyplace her eyes fell. A stream gurgled nearby.

A puzzled line creased her forehead. The light was strange. It wasn't daylight, but it was bright and even. Almost as if she were in...

A voice interrupted her thoughts, "Welcome back to the land of the living."

Val turned her head to find Rosa sitting in a white armchair within easy reach. A black dog curled on a braided rug at her feet. The scent of berries and flowers rose from a steaming mug cupped between the young woman's palms.

"Would you like some tea?"

Val nodded mutely, her mind still wrapped in cottony sleep. Yes.

Tea sounded nice. She started to sit up, but Rosa put a hand on her shoulder and pressed her back down.

"Don't get up. I'll bring it to you."

Val let herself be restrained, but as soon as Rosa was gone, she sat up and swung her legs over the edge of the couch. The dog's head popped up, eying her warily.

"Easy boy. It's OK." She tried to make her tone reassuring.

The dog didn't take its eyes off her, but neither did it start barking, instead adopting a wait-and-see attitude.

Val marveled as she ran her fingers over the cushion beneath her thighs. The couch was shaped like any other, but it seemed to be upholstered in a light-green moss, thick and soft as alpaca wool beneath her fingers.

As her gaze traveled around the room, her perplexity grew.

Plants covered every square inch, a riot of twisting vines and blossoms. Yet the dimensions of the space around her were intimate and close. It felt like she was in a large room rather than an outdoor garden. Surely such a proliferation of greenery meant they were outdoors?

Rosa returned before she could puzzle it out, emerging through a wall of trailing honeysuckle.

"Naughty, naughty. I told you to rest." Rosa placed a cup and saucer on a small stump-table beside Val's knee.

"I didn't know you had a dog."

"He belongs to himself."

While she tried to puzzle out that statement, Val lifted the mug and held it beneath her nose, inhaling the scents of rose hips and honey. The cup was warm against her fingers, and she blew across the surface of the tea before taking a cautious sip. It was the perfect drinking temperature. Val took a larger sip, relishing the warmth as it slid down her throat, filling the space behind her ribs.

Her ribs.

She wiggled her torso experimentally. There was no pain.

"My ribs are better. Did you heal my ribs?" Her mind was finally coming awake, and it viewed this new fact with alarm. "What are you?"

Rosa smiled. "I told you. Magic runs in my family."

"I thought you meant tarot cards and tea leaves." Val prodded her ribs with a finger. No pain. "This is real magic."

Rosa cocked her head to the side. "I'm not sure whether to be amused or offended."

Val felt her cheeks color. She dropped her eyes to her tea.

"I only meant..."

Rosa laughed, a high, tinkling sound. "I know what you meant. And I get it. I wouldn't believe every random person that told me they could do magic either."

"Did you tell me that?" Now it was Val's turn to tilt her head. "I don't think you did. You only told me you had an aunt that did magic."

"Well... I never told you I couldn't do magic." Rosa took a sip of her tea and winked.

Val ground her knuckles into her eye, scrubbing sleep from the lashes. There was something else bothering her, but she was having trouble putting her finger on it.

Fingers.

She examined her petrified fingers critically. Her hand didn't hurt, and the grayness didn't seem to have spread.

"That won't be getting any worse." Rosa casually crossed one leg over the other, her slim ankles wrapped in green stockings.

Val stared at her.

"What do you mean?"

"Just what I said. I was able to stop the spread."

Val's mouth worked, but no sound came out. That was more than a simple healing. Something like that required major power.

She realized what had been bothering her.

"Mister E!" She felt within her for the demon-cat, but found nothing. Panic gripped her as she surged to her feet.

No. There.

She could hardly feel his presence. It was tenuous, as if he were floating at the end of a long tether. She tried to reel him in, but something was in the way.

Val reached for her knife, but it was not at her hip. She turned on Rosa in a rage.

"What have you done?"

A low growl rumbled up from the black dog. Rosa's eyes became opaque.

"Sit down. We have things to discuss."

"Not until you tell me what you've done."

Val started to step toward Rosa, intending to wring the answers out of her, but could not. She looked down to find vines winding around her legs. She struggled and thrashed, but she might as well have been fighting the earth itself. The vines pulled her down with implacable power, until she was sitting on the couch once again, wrapped so tight she could hardly move.

Rosa smiled, and the thing that looked out of her eyes was no simple shopkeeper. When she spoke, her voice was as cold as winter.

"Now, as I was saying. We have a lot to talk about, Valora Keri."

46

V al struggled against the vines binding her, but they might as well have been steel cables. She was helpless as a kitten.

"You're not Rosa. Who are you?" she snarled.

Not-Rosa bared teeth that gleamed like ice. Her features stretched, her ears becoming long and tapered, her face pale. Cheekbones sharp enough to cut.

Val's eyes widened in recognition.

"You're one of the fae from the speakeasy."

"Who I am is not the important question. What you should be asking is, 'What can we do for each other?'"

"What do you mean?"

The fae crossed long legs and took a sip of her tea.

"You have a problem that is beyond your abilities, Valora Keri. As do we. I propose we help each other."

"The only help I want is for you to release me so I can get out of here."

"Oh?" The fae arched a delicate eyebrow. "You are happy with your fingers being stone? You would not wish them flesh again?"

Val went still.

"You can do that?"

"We can do many things."

Val's mind went from her fingers to Sandra, and then to all the people the Puca had transformed. Could this fae give them their humanity back?

"What would you want from me in return?" she asked slowly.

"There. That wasn't so hard, was it?" The fae's smile was all teeth. "An object has been stolen from us. We want it returned."

"You want me to collect it."

"Precisely. We propose a bargain. A favor for a favor. Retrieve this item for us, and we will grant you a boon. Anything you desire that is within our power to grant, we shall."

"That's an awfully big reward. You must really want this thing back. What is it?"

"Before we may tell you any more, we must strike our bargain. Do you agree to our terms?"

Val licked her lips. The size of the reward all but guaranteed the task would not be easy. Rule number one of dealing with the fae was: If you think you're getting a good deal, count all your fingers and toes first.

For Val, that was easy. She only had three fingers that mattered. She ran her thumb over the rough, frozen fingers on her right hand. She would risk almost anything to undo the petrification.

She swallowed and took a deep breath.

"Fine. You've got a deal."

"Wonderful." The fae waved her fingers and the vines that held Val in place relaxed their hold. She plucked a drawing from the table beside her with long, delicate fingers and slid it onto the couch beside Val. "This is the thing you are to retrieve."

The picture was a vivid watercolor with swirling lines and a misty, dreamlike quality. In it, a clear pool huddled within a shadowed glade, fed by a tiny waterfall tumbling down mossy rocks. Beside the pool stood a round table and a single chair with a green cushion. On the table was a wooden box with a curving top. The box was no bigger than a cat and beautifully wrought, the smooth wood stained a rich amber and banded with iron. The lid was fastened by a lock of pure silver.

Val raised an eyebrow.

"A box banded with iron? Are you sure this belongs to you? You wouldn't be trying to use me as a common thief, would you?"

"Do you doubt our word, Valora Keri?" the fae replied icily.

Val noticed the fae didn't answer the question. She scowled and shook her head. Perhaps it was better to let it go.

She'd known she wasn't going to like whatever the fae proposed. She'd already agreed to the bargain. Val didn't know what unpleasant penalties trying to back out of the deal now would carry, but she was sure she didn't want to find out. It was better to just hold her nose and get on with the job. The reward would be worth it.

"What is the box?" she asked.

"You do not need to concern yourself with that. You only need to fetch it."

"I'm not in the habit of retrieving objects I know nothing about. Especially magical ones—which I assume this is. That's a good way to get yourself killed. Or cursed. And I've got too much of that already." She held up her stone fingers. "Start talking."

The fae leaned back and crossed her long legs, unperturbed by Val's ire.

"The box itself is unimportant. What matters is the thing it contains. You may transport the box safely. It will not harm you unless you try to open it."

"What's in it?"

The fae waved away her question.

"More than that, I will not say. All you need know is that the box was stolen, and it must be recovered. You must fetch it and bring it to me. When you have done that, our bargain will be complete."

Val's lips pressed into a thin line. The dog watched her intently, its liquid eyes laughing. She tore her gaze away with an effort, focusing on the fae.

"I get the box, bring it to you, and you grant me a boon. It's that simple?"

The fae inclined her head.

"Why can't you get it yourself?"

"There are compacts. Rules. Direct action is forbidden."

Direct action. Val almost laughed. If the fae were known for one thing, it was indirect action. They were legendary schemers and manipulators. Pretty much the exact opposite of Val.

"And if I fail?"

"You must not fail."

Val puffed in exasperation.

"You make it sound like I've been given a quest. Is some watery tart going to toss me a sword from a lake too?"

"We do not understand."

"Never mind."

She ground her teeth, trying to stay calm. Everything about this felt perilous, from the vague evasions of the fae regarding the contents of the box to the casual way the creature had locked Mister E outside the flat. Val had never been separated from Mister E before. She hadn't known it was possible. That this creature had done it was terrifying.

But it also spoke to the fae's immense power. If she could drive a wedge between Val and Mister E, she could deliver on her promised reward as well. She would be able to fix Val's fingers. Reverse Sandra's transformation. Restore humanity to all those poor souls shifted by the whim of the Puca and the power of the Wild Storm.

She took a deep breath and straightened her shoulders. The risk was worth the reward.

"It's a deal. Now, where do I find this thing?"

The fae smiled.

"The box is currently in the possession of Padraig O' Ceallaigh."

47

"You've got to be kidding me." Val glared at the fae.

The creature didn't even have the good grace to look embarrassed.

"We do not kid."

"Padraig is a friend of mine. I'm not stealing from him."

"His operatives stole the box. Stealing it from him is fair play." The fae shrugged, a barely discernible rippling of her narrow shoulders. "This is the way things are done."

"Can't you just ask for it back?" Val's face reddened at the fae's musical laughter. She set her jaw and pressed on, "Or, I don't know, buy it from him? He's in the import business."

"We assure you, the box is not for sale." She raised her hand to forestall Val's next argument. "And even if it were, we could not buy it. As we have said, that is not the way things are done."

"I can't steal from my friend." Val crossed her arms over her chest.

"You humans are so naive. Do you think this 'friend' would hesitate to steal from you if it suited his needs?"

"No, I don't think he'd steal from me."

"And this is why, since time immemorial, the fae have always emerged as the winners when dealing with humans. You stubbornly cling to your own simplistic notions of morality and believe that all other creatures must subscribe to your views as well. When in reality nothing could be further from the truth. Your ideas of right and wrong are infantile, and any member of the Courts who tried to live by such would be swindled out of everything they own the instant they came of age." The fae took a sip of tea, a smile playing at the edges of her lips. She leaned forward in her chair. "Listen well, Valora Keri, and pay heed to these words. The universe does not play by human rules. You must understand this if you are to survive."

Val scowled, but kept her peace. She wasn't going to waste words arguing with this creature. They would have to agree to disagree.

"Fine," she said. "Are we done here?"

"Yes." The fae inclined her head. "That path will take you to the door. Good hunting, Valora Keri."

Val took three steps down the path before a thought occurred to her. She turned.

"What did you do with the real Rosa?"

"How do you know there is a 'real' Rosa?"

Val narrowed her eyes for a moment, then shook her head.

"No. The first time I met Rosa in the market, she wasn't you. I'm sure of it. If you've hurt her..."

The fae's laughter rang like wind chimes. "You are so forceful, Valora Keri. We have chosen our champion well."

Val glowered, and the fae raised a delicate palm.

"To answer your question, Rosa has not been harmed. She is... sleeping."

"In the same way that Sleeping Beauty was 'sleeping'?"

The corner of the fae's mouth curled up.

"Something like that."

"Let her go."

"Perhaps. In good time."

"Let her go now." Val stepped back towards the fae.

The dog lifted his head and growled. The fae remained glacially cool.

"At present you have nothing to bargain with, Valora Keri. We will talk again when you have completed your task."

The fae waved her pale fingers. Val was seized by dozens of vines and carried swiftly away through the garden. The door opened, and they deposited her unceremoniously on the front steps of the house.

Two things happened as soon as she crossed the threshold.

First, the full force of Mister E came rushing back into her. The demon-cat was ready to fight, but there was nothing to fight, so he ended up stalking angry circles around her, fur standing on end, hissing and snarling while his golden eyes smoldered with rage. Val had never been so happy to see him in her life.

Before she had a chance to process that, the second thing happened: She almost walked into a figure in mirrored sunglasses and a baggy hoody standing just outside the door with an arm raised as if they were about to knock.

The figure glanced at her in surprise, and Val saw her own face reflected back at her. The figure gasped and quickly looked down.

"Sandra? What are you doing here?" The realization of what had just happened hit Val, and she flinched. "Did you just look at me?"

"I'm sorry. You startled me. It was a reflex. I'm sorry!"

Val braced herself for pain as more of her flesh turned to stone... but nothing happened. Cautiously, she checked her extremities.

"Um. You did look at me, right?"

"Yes. I'm sorry..." Sandra's words trailed off as she realized that Val was not turning to stone. "You're OK?"

Val flexed her fingers. "It seems that way."

Sandra broke out into a grin.

"It must be the glasses! Hillary was right!"

"Vampire Hillary?"

Sandra nodded excitedly.

"Hillary had the idea that if I wore mirrored sunglasses, it might keep people from making eye contact with me and keep my power from turning them to stone. We didn't know if it would work, though." A huge smile split her face. "But it does!"

"I'm glad I could serve as your human guinea pig."

Sandra's cheeks reddened.

"Sorry. You startled me. I didn't mean to look at you." Her smile broke through again, her enthusiasm too powerful to tamp down. "But it worked! Do you know what this means? This changes everything. I can look at people again!"

Sandra's enthusiasm was infectious, and Val almost smiled despite herself.

"That's great, Sandra. I'm happy for you. But what are you doing here?"

Sandra avoided her eyes.

"I followed you here. I didn't mean to. I was out walking and I saw the woman from the market bring you here. You looked like you were sick or something. Then she took you inside and... I've been standing out here ever since, trying to decide what to do next."

"So you were thinking about what? Bursting in to rescue me? Turning my captors to stone?"

"Maybe," Sandra said defensively. Then she deflated. "No, not really. I'm not a fighter, like you. First, I was thinking about going for help. Coming back with someone tough. Hillary, maybe. But I was afraid if I left, they might move you somewhere else while I was gone, and we'd never be able to find you."

"So you ended up standing here on the steps, paralyzed by indecision?"

"Pretty much." Sandra nodded sadly. "I've been going round in circles in my mind for a while. I'd finally decided to knock on the door just before you opened it. But you're out now. Are you all right? What happened in there? Where's Rosa?"

"I'm fine. The rest is complicated. It turns out Rosa is one of the fae. Or she's been replaced by one. Anyway, I made a deal with her. After I retrieve something for her, she's going to grant me a boon. If we're lucky, I might be able to use the boon to undo all of this." Val held up her petrified fingers and gestured toward Sandra. "And fix all the other people the Puca messed up."

Sandra's voice choked down to a whisper. "Really?"

Val nodded while mentally kicking herself and her big mouth. She shouldn't have given the girl hope. Now Sandra would be crushed if Val failed.

She took a deep breath and squared her shoulders. One more reason not to fail.

48

Val left Sandra outside not-Rosa's house and stalked across the city. No matter what the fae said, stealing from Padraig was out of the question. Val didn't betray her friends. And she certainly didn't steal from them.

"Then how do you intend to retrieve the box?" Mister E asked. He'd recovered some of his equanimity and floated at eye level as she strode down the street, his candy cigarette held in one paw. He was still agitated from their separation, however, and wasn't blowing his customary smoke rings, instead using the cigarette to stab the air as he spoke.

"I'm going to ask him," Val replied.

Mister E stopped floating along with her and hung there in amazement, watching her walk away for a full five seconds before recovering himself. He zipped back up to float directly in front of her.

"You're going to do what?"

"I'm going to ask him. It's what friends do. They don't steal from each other. They talk to each other."

Mister E burst out laughing and stopped moving again, forcing her to walk right through his insubstantial body.

Val grimaced. She really hated it when he did that.

"And here I thought you were a jaded and cynical old witch. Apparently you're as innocent as a schoolgirl."

"I'm not naïve and I'm not stupid. I know asking is a long shot. But he's a friend, and he deserves my honesty."

"And when you've done that, maybe we can sign some petitions and try to save the penguins." The cat chuckled.

"Just because the right thing is difficult, doesn't mean you shouldn't do it. In some ways, the difficulty makes a thing even more worth doing."

"You sound like one of those unbearably self-righteous people who always takes the stairs instead of the elevator and never puts sugar in their coffee."

She shot him a look.

"You know that's not true. Coffee should be sweet as cake and twice as light."

"Well, that's a relief. For a minute there, I thought they'd done something terrible to you inside that house while I was locked out." He gave her a tentative look. *"They didn't do anything terrible to you, did they?"*

"Not unless you call roping me into a contract with a fae something terrible."

Mister E chuckled.

"That does qualify. But that's not what I meant."

She caught a look in his eyes she'd never seen before.

"Were you worried about me?" He huffed and rolled his eyes, but she could see she'd hit the mark. "You were, weren't you."

"Of course I was worried about you. If something happened to you, where would that leave me?"

"How did she separate us like that? I didn't know that was possible."

Mister E grimaced.

"It was a combination of things. First, you were drugged and unable to use your magic. But the real culprit was the threshold of the house. As you know, thresholds have power, and many creatures and spirits cannot pass them without permission. Normally, we are immune to such tricks because we come as a package deal. If someone allows you to cross their threshold, they are by default allowing me to enter as well. But with you drugged, the fae was able to use her threshold as a

surgical tool. Obviously, she couldn't sever our connection entirely. Our contract can only be ended by death. But she was able to keep me outside her threshold, where I was unable to help you or know what exactly was happening to you."

He lapsed into a brooding silence, his tail lashing the air.

Val was taken aback. She didn't think she'd ever seen Mister E so upset.

"I'm sorry," she said finally. "That must have been hard for you."

"Before you came along, I spent a long time trapped in that mountain. I'm not eager to return anytime soon."

"Is that what happens to you when I die? You end up trapped in the mountain again?"

"I'm not certain. It depends."

"Depends on what?"

"Many things. None of which need concern us at the moment," he said dismissively. *"Padraig's house is just ahead. It's time to get your game face on."*

Padraig's mansion loomed out of the fog ahead of them. It was a gorgeous French chateau made of white limestone, with columns flanking the entrance and huge windows draped with heavy white curtains. After the doorman let her in, Val descended into the open salon at the back of the house. Polished hardwood floors rang beneath her heels. Floor-to-ceiling windows revealed the distant lights of Angel Island sparkling in the dark expanse of the bay.

Padraig's voice rang out behind her.

"It's rather late for a social call, don't you think?"

She turned to find him draped in a thick golden robe belted at the waist. It shimmered as if it were made of real gold thread. Expensive-looking leather slippers covered his feet. Tousled auburn hair above hazel eyes and a rugged jawline. In short, Padraig looked stunning, as always, though Val didn't know if that was due to natural good looks or some kind of glamour.

She raised an eyebrow.

"Playing King Midas today, are we?"

Padraig had the good grace to look slightly embarrassed.

"The robe was a gift from my mother, if you must know. Yes, it's a bit gaudy, but it's warm and comfortable." He fixed her with a stern look. "I also wasn't expecting visitors. I hope this is important."

"It is. But you're not going to like it."

"Wonderful. Not only have you interrupted a perfectly pleasant evening, but you're going to ruin it with bad news as well. You're a terrible houseguest, Valora Keri."

"So I've been told."

He sighed.

"I suppose you'd better come out with it then. Bad news is never made better by waiting."

Val squirmed under his gaze. Now that she was here, part of her wished she'd just tried to steal the box after all. Honesty might be the best policy, but that didn't make it any easier.

She cleared her throat and took a deep breath.

"I need something from your family's hoard."

The corner of Padraig's mouth quirked.

"Our hoard? Do you think we're a clan of dragons now?"

"Well, I mean..." She gestured to his golden robe.

Padraig laughed.

"Touché. I guess I deserved that."

His laughter died at the tension on Val's face.

"What is it? Just come out and say it. You know I'm happy to help, if I can."

She grimaced and pulled the watercolor out of her pocket. Delaying wouldn't make things any easier. The best way was to plunge right in. She flattened the paper and handed it to him.

"I need to retrieve this box."

Padraig's face went white.

49

"Where did you get this picture?" Padraig's voice was low and urgent.

"I've been contracted to retrieve this box. My client says it was stolen. They want it back." Val's reply was cool and professional. This was just a job. A contract. None of it was personal.

Padraig, on the other hand, was not calm at all, running his hand back through his hair in agitation.

"Stolen? That's impossible. My family have been the guardians of this box for generations."

"Maybe it was stolen generations ago," Val suggested. "You told me yourself that you don't always know where the artifacts your family collects come from."

"I know where this one came from. It was entrusted to us. We were tasked with keeping it safe." He grabbed her by the shoulders, his eyes intense. "Where did you get this picture?"

Val knocked his hands aside.

"Keep your hands to yourself. Have some manners."

Padraig restrained himself with a visible effort.

"My apologies. That was out of line. I ask you a third time. Where did you get this picture?"

"My client gave it to me."

"And who is your client?"

"That's confidential." Val crossed her arms over her chest. "Are you going to give me the box, or not?"

"Absolutely not. You're mad for even coming here and asking."

"I came as a courtesy. Because you're my friend. I don't steal from my friends."

Padraig laughed.

"Is that what comes next? You trying to steal from me?"

"No. I just told you. I don't steal from my friends."

"So what happens now?"

She sighed and drew her shoulders back. Stood up straight and looked him in the eye.

"Padraig O' Ceallaigh, I challenge you to single combat."

He gaped at her.

"You really are mad."

"You stand accused of theft," she continued, working to keep her tone official so her voice didn't shake. Challenging Padraig was risky. Doubly so because he was a friend. "I have been contracted to retrieve the item in question. It is my right to challenge you, and I do so now."

Padraig's face went from incredulous to annoyed.

"You don't want to do this, Val."

"It's the only option I have left. I will not steal from a friend, and you will not voluntarily relinquish the item. Yet I must retrieve it. So we fight for it. If I win, I get the box. State your terms, if you win."

Padraig's mouth pressed into a hard line, his jaw bulging with anger. When he spoke, the easygoing man who had nursed her back to health was gone, replaced by a cold being Val had never met.

"If I win, you will leave this city, Valora Keri, and never return."

It was Val's turn to gape. Leave the city? Forever?

She felt like she'd just gotten here. In two short years, this city had become the home she'd never known.

The thought of leaving it all behind made her unfathomably sad. She'd been a nomad her entire life. Running from her past. Trying to escape herself.

She couldn't leave now. Things were just starting to get good.

Val shut down that line of thought.

"I'm not going to have to leave. I'm not going to lose," she told herself.

"You'd better not," Mister E added. *"Because if you don't get the box, you'll be in breach of contract with the fae. And I don't think she'll accept failure."*

She turned her attention back to Padraig.

"I accept your terms."

He nodded shortly, his eyes hard, face all business.

"As the challenged party, I get to choose the terms of the duel," he stated formally. Val nodded, and he continued, "We will fight until one of us surrenders, is unable to continue, or is killed. Quarter will neither be asked for, nor given. Melee weapons shall be permitted. No projectiles. You may choose any weapons you like from my armory prior to the bout."

Val opened her mouth to accept the terms, but Padraig was not finished.

"Finally, no elemental magic shall be permitted."

"That's ridiculous!" Val burst out.

Padraig gave her a thin smile.

"Those are the terms. Accept them, or walk away. The choice is yours."

For a dozen heartbeats Val stood there, hands balled into fists, shaking with rage. Padraig was taking away her magic. Her strongest weapon. It was all she could do to keep from launching herself at him where he stood.

Finally, through gritted teeth, she snarled, "I accept. Take me to your armory and let's get it over with."

"My butler will take you there. I must change into something more suitable. We will begin in thirty minutes."

"Fine."

Padraig swept stiffly up the stairs, his golden robe billowing behind him like a cape. His clothes and the grandness of his home made him appear a king.

"I guess that makes me the upstart peasant girl," Val muttered.

"Excuse me, miss?" Padraig's butler was watching her expectantly. "If you'll please follow me."

She set her shoulders and inclined her head.

"Lead on."

50

"This really is quite the pickle, even by your standards." Mister E floated beside Val, his expression not at all mocking for once.

"What's that supposed to mean?"

"It means that, for a girl who regularly finds herself fighting monsters of all shapes and sizes, managing to get yourself into a duel with a fae prince still counts as a noteworthy achievement."

She eyed him askance.

"Padraig is a fae prince?"

"Well, he's certainly snooty enough to be one. But no, I don't mean that he's a member of one of the Courts. I was referring to his position in the O' Ceallaigh family."

She nodded. "He's certainly that."

"Do you have a plan for winning this duel?"

"No, I thought I'd play it by ear."

"Play it by ear? With no elemental magic allowed? You do recall the way Padraig fought against the vampires?"

"No, that completely slipped my mind," she said dryly.

The first and only time she'd seen Padraig fight was on the day he and his men had helped her take down the vampire queen and her pet necromancer. Padraig had wielded an old-fashioned sword and moved like the wind, fighting the top lieutenant vampire to a standstill.

That was when she'd realized Padraig was at least part fae. No human could move like that.

And now she was going to fight a duel against him.

"Brilliant plan, Val," she muttered, following Padraig's butler down a set of stairs. "What could possibly go wrong?"

The armory had a thick wooden door, and would have been right at home in a medieval castle. Inside was a rectangular room with racks of weapons hanging along stone walls. There were spears, quarterstaffs, crossbows, longbows, halberds, pikes, and swords of every shape and design.

Val moved slowly around the room, picking up weapons and testing them for weight and balance. She assumed Padraig would use a sword, as he had before, and she already knew he was deadly fast. She examined the weapons with an eye toward countering that.

She considered weapons that might keep him at a distance. She picked up and discarded a spear, a pike, and a quarterstaff. She even examined a massive halberd which stood twice her height, but she could tell without even picking it up that the cumbersome thing was far too heavy and slow. Padraig would have his blade through her guts before she could bring the head around to face him.

Val finally ended up back at the quarterstaffs. They were the lightest option and had two ends that could be used to both defend and attack. If she had any hope of keeping Padraig at bay, the quarter-staff was it.

She strapped a knife to her hip for good measure.

Thusly armed, she let the butler guide her to the sparring chamber.

The room reminded her of many dojos she'd seen. It was open and spare, several dozen paces across, with clean hardwood floors and walls covered in mirrors. Blue floor mats lay stacked against one wall.

Padraig hadn't arrived yet, so she paced the room and started to warm up. It was soothing to let her body fall into old physical patterns, the centering calm of movement. Her anxiety didn't disappear entirely, but she was able to let it recede into a low background buzz.

She focused on the movements, the physical meditation. Muscles flexing and stretching. Limbs bending. Breath hissing in and out of her lungs.

Once she'd gotten her body warmed up, she practiced with the quarterstaff, going through forms of attack and defense, snapping the staff in whistling arcs that ended in clean lines. The petrified fingers on her right hand made gripping difficult, forcing her to figure out how to make do with the fingers she had. It was sub-optimal, but after a little experimentation, not as bad as she'd feared. It was a two-handed weapon, so Val compensated with her other hand as best she could.

The quarterstaff wasn't her best weapon, but it wasn't her worst either, and she mentally thanked old George at the gym for insisting she get a well-rounded martial education. Left to her own devices, Val would have tried to get by with only her fists and spells. But George had nagged and cajoled her into getting a basic familiarity with every weapon he could put his hands on.

Now she was glad he had.

A sheen of sweat shone on her brow by the time Padraig entered the room. A stiff formal robe of green and gold hung from his shoulders, and his lips held no trace of their usual smile. His blade was naked in his hand. For her part, Val had shed her leather jacket and wore black boots, black pants, and a sleeveless black shirt.

He faced her stiffly.

"It's not too late to withdraw your challenge," he said. "You can still stop this foolishness."

"It's not too late to give me the box," she replied. "You can stop it just as easily."

He scowled and nodded sharply, as if she'd given him the confirmation he expected.

"There's nothing else to say then." He locked eyes with her and took up a fighting stance. "Shall we begin?"

Val hesitated before readying her quarterstaff.

"Padraig?"

"Yes?"

"I'm sorry it had to come to this."

His lips pressed into a grim line.

"Not as sorry as you're going to be."

51

Padraig came at her in a blur, steel shining, his formal robes swirling around him.

Val barely raised the quarterstaff in time to block his first strike, and his second sent chips flying from the smooth wooden shaft. She gave ground with each strike, buying herself time to react to the next.

He was as fast as she remembered, though his blade seemed faster when it was flashing at her face instead of someone else's. She didn't try to do too much, staying balanced over her hips and light on her feet, working to understand Padraig's fighting style and keep his blade away from her body rather than counterattack.

He fought the way she would have expected given his slightly curved blade, with lots of slashing cuts and very few straightforward stabbing motions. It reminded her of the way samurai fought with katana swords, or pirates wielding cutlasses. She wondered if he had ever been a pirate, which made her consider how long he might have been alive. Padraig looked young, but that meant nothing—all fae looked young if they wanted to. With the fae's penchant for using glamour to disguise themselves, trying to judge one of them on their looks was as useful as trying to find the real Sailor Moon at an anime convention.

Padraig's attacks flowed smoothly from one into the next. He varied their angle and speed, high to low, left to right, slashing at her ankles one moment only to loop the blade up into a vicious head cut the next. Val circled her retreating steps to the left, staying away from the walls. In order to maximize the defensive capabilities of her staff, she needed to keep Padraig at a distance, and in order to do that, she needed room to maneuver.

The fae used three quick slashes to drive her towards the corner of the room, where he could close in and dart past her longer reach. Val responded with a whirling counterattack, creating enough room for four quick side-steps that carried her out of danger again.

And so it went, attack and parry, move and countermove, attack and retreat.

Val was surprised she was doing so well. She'd expected Padraig to overwhelm her with his speed and skill, but she was keeping up with him, matching him move for move. It felt more like a friendly sparring match than a high-stakes duel.

"Don't get cocky," Mister E warned. *"This is just the opening act."*

His words proved prophetic as Padraig shifted into another gear. His attacks became faster, the impacts against her quarterstaff more forceful. His blade touched Val's skin for the first time, and within thirty seconds she was bleeding from a trio of shallow cuts. Fresh sweat trickled down her temple.

Padraig smiled at the surprise on her face.

"Surely you didn't think that was all I had?"

Val grimaced. "I was kind of hoping that, yeah. I suppose next you'll be telling me you're not lefthanded."

He frowned at that, not understanding the reference.

Val took the opening created by his confusion to launch an attack of her own. In an attempt to limit her power, Padraig's rules had specified no elemental magic. And to be fair, her wind magic was by far the flashiest she'd mastered, but not the only magic she had. And the rules said nothing about other types of magic.

In addition to her elemental magic, Val also knew a bit of ritual magic, like the burning of hairs she had used to track down Sandra.

Ritual magic was slow and careful and required great concentration. It was the exact opposite of what she needed in a fight.

But ritual magic wasn't the only tool in her bag of tricks.

For better or for worse, Mister E was part of her being. This meant that his power was as much a part of her as blood or bone. The air that she breathed. She'd never needed to consciously access that power. During times of great duress, Mister E's magic welled up within her of its own accord, making her faster and stronger than any human had a right to be. This was the reason she went through so many sparring partners at the gym. When her blood got flowing, the power inside Val put her on a level other humans simply couldn't match.

As Padraig's blade nicked her for a fourth time, Val's lips peeled back from her teeth. Mister E hissed inside her, and she felt his blood-lust kindle. Power and anger surged beneath her skin.

Her attack was twice as fast as her defense had been, and three times as powerful. In the space of three heartbeats, she'd tagged Padraig with her quarterstaff three times, the last strike cracking him in the ribs and sending him staggering.

"You want to play?" Val snarled at his wide-eyed surprise. "Fine. Let's play."

52

Val and Padraig swept back and forth across the floor of the training room, their movements almost too fast for an observer to follow. There was no more time for banter, just grunts and curses and the sound of weapons connecting. Blood splattered the floor and created growing spots of darker black on Val's clothing. Padraig's golden robes were stained with sweat. They were both breathing hard.

No quarter was asked and none given. Two predators going at it tooth and claw.

Val was impressed with herself. Even without her wind magic, she was holding her own in a duel with a fae. Before today, she never would have guessed that was possible.

Give the girl a gold star.

But as the fight went on, she slowly realized it wasn't going to be enough.

Her power might make her a match for Padraig in strength and speed, but power alone couldn't close the gap in technique. The sword was his chosen weapon. He'd been training with it his entire life.

Val was no more than adequate with the quarterstaff, and against an opponent as skilled as Padraig, no amount of power could make up for that fact.

Little by little, he was finding the gaps in her defenses. Wearing her down.

Taken individually, none of her wounds were debilitating. But each scratch released a little more blood. Every lost drop of blood sapped her energy a fraction more. Despite the magic running through her veins, if she lost enough blood, she would tire and slow.

When that moment came, her defenses would slip.

And Padraig would slide the tip of his blade between her ribs.

As if sensing her thoughts, Padraig said, "Give up, Val. You can't win. I don't want to hurt you."

She snarled and launched a complicated attack in reply.

In the back of her mind, Mister E was chanting, his civilized veneer lost in bloodlust. *"Cut him. Tear him. Give me blood."*

A thought occurred to her.

Maybe she was going about this all wrong.

Val was a mixed-martial-arts brawler, accustomed to getting up close and personal. Using her fists and her feet. Perhaps by focusing too much on their weapons, she was playing her opponent's game. Padraig was a master of his blade. She couldn't hope to match his skill.

She started to leave tiny holes in her defenses. Let her reactions slow just a fraction.

Padraig picked up on it instantly, as she knew he would. He pressed the attack, his blade flickering past her quarterstaff, nicking her skin as he drew closer, preparing for the strike that would end it.

Her parries grew sloppy as she allowed him to get closer and closer, waiting for her moment.

Finally, he committed. Padraig lunged forward, extending his blade in a thrust designed to pierce her neatly between the ribs.

Instead of trying to dodge, Val stepped into the thrust.

She twisted as she moved, so the blade scraped down her side instead of sinking between her ribs

Val clenched her teeth. It still hurt like hell.

But by accepting the thrust, she'd brought Padraig within arm's reach. Right where she wanted him.

Releasing her quarterstaff, Val seized Padraig's sword arm with both hands. Dragging and twisting, she fell backwards, yanking him off balance as she kicked a foot up and flipped him over her head.

Padraig yelped in surprise, his sword clattering to the hardwood beside him as his back slammed onto the floor. Before he could recover his weapon, Val kicked out at the sword, sending the blade skittering away.

She turned the kick into a roll, and in a blink she was on top of him, pinning him to the floor. She slammed her elbow into his nose.

Mister E was exultant, *"Yessssssssssss..."*

Her fists rose and fell, rose and fell. His speed and skill were no use now. A red haze filled her vision. She was beyond strategy, beyond thought. Mister E's bloodthirsty exhortations filled her ears. A primal roaring filled her mind as she smashed Padraig's face into pulp.

Blood dripped from her knuckles. It spattered her lips.

Everything was blood.

After what felt like a long time, Padraig's voice finally broke through the roaring in her head.

"Yield. I yield." His words bubbled.

The world slowly came back into focus. Val was horrified to find Padraig's handsome face unrecognizable. Both his eyes were swollen shut. His breath bubbled and rattled in his throat. His mouth was full of blood and he was missing several teeth. One cheekbone was caved in, his face horribly deformed.

In the back of her mind, Mister E was chuckling. She could feel his self-satisfied contentment. Like a cat that drops a half-eaten bird on your pillow for your admiration.

"I'm sorry," she gasped. "I'm so sorry."

"Take the box," Padraig bubbled. "And get out." His butler appeared, holding the box in white-gloved hands.

"I only..."

"Get out!" Padraig roared.

Val took her prize and fled.

53

"It doesn't look like much, does it?" Sandra materialized from the shadows as Val approached Rosa's house. Her hood was up, the streetlight glinting off her silvered sunglasses. A snake's tongue flickered at her temple.

Val jumped and scowled at the girl.

"Have you been waiting out here this whole time?"

Sandra shrugged. "It doesn't bother me. I spend a lot of time sitting and observing. It's the way I move through the world."

"Well, move through the world a little more loudly next time."

"You're hurt." Sandra reached toward her, but Val flinched away.

"It's nothing. Just a flesh wound."

"It looks like twenty flesh wounds."

Val grimaced. "You're right. It's more like twenty flesh wounds."

"Is that it?" Sandra cocked her head at the box.

"Yes. That's it."

Val examined the box in her hands. It looked exactly the way it had in the painting, dark wood about the size of a breadbox, with three black iron bands enclosing the smooth surface. The box was strangely warm beneath her fingers, as if hot coals smoldered within it. A silver padlock fastened the hasp.

"What do you think's inside it?" Sandra asked.

"I don't know."

"Aren't you curious?"

Val's scowl deepened. "Of course I'm curious. I entered into a contract with a fae over this box. That's a big deal. The contents might be important."

"Are you worried about what's in there?"

"Yes, if I'm being honest."

"Why retrieve the box then? If it worries you?"

There was no recrimination in Sandra's voice, just curiosity. It was this, more than anything, that allowed her words to reach Val. If Sandra had come at her with accusations, Val's defenses would have snapped up, and she would have lashed out in response. But Sandra's simple, childlike curiosity allowed Val to respond in kind.

She stared into the swirling fog, her fingers tracing the lines of the box.

"I couldn't see any better options. The Puca. The Wild Storms. My hand. You and all the other transformed people. Even the real Rosa, kidnapped and replaced. It was too much. I couldn't find a way to undo it all. This was the only way."

"Isn't it dangerous to make deals with the fae?"

Val snorted. "Of course it's dangerous. Everything I do is dangerous. I have to choose between things that are certain to kill me and other things that are only 99% likely. When you fight monsters, there are no good choices. Only less bad ones."

They stood in silence for a minute while Sandra digested that.

Val turned up the walkway to Rosa's door and Sandra fell in behind her.

"You should stay here," Val said.

"No. I'm done missing all the good stuff. I'm coming with you."

Val sighed but didn't argue. "Suit yourself."

The door opened before Val had a chance to knock. The fae's eyes lit up when she saw the box.

"Come in," she purred. Her eyes hardened as she noticed Sandra. "A gorgon."

"She's a friend," Val said. "She's coming in with me."

The fae's expression went flat. "If she breaks hospitality, it will be on your head."

"Understood."

The fae ushered them to the mossy couch and tutted over Val's battered appearance.

"Let me see to your wounds."

"My wounds are fine," Val snapped.

The wince when she lowered herself onto the couch gave the lie to her words. Sandra hovered uncertainly for a moment, then perched on the far end of the couch.

"Well done, Valora Keri." The fae's gaze smoldered upon the box. "I did not expect you to retrieve the prize so easily. Had I known how effective you are, I would have hired you as my agent years ago."

"Easily?" Val displayed her bloodstained clothing. "You call this easy?"

"Scratches, nothing more. If that is the only price you paid for such an item, the retrieval was quite easy indeed."

The fae pulled on elbow-high silk gloves to protect her hands from the cold iron bands and unfurled a silk cloth.

"Give me the box."

"What about my boon?"

"As agreed, I will grant you a boon once the box has been delivered. The box has not yet been delivered." She gestured impatiently.

Val hesitated, scowled, and finally handed over the box.

The fae took it reverently, carefully wrapping it in the silk cloth, her eyes alight with avarice. "The things you and I will do," she purred.

"Now that's over, can I drop the charade? I'm tired of lying on the floor, scratching fleas." The dog shimmered and shifted and became the Puca. He was dressed in an ochre vest, a yellow silk scarf and a silver shirt. A fedora perched jauntily over his black curls and long face.

"What's he doing here?" Val leapt to her feet, power crackling at her fingertips. Even as she asked the question, she thought she knew the answer. "Have you been working together all along?"

The fae ran her slim fingers through the Puca's hair.

"You can never resist your flair for the dramatic, can you?" she admonished him lightly. "You had to make your grand reveal."

"What does it matter now? You've got the box. The game is over."
He grinned at Val. "And I'm tired of playing the hound."

"I don't understand," Val said. "Why the subterfuge?"

The fae's laughter rang like chimes. "Why the subterfuge? You really know nothing about fae, do you."

"Why walk a straight line when a stroll through the garden maze will get you there all the same?" the Puca agreed.

"But... you caused all of this," Val said, gesturing to Sandra, who sat frozen on the end of the couch, her hands clenched in her lap.

The Puca laughed. "You give me too much credit, witch. The Wild Storm provided the power. I only helped to sculpt things into a more pleasing shape."

"A more pleasing shape?" Sandra's voice was so quiet, Val almost didn't hear her, but there was unexpected steel in her tone. "You call this a more pleasing shape?"

The Puca was unperturbed.

"Certainly. Who were you before? A mortal nobody. Forgettable. Unexceptional in every way. Now look at you. Nobody will ever forget you again."

54

"My boon," Val growled. "I demand my boon."

The fae's lips twisted in amusement.

"So forceful. There's no need to demand anything, Valora Keri. You have been promised a boon, and a boon you shall have. All you need do is ask."

"I want you to put everything back the way it was before the Puca started transforming people."

The fae gave her a slight frown, like a disappointed parent. "They told me you were clever, Valora Keri. 'Everything' is so terribly vague. You are asking me to rewind time. Restore the world to the exact state it was days ago. That is beyond my power. Be specific."

Val clenched her teeth. "Fine, restore the people then. All the people who have been transformed or affected by your machinations. Undo the changes. Return them to their natural state."

"You're getting warmer. It's rather like watching a toddler learn to walk, don't you think?" she said to the Puca. The dog-faced man laughed.

Val ground her nails into her fists. "What was wrong with that one?"

The fae put on a lecturing tone. "First, there was no time frame. 'All the people' when, exactly? Over the course of my entire life? Given that many of them are dead, that timeline is far too broad."

"Over the past week, then."

"And second,"—the fae raised a cautionary finger—"saying 'all the people' is still far too general. A boon is good for a single thing. If you want me to reverse someone's transformation" —her eyes lingered on Sandra, a smile playing at the corners of her lips—"you must pick a person."

"What? The boon can only be used to help one person? You've got to be kidding me." Val glared at the fae. She'd expected trickery, but this was too much. Who knew how many people the Puca had transformed?

She ran a thumb over her petrified fingers. Plus, she was one of them.

The fae's slim shoulders rose and fell in a graceful shrug. "I do not make the rules."

"No, but you enjoy twisting them to suit your whim," Val snarled. "If I'd known you were only going to help one person, I wouldn't have fetched your stupid box. I would have found some other way."

"The paths not taken are the lies upon which you humans build your lives. If I'd only done this, everything would be better. If I hadn't done that, I would be content." The fae's voice dripped with scorn. "You have done the things you have done. Your life is what it is. These foolish attempts to comfort yourself with fairy tales of what might have been achieve nothing. You deceive only yourself."

"I want you to help Sandra, then," Val ground out. "For my boon, I ask that—"

"No," Sandra interrupted. Val turned to find her perched on the corner of the couch, spine straight, hands pressed together in her lap.

"What do you mean, no?" Val said. "I can undo what's been done to you. No more snakes in your hair. No more mirrored shades."

"No," Sandra repeated. Her voice was soft, but firm, the steel Val had detected earlier still present. "I can't be the only one. I'll feel guilty. Help someone else."

"You'd rather be a gorgon for the rest of your life than live with a little guilt?" Val asked in exasperation.

Sandra nodded, her mouth set in a determined line.

Val pressed her fingertips into her temples. She could feel a headache coming on.

"Who then?" she asked wearily. "We don't even know how many people the Puca has transformed."

Sandra hesitated for a moment, before saying a single word, "Rosa."

"Rosa?" Val looked from Sandra to the fae, her brow creased in confusion.

"Rosa," Sandra repeated. "The real one. They've done something to her. Wherever she is, she's innocent. Use your boon to help Rosa."

Val considered Sandra's words. The girl was right, Rosa was an innocent. The shopkeeper had been in the wrong place at the wrong time, and the fae had swooped in and stolen her identity in order to gain Val's trust.

She thought about the other people she could help instead. All of those terrified new shifters being stuffed into the Mission District Shifter Settlement. She didn't know any of them personally, though. How could she choose only one of them?

Also, they were under the care of Alain and the other shifters. At least they had a community to protect them.

Rosa didn't have that. In fact, who knew where Rosa was? If Val didn't free her, would the fae take Rosa's place indefinitely? Would the world ever see the real Rosa again?

Val looked at Sandra. "Are you sure? I can make you normal again. This might be your only chance."

"Normal again?" Sandra said the words like she didn't know what they meant. "I've never been normal. I've always been the girl sitting in the corner, hiding behind my sketchbook. Watching the world, but never truly a part of it. I've never been normal." Sandra met Val's gaze squarely. The artist's mirrored glasses reflected Val's questioning face back at her. In contrast, Sandra's words held granite resolve. "I'm sure. Rosa needs it more than I do."

Sandra was right. Rosa was innocent.

Grief tugged at Val's heart as she looked at her petrified fingers. Last chance. If she used her boon on Rosa, her fingers would be stone forever.

No. She had plenty of sins to atone for. Stone fingers were simply one more part of her penance.

Val took a deep breath. Her golden eyes caught and held the fae's ice-blue gaze. "I want you to undo whatever you've done to Rosa. Stop impersonating her and free her. Give her life back."

The fae smiled. "As you wish."

A cracking sound came from the couch, and Sandra started to her feet. A seam appeared, the moss peeling open like a flower petal. It exposed a shallow, coffin-like chamber made of living wood inside.

Rosa lay on her side within the chamber, nude, her body curled like a seed. Roots twined around her brown limbs—though whether the roots were feeding her or feeding off of her was unclear. Her ribs rose and fell, and her face scrunched up as a great yawn cracked her jaw open. Her eyes blinked.

"Where am I?" she asked, roots falling away as she levered herself up.

Val helped her step out of the living chamber. "You're safe now. Here." She handed Rosa a blanket from the foot of the couch.

Rosa wrapped the blanket around her shoulders calmly, though she seemed unbothered by her lack of clothing.

"I was having the strangest dream..." Her words trailed off, her forehead creasing as her eyes took in the garden that had swallowed the room. "Is this my living room?"

55

Rosa's eyes followed the vines stretching across the ceiling. The moss-covered floor. The flowers dripping down the walls. Her brow creased as she finally noticed the Puca.

"You were in my market when those grafters turned into monsters."

The Puca grinned and tipped his cap. "Some of my finest work, that was. Hooked this one like a fish."

Val glared at him. "What does that mean?"

"It means you swallowed the bait like a prize trout. Hook, line, and sinker. Followed the line whichever direction I pulled. It was great fun."

"What does that mean?" she demanded again, stepping towards him.

The Puca pulled a grape from a vine and popped it into his mouth. He winked at her while he chewed the fruit.

The fae rolled her eyes. "Are you really going to do this? We've got what we wanted. You don't need to impress us with your cleverness."

The Puca ignored her.

"Sometimes you do the job yourself, and sometimes you need to find the right tool for the job. And you, Valora Keri, were the right tool for this job." He patted the silk-wrapped box affectionately. "Padraig

O'Ceallaigh would have never given this to either of us, he distrusts us too much. No, prying it from his grasp required a friendly touch. One might say, a woman's touch."

Val balled her fists. "I'll give you a woman's touch. Are you telling me that all of this was a setup? All the transformations, all the chaos, was just a ruse to lure me here? To get me to fetch that box for you?"

The Puca shot her with a finger gun. "Give the lady a prize, she got it in one."

A roaring sound filled Val's ears. Red hazed her vision. She'd been a pawn.

Hot wind swirled around the room, whipping the leaves and branches into a frenzy.

The Puca raised his hands in a calm-down gesture. "No need to get worked up. A bargain was struck and executed. Everyone got what they wanted."

"Everyone got what they wanted?" Val punched out with a fist of wind, pinning the Puca against the wall. "Did the people you transformed get what they wanted? Did Sandra? Did I?" She pointed her stone fingers at him like an executioner's ax.

"Stand down, Valora Keri." The fae's voice was icy. "The Puca may have put it inelegantly, but the substance of his statement is correct. Our bargain is complete. Antagonize us at your peril."

"At my peril?" Val turned her rage on the pale woman. "What are you going to do? Kidnap my friends? Transform them into monsters? Turn my fingers to stone? Oh wait, you already did all that."

With a cry, Val sliced a whip of air across the fae's hands, sending the box spinning out of her grip. It slammed into the wall, punching a hole through the greenery that clung there. The impact snapped one of the hinges with a loud crack, leaving the lid slightly crooked. Where the cold iron bands touched greenery, the vines blackened and hissed. Rising smoke curled across the ceiling.

The fae gasped in pain. "You will pay for that, Valora Keri."

More vines rose from the floor, twining around Val's legs. Val sliced at them with blades of air, but they multiplied faster than she could cut them down. In seconds, the vines had her wrapped tight, pinning her arms against her sides.

"There. Now we can talk like civilized beings." The fae's cold smile was back.

The Puca straightened his vest indignantly. "No need to be rude."

"Rude? I'll show you rude." Val spun a tight whirlwind around her body, vines shredding as it spun faster and faster.

"I think someone needs to go for a little ride. But first we need to get rid of this." The Puca plucked her knife from its sheath and tossed it away. "I had quite enough of that last time."

His body twisted and stretched as he transformed into a black horse.

Steam snorted from his nostrils. His eyes shone red. In a blink, his back was beneath Val, lifting her up into the air. The greenery parted before them as he carried her into a gnarled forest.

The thick canopy obscured the sky, the light at ground level a brooding twilight. Branches whipped at Val's face and legs as the Puca sped through the undergrowth. She'd seen this movie before.

"Not this time." She pulled the chain from her jacket.

The collar would not fit around the Puca's neck while he was in his horse form. But Val had a plan.

She slipped one end of the chain through the metal collar, turning the entire chain into a large noose. Then she lunged forward and tossed it around the Puca's neck.

The Puca screamed.

He reared up and bucked, and Val was airborne. But she clung to the chain, and her momentum pulled the noose tight. The skin of the Puca's neck sizzled and smoked around the cold iron.

The Puca began to shift forms. His skin became slick and scaled, making Val slide across his back.

She set her jaw and held on. "You're not getting away that easily."

The Puca writhed and changed, his form flowing like liquid. One moment he had a long, serpentine body. The next, coarse black fur covered his hide and a thick mane sprouted around his neck. He became a black albatross, leaping into the air, and for a heart-stopping moment Val thought he was going to carry her up into the sky. But the Puca only managed to flap his massive wings a few times before he collapsed to earth and sprouted legs again. From breath to breath, he shifted and writhed, trying every form to escape the cold iron noose.

Val refused to let up. When his neck grew so big it strained the limits of the chain, she set her feet and put every ounce of strength into holding the circle closed. When he shrank and tried to slip free, she cinched the noose tight in one motion.

But she wasn't quite fast enough.

The Puca became a tiny black garter snake, wriggling free of the chain as Val tried to tighten the noose in vain.

56

S andra gaped as the Puca took the form of an enormous black bear. He towered over Val, his head nearly scraping the ceiling. He roared and swatted at the witch with a massive paw, sending her crashing headfirst into the wall.

Val tried to push to her feet, but she sagged drunkenly against the ivy, her limbs refusing to respond.

The Puca stalked her with yawning jaws, madness in his eyes. He wasn't simply going to take her for a ride this time.

As the creature closed in for the kill, Sandra stood frozen, unable to breathe. She watched Val try to gather her strength. The witch got to her feet with effort, raising her hands in vague defense.

Sandra silently willed her to wake up. To get it together. To fight!

But Val's eyes were unfocused, her head bobbing on her neck like a rubber doll's. She was done.

As the Puca's teeth bent toward Val's neck, Sandra teetered on the edge. She'd always been an observer. Floating around the edges of life. Hiding behind her pencils and paper. Safe inside her fantasy worlds. Participating only as much as she had to.

But she was about to see her friend die. Watch her be torn apart by the same creature that had locked Sandra inside this monstrous gorgon body.

Enough was enough. Sandra couldn't sit back and watch anymore.

The Puca had made her a monster. It was time to reap what he'd sown.

"Stop right there," Sandra's tone was quiet but commanding. The steel she'd been cultivating was razor sharp now.

The Puca glanced over at her... and Sandra's sunglasses were off, exposing orbs as black as night. Her stomach fluttered and twisted inside her as his eyes met hers. Like a thousand moths taking flight.

The Puca's mouth stretched into a silent scream.

And froze that way. Forever.

The trickster's skin was cold and gray. In the middle of the room, where the menacing fae had stood, now towered the statue of a bear, every detail hauntingly preserved and perfectly lifelike.

Val gasped in shock. "Sandra!"

Sandra blinked as the awareness of what she'd done hit her. Her cheeks colored and she dipped her head, but an unfamiliar pride swirled in her chest. She'd done it. She'd stopped the creature that had transformed her.

"He made me a monster," she breathed. "He didn't expect that monster would come back to devour him."

"That was brilliant," Val said. "Well done. Are you all right?"

Sandra nodded dazedly. She was still figuring it out, but something important had shifted inside her. A smile pushed at her lips. She was better than all right. She had found her power.

"Good." Val pushed away from the wall and turned her attention to the remaining fae. "I suggest you leave before something happens to you as well."

The fae's voice was as cold as winter. "Is that a threat?"

"No, it's a promise. If you touch my friends again, I promise you'll regret it for the rest of your life."

"You humans have such an inflated sense of your own importance." A thin smile slipped over her features as she reached to retrieve the box.

Val ripped it from her grasp.

"I don't think so. For all the pain and suffering you've caused, this box belongs to me now."

"That was not the deal, Valora Keri."

"No, the deal was that I deliver the box, and you provide a boon in payment. Both of which have been accomplished. Our bargain is complete." Val smiled a shark's smile. "But nobody said I had to let you keep the box afterwards."

"Do not make an enemy of me, witch. You will regret it."

"Funny, I was about to say the same thing to you."

Their gazes locked, the fae's eyes glacial, Val's golden orbs burning hot as the sun. Sandra felt the air crackle and spark between them.

The fae smiled. "It matters not. I have already won."

Dread yawned in the pit of Sandra's stomach. What tricks did the fae still have to play?

Val said, "What do you mean?"

"As I told you, the prize was not the box, but that which the box contained. Look."

Sandra watched Val examine the box. One of the hinges had broken when it smashed into the wall, and now the lid was hanging crooked, leaving a sliver of space between the body of the box and the lid.

"It's just a crack," Val said. "Whatever's in there couldn't have fallen out."

"That's where you are mistaken." The fae's smile grew. "That box contained chaos."

"Chaos?" Val pushed the box out to arm's length, as if it were a viper about to strike.

"Pure chaos. That box once belonged to a woman named Pandora. You may have heard of her."

"Pandora's box?" Val looked skeptical. "You can't be serious. Wasn't that opened a long time ago?"

"Indeed, it was. But over the centuries much of the chaos was collected and trapped in physical form, as sand. That sand was put into this box and sealed away, taking much of the world's magic with it." Now her smile was wide and feral. "That magic has leaked back out into the world."

Sandra peered inside the box over Val's shoulder. Sure enough, there were a few grains of sand still sticking to the corners. But the box was mostly empty.

"I don't see how this will make a difference. We've got plenty of chaos already." Val snapped the lid tight and held it closed with her fingers. "The Wild Storms are getting worse every day. Look what the Puca was able to do with them."

"And because you have vanquished the Puca, you believe you have won? You think chaos is banished so easily? I hold our victory in my hand." The fae raised her hand and sand trickled between her fingers. Tendrils of green and gold energy swirled up from it, and a glowing gold circle appeared in the air behind her. "Magic returning to this world is no coincidence. We have been working to make it so. The Courts have been banished from the human realms for too long. With the power of the box, we will return. And there is nothing you can do about it."

57

C haopter Fifty-Seven

Val sucked in a breath as the golden portal behind the fae grew. Dark shapes were in there, vague and indistinct but getting closer.

"No longer must we travel through the twilight realms to reach the mortal plane." The fae's icy smile was triumphant. "No longer will the doors between realms be few and fickle. I am a Harbinger of Winter, and I am bringing my home here. The Winter Court will rule the mortal plane once more."

Guilt pierced Val as she realized what the dark shapes were. The Winter Fae, coming to take over the city. The harbinger was using the wild magic from Pandora's Box to tear down the walls between San Francisco and winter.

This was all her fault. She had fought Padraig for the box and delivered it to the harbinger. She'd given the fae exactly what she wanted.

Val had thought she was doing the right thing. Fighting to stop the Puca. Undo the changes the trickster had unleashed on the city.

But she'd been set up. Manipulated into retrieving Pandora's Box for them. And she'd played right into the fae's hands.

"Not if I have anything to say about it." She growled and punched out with a fist of wind. If she could distract the fae, disrupt her concentration, the portal would close.

The harbinger flicked her chin contemptuously, and a heavy golden mist flowed past her like fog coming in over the hills, pushing Val's wind into the ground before it reached her. Not so much as a single lock of the fae's hair was stirred.

"Your magic is nothing before the power of the box," she mocked. "You cannot stop me. Prepare to kneel; the Winter Court will be here soon."

"Look here!" Sandra called out.

Instead of looking, the harbinger stretched out a hand and made a pinching motion. Sandra yelped as her hood was yanked down, cinching tight over her face.

"Do you really think I would be caught as easily as a brainless Puca?"

The fae crooked her finger and the drawstring on Sandra's hood looped tight around her neck. Sandra fell to her knees, clawing at the string as her own hoodie started to strangle her.

"Let her go!" Val used the only weapon at hand. She tossed Pandora's Box at the harbinger's face.

The wicked fae's dodge wasn't quite fast enough. The box's iron bands clipped her cheek, and she cried out, raising a hand to her sizzling flesh. A trickle of sand escaped between her fingers. Behind her, the golden portal flickered, blurring into a translucent mist. For a moment, Val could see the living room wall behind it.

Then the harbinger closed her fist and straightened once again. The portal solidified.

Val could see what the dark shapes inside the portal were now. They were soldiers of winter. Monstrous fae with long arms and gaping mouths, all teeth and claws. She saw red caps among them, and dark, bestial shape changers. At their forefront burned the ice blue eyes of the Winter Wolves.

But the harbinger's falter had given Val an idea.

She reached into her pocket and pulled out a handful of the holly berries she'd collected in the twilight realm. She held her other hand flat and spun them up into a little whirlwind over her palm.

The harbinger narrowed her eyes. "What are you doing?"

Val grabbed her middle finger with her thumb then released, flicking it toward the wicked fae. A red berry shot forward as if she'd hit it with her nail.

The harbinger flinched, but the berry flew harmlessly past her shoulder. She sneered.

"Holly berries? You'll have to do better than that, little witch."

But Val hadn't been aiming at the harbinger.

The portal rippled as the holly berry pierced the golden surface.

The fae snapped her head around as if struck.

"Don't do that."

Val flicked her nail again and again, berries peppering the portal like buckshot. The golden surface became translucent again, the wall behind it coming into focus more and more with every berry that passed through. It was working. The portal was weakening.

"I said, stop that!" the fae roared.

Vines clutched at Val from every direction, dragging her down to her knees, pinning her arms to her sides.

But her training sessions with Mister E paid off. Even without her palm as a focus point, she was able to keep the little whirlwind spinning in front of her. Her arms were bound by her side, but her finger continued to flick, shooting berries faster and faster, making the portal waver like the surface of a pond in the wind.

The harbinger held out her hands, one on top of the other. A thin stream of Pandora's sand ran down between them, as if her hands were the two halves of an hourglass. The sand flared bright gold, burning incandescent, and the portal flared with it, solidifying behind the fae once more.

Inside the portal, the other dark shapes had almost reached the surface. Val could clearly see the wolves now, with the red caps and shape shifters right behind them. In moments, the creatures of winter would pour through the portal and into the city.

"Not today," she swore.

A hail of holly berries struck the harbinger's hands and face.

The fae screamed and jerked her hands up, opening her fingers wide as she instinctively tried to protect her face.

A cloud of sand released into the air in front of her.

With a thought, Val caught the sand in a downdraft, funneling it toward the crack in the lid of Pandora's Box.

"No!" the fae shrieked.

She lurched toward the box, but it was too late.

Val whirled the sand back into the box like water spinning down a drain. As the harbinger reached for it, Val grabbed the box with a firm gust and yanked it across the floor. It skidded to a halt just below her boot. She stepped down, shutting the lid tight.

The fae turned to her with murder in her eyes.

"You will pay for that, witch."

"Maybe," Val acknowledged. "But not today."

She hit the harbinger with everything she had. A storm of holly berries inside a hurricane wind lifting the fae off her feet, throwing her through the golden portal.

In the blink of an eye, the portal winked out. The harbinger was gone.

58

P eople shied away from the life-sized bear statue towering over the sidewalk outside Rosa's apartment. The bear was snarling and fierce, but that wasn't what made them cross the street to avoid it. What bothered people was the look of terror in the bear's eyes. As if it had come face to face with a predator even it could not handle.

"Are you sure you don't want us to get rid of it?" Val asked.

She and Rosa stood squinting up at the petrified Puca. It was a warm, sunny November afternoon, and Val's leather jacket hung open, revealing the worn black t-shirt beneath.

The Ural sparkled beside her at the curb, and Val fondly ran her fingers over the old motorcycle's sidecar. After the Puca had turned it into a black stallion, she hadn't known if she'd ever see the Ural again. But to her shock, SFPD had found it out near the old zoo. The metal beast had some new scratches, but otherwise it seemed no worse for the wear.

"Nah. It was hard enough just getting it outside. That bear must weigh a thousand pounds," Rosa said. "Besides, I kind of like it. It keeps the crazies away. I haven't had one stranger knock on my door since we put it out here."

"Whatever works for you." Val smiled, but her face turned sober as she searched Rosa's face. "How about you? Are you OK?"

Rosa shrugged one shoulder but didn't meet Val's eyes. The shopkeeper's expression was haunted.

"Sure. Fine. The nightmares of being trapped in my couch are getting better. I only woke up screaming twice last night."

Val winced. "I'm sorry about that. If there's anything I can do..."

"No," Rosa said quickly. "I'm good."

An awkward silence rose like mist between them.

Val licked her lips and took a nervous breath.

"If you ever need a friend..."

"No. Thank you, but no. I know I said I was used to magic in my family, but..." Rosa retreated a step toward her front door. "No offense, but the crowd you run with operates on a whole different level. I don't think I can handle that kind of crazy in my life."

Val swallowed the lump in her throat. She blinked back the tears. Cleared her throat.

"Understood. I'm sorry about everything. Take care of yourself." She held out a hand.

After a moment, Rosa took it. Her fingers were dry and strong.

"You too, Val."

Rosa squeezed once and released, then went back inside without another word. Val hugged her jacket shut, alone with the Ural and the bear, staring unseeing at the empty street. She shivered. The sun didn't feel nearly as warm as it had a moment before.

Saying goodbye to Rosa had been hard, but Val's next stop would be the hardest. She took a deep breath, squared her shoulders, and knocked on the polished front door of Padraig O'Ceallaigh's mansion. The bay wind ruffled her hair as she waited, and she buried her hands in her pockets against the chill. The views were nice, but it was always cold up on the hills where the rich people lived.

Val was about to knock again when the butler finally opened the door. He did not step aside to invite her in.

"Miss Keri. I regret to inform you that the master does not wish to see you."

Val winced. She'd expected it, but it still hurt to hear.

"I just wanted to return this to him." She held out Pandora's Box. She'd wrapped a blue bungee cord around it to keep the lid on tight.

The butler frowned at it for a long moment. Finally, he stepped aside.

"Come in, Miss Keri. I have a feeling he may want to see you after all."

She followed him into the cavernous living room and perched nervously on the arm of the couch while he went to fetch Padraig, balancing the box across her knees. The bungee cord was a terrible solution to the broken hinge, but what was she supposed to use? Zip ties? Duct tape?

"It doesn't have to look pretty." Mister E prowled around the room, peering under the furniture. *"It only has to get the job done."*

"I feel like that should be inscribed on my tombstone."

He turned to regard her with his golden eyes half-lidded. He puffed on his candy cigarette and blew a pair of smoke rings. A crescent moon grin split his face.

"Yes, I believe that would be appropriate."

Before Val could retort, footsteps rang on the marble floor behind her.

A surly voice said, "You've got some nerve showing your face after what you've done, Val Keri."

She turned to find Padraig glaring at her. His face showed no signs of the beating she'd given him, and she wondered if the bruises were hidden behind a glamour, or if he'd healed so quickly? His arms were crossed over his golden robe, his hair as artfully tousled as ever.

A pang stabbed through Val's breast. Even scowling at her, he was achingly beautiful.

"I'm sorry," she said. "I know I have no right to be here. If you never want to see me again, I understand. I just wanted to return this to you." She held out the box.

His frown deepened when he saw the bungee cord.

"What have you done to it?"

"It kind of... it broke."

"Broke?" He snatched it from her, his eyes widening as he noticed the broken hinge. "Did the troubles escape?"

Val couldn't meet his eyes.

"Yes. I got a lot of them back, but... some of them got away."

"Do you know what you've done?"

She nodded miserably. "I've got a pretty good idea."

Padraig paced the floor in fury, his robe swirling behind him.

"My family has kept this box safe for centuries. You've undone all of that in a day. Why? What on earth made you challenge me for it?"

"I made a bargain with a fae. Once the bargain was made, I had no choice but to follow through. You know what the consequences would have been if I didn't."

"Better the consequences fall on you than the whole world!"

She winced. "The bargain was only to retrieve the box. I didn't know what was in it."

"The name Pandora's Box didn't give you a clue?" he sneered.

"She didn't tell me the name of the box. She only described it to me."

"She?" Padraig's hazel eyes pinned her with the intensity of a hawk's. "She who?"

"I don't know. She didn't tell me her name."

"Describe her to me."

Val did, with Padriag pressing her with questions, prying out every detail she could remember.

Finally, he shook his head. "It's not enough. She's from the Winter Court, but beyond that, she could be anyone."

"I'm sorry," she said softly.

"Not as sorry as we're all going to be, now that you've opened the box."

"Tell me how to make it right. I'll do anything you ask."

"No. You've done quite enough already." Padraig's voice was hard, his expression stiff and unyielding. "The butler will see you out. Do not come here again, Valora Keri."

"Padraig..."

But he was already gone. Striding away in a swirl of golden robes.

59

"You opened Pandora's Box?" Malcolm tutted. "Girl, you really are bad news."

The afternoon sun slanted in through the bay windows, warming Val's legs on the window seat. Hillary sat in the old recliner across the room, keeping her sensitive skin far from the intruding beams, while Malcolm and Sandra shared the couch.

They were all drinking coffee, and the delicious smell of baking bread filled the apartment. Baking was Malcolm's latest obsession; he'd been stuffing them all with bread at every opportunity. Not that anyone minded. Warm bread was the perfect thing for those cold San Francisco evenings. He'd even tried making gluten-free bread for Hillary, with very mixed results.

It was a beautiful day, showing no indication that a horde of troubles had escaped into the world.

"I didn't know it was Pandora's Box," Val said defensively. "And I didn't open it. The hinge broke."

"Tomayto, tomahto," Malcolm said. "Your actions caused the box to be opened, and now we've all got to deal with the shit that fell out."

"We?" Val cocked an eyebrow at him. "I didn't see you out there fighting the fae, Malcolm."

"We all fight in our own way," he said airily, though his face paled a little. "I've decided I'm not really cut out for that action and adventure stuff. I'm better in a supporting role. If you need any research done at the Library or bread baked, just let me know."

"Gee, thanks." Val rolled her eyes as she sipped her coffee.

In reality, she was thankful for the role Malcolm played, and equally thankful that he'd given up wanting to be on the front lines. He wasn't cut out to be a fighter, and trying to protect him made her job more difficult.

But that didn't mean she was going to stop giving him a hard time about it. What were friends for, after all?

"Do you think you can find the escaped troubles and put them back in the box?" Sandra asked. She was wearing her fox onesie with the hood up and her mirrored aviator sunglasses, making her look like some kind of weird cosplayer/fighter-pilot hybrid. Occasionally, one of her little snakes would venture down over her forehead, its pink tongue flickering.

"Sure, I'll add that to the list." Val frowned as she ran her thumb over her petrified fingers. "Right after I deal with the stray monsters still at large from the Puca's mischief spree, the vampires, and the witches still trying to kill me."

"Don't forget, you're on probation too," Hillary said.

"And there might be a gang war brewing," Malcolm added. He nodded toward the invitation for Andrei Vasilevski's funeral, which was still lying on the coffee table.

"Thanks for the reminder." Val shot them both dark looks.

"I mean, it is possible to put things back in the box, right?" Sandra insisted. "You did it before."

"Yeah." Val sighed and stared out the window.

She'd spent the week running around the city, dealing with one crisis after another. From fighting newly made shifters and tracking down Sandra and the Puca to making a foolish bargain with one of the Winter Fae. Opening Pandora's Box felt like the cherry on top.

The truth was, she was tired. Exhausted, really. She wanted to crawl into bed and sleep for a week.

"The thing I don't understand," Malcolm said. "Is why it was a box.

Everything I've read says that 'box' was a mistranslation from the original Greek. The original wasn't a box, it was a clay jar or something."

"Maybe they replaced it when they put the troubles back inside," Sandra suggested. "Or maybe the original was broken when Pandora first opened it."

"I suppose that's possible," Malcolm took a sip of his coffee and frowned. "I still don't like it, though. It's not supposed to be a wooden box."

"Aww, does the world not match up to your expectations? Join the club," Hillary mocked.

"Cheers to that." Val raised her mug.

"Are you allowed to toast with coffee?" Malcolm wondered.

"Why wouldn't you?" Hillary asked.

"Well, it's bad luck to toast with water. I just wondered if coffee was bad luck too."

"You worry too much. Relax your tight ass once in a while," Hillary said. "Coffee is fine for toasting."

"My tight ass is round and firm," Malcolm shot back. "You're just jealous."

"A gorgon, a vampire, a faerie and a witch walk into a bar." Mister E sprawled lazily in the sunbeam. *"What's next? A minotaur?"*

"I hope not," Val muttered. "Those horns would be murder on the ceiling. We'd never get our security deposit back."

"So, about the basement," Malcolm started. Sandra tensed, her shoulders drawing up toward her ears. "I think it's a sin to let Sandra live down there in all that clutter. And that couch is not a proper bed. Just because she's a gorgon now doesn't mean she shouldn't have proper back support."

"I'm sorry, I haven't had time to find a better place for her to stay. I've been a little busy," Val snapped.

"Relax, that's not what I'm suggesting."

Val narrowed her eyes at him while she sipped her coffee. "What are you suggesting?"

Malcolm glanced at Hillary, who nodded conspiratorially. Val tensed, dreading whatever was coming next.

"We should fix the basement up," Malcolm proposed. "Turn it into a proper apartment. Make Sandra officially part of the family again."

Val scowled. "Sandra and I don't live well together. We've established this."

"Which is why she'd be living in the basement," Hillary said. "Far enough away to stay out of your hair, but close enough to be part of the gang."

"So... what? We'd get rid of the junk and paint the walls? Put a little kitchen and bathroom down there for her?"

"Exactly!" Malcolm turned to Hillary. "See, I knew she'd be on board."

"Wait... but I..." Val sputtered.

Malcolm rode right over her. "I was thinking that for now we could paint that old workbench and get a hotplate and a little refrigerator. We can replace the couch with this great futon my friend is giving away. Once we clear out the junk, we can paint the walls and put up a disco ball..."

It was too late; Malcolm was off and running. Val could see which way the wind was blowing, so she decided to just let him go. It was easier than trying to fight the inevitable.

"A disco ball?" Sandra looked horrified.

They all laughed, and Val felt warm inside. She took another sip of her coffee, swishing the butterscotch over her tongue with satisfaction.

The outside world was filled with chaos, and tomorrow would likely bring new horrors. Dangers both old and new.

When they came, Val would go out and face them, as she always did.

But in here, for this fleeting moment, there was warm sunshine, hot coffee, fresh bread, and good friends. Looking at the animated faces around the room, Val realized they'd put together an improbable misfit family. What more could a witch ask for?

"A body," Mister E mused. *"I think I'd like my own body..."*

Val choked on her coffee.

When she could breathe again, she muttered, "Absolutely not. The world does not need another serial killer."

<<<<>>>>

Thank you so much for reading Twilight Storm. I hope you enjoyed
reading it as much as I enjoyed writing it.

Before you go, please take a moment to leave a review. Even just some
stars or a few words can make a huge difference in helping other
readers discover the world of The Keri Chronicles.

Thank you very much.

Yours,
A.C. Arquin

P.S. I'll see you in the next Keri Chronicles Adventure: JADE SECRETS.
Coming Soon!

GET YOUR FREE STORY!

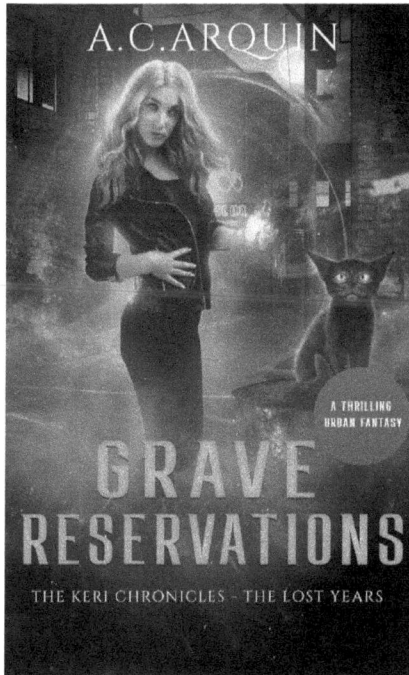

Join the Arquinworlds Reader Group to get your free story from The Keri Chronicles - The Lost Years!

ABOUT THE AUTHOR

A.C. Arquin lives in his own worlds. At least, that's what his teachers always told him when they caught him reading a book in class instead of paying attention to the lesson.

Now all grown up, he still prefers realms of imagination to reality. The only difference is that nowadays, he writes down his adventures and shares them with the world.

When not writing, he is also a very busy audiobook narrator, under the name J.S. Arquin.

He is hard at work on the next book in The Keri Chronicles.

Get a FREE KERI CHRONICLES PREQUEL STORY as well, as all the latest news and deals, by joining his Reader's Group at www.arquinworlds.com/

BOOKS BY A.C. ARQUIN

THE KERI CHRONICLES

Dead Wrong

Pale Midnight

Twilight Storm

Jade Secrets - Coming in AUGUST 2023

Grave Reservations (Val Keri, The Lost Years)

The Itch (A Stand-Alone Gaslamp Fantasy Thriller)

THE CRIMSON DUST CYCLE (A Dystopian Space Adventure. Published as J.S. Arquin)

Ascent (Book 1)

Slide (Book 2)

Peak (Book 3)

Twist (A Crimson Dust Prequel)

The Crimson Dust Cycle Box Set

COMING IN AUGUST 2023

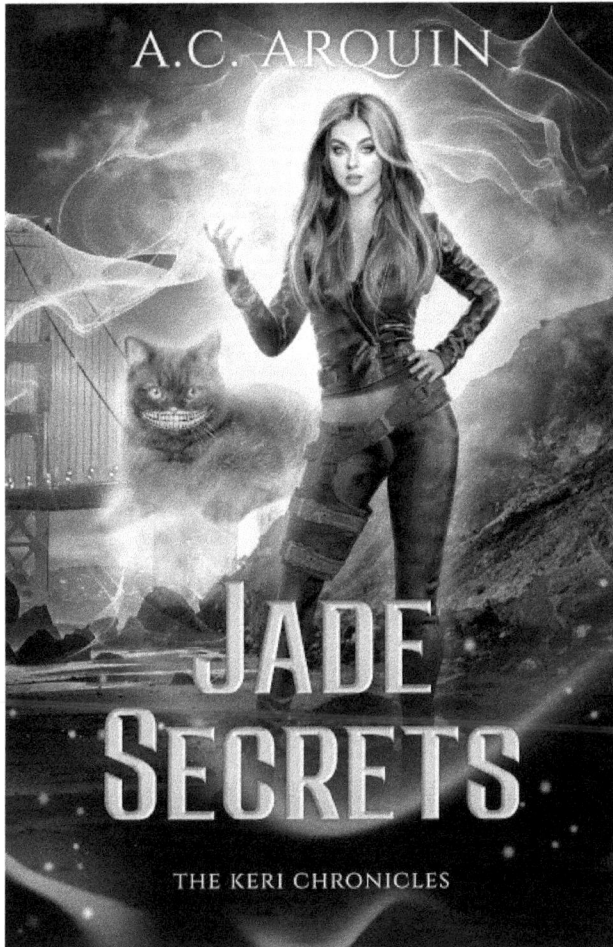

A.C. ARQUIN

JADE SECRETS

THE KERI CHRONICLES

PRE-ORDER NOW!

www.ingramcontent.com/pod-product-compliance
Ingram Content Group UK Ltd.
Pitfield, Milton Keynes, MK11 3LW, UK
UKHW061448131025
8355UKWH00046B/1717